THE
HEARTBREAKER

*Also by Carly Phillips
in Large Print:*

The Bachelor
The Playboy

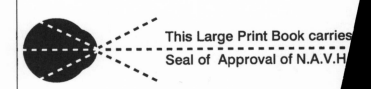

This Large Print Book carries
Seal of Approval of N.A.V.H

THE
HEARTBREAKER

CARLY PHILLIPS

WHEELER
PUBLISHING

Published in 2003 by arrangement with Warner Books, Inc.

Wheeler Large Print Hardcover.

The text of this Large Print edition is unabridged.
Other aspects of the book may vary from the original edition.

Set in 16 pt. Plantin by Ramona A. Watson.

Printed in the United States on permanent paper.

Library of Congress Control Number: 2003108598
ISBN 1-58724-517-5 (lg. print : hc : alk. paper)

THE
HEARTBREAKER

As the Founder/CEO of NAVH, the only national health agency solely devoted to those who, although not totally blind, have an eye disease which could lead to serious visual impairment, I am pleased to recognize Thorndike Press★ as one of the leading publishers in the large print field.

Founded in 1954 in San Francisco to prepare large print textbooks for partially seeing children, NAVH became the pioneer and standard setting agency in the preparation of large type.

Today, those publishers who meet our standards carry the prestigious "Seal of Approval" indicating high quality large print. We are delighted that Thorndike Press is one of the publishers whose titles meet these standards. We are also pleased to recognize the significant contribution Thorndike Press is making in this important and growing field.

Lorraine H. Marchi, L.H.D.
Founder/CEO
NAVH

★ Thorndike Press encompasses the following imprints: Thorndike, Wheeler, Walker and Large Print Press.

Special Acknowledgments

These acknowledgments are for the most special people in my life, who show it every single day.

To my family, the people closest to my heart. Phil, Jackie, Jen, and Buddy, for living with me through the madness that followed *The Bachelor's LIVE with Regis and Kelly* pick and loving me anyway, and to my parents for raising me to believe all things are possible. I love you all.

To Janelle Denison, a best friend who feels like family and who weathered the ups and downs along with me as if they were her own. You're special, unique, and I'm lucky to have you in my life. I'm more grateful than you'll ever know!

To Shannon Short, a best friend with wisdom beyond mine, who's able to see through the forest when I can't, who guides me when I'm confused and nurtures my ambition with common sense and reason. You'll be beside me when we're old and infirm, our Louis' in one hand and our memories of Mets and monkeys to keep us laughing.

To Theresa Meyers, for not laughing when I said, "Let's send *The Bachelor* to Kelly Ripa," and for your tireless and never-ending support. You're more than a business associate, you're my *friend. Everything happens the way it's supposed to.* Words to live by.

To Julie Elizabeth Leto, who understands plot and my lack of it and who can change the direction of a story in one simple phone call. You're extraordinary, my friend. Thank you!

And last but certainly not least:
To Kelly Ripa, wonderful actress, savvy talk show host, and a woman with vision. Thank you for picking *The Bachelor* for your book club and for changing the course of my career, and thus my life. I wish you only good things in return.

Chapter One

Chase Chandler walked out of the gate into Dulles International Airport and inhaled deeply. Each breath of air outside his hometown of Yorkshire Falls, New York, presented true freedom. At last.

"Hey, big brother!" His youngest sibling, Roman, pulled him into a bear hug. "Welcome to D.C. Good flight?"

"The best kind. Short and on time." Chase hiked his duffel bag over his shoulder and started toward the exit. "How's the wife?"

A ridiculous smile settled on Roman's lips. "Charlotte's amazing. Getting bigger by the day. My kid's growing inside her," he added, as if he hadn't reminded them all of Charlotte's pregnancy one hundred times before. "One month to go." He rubbed his hands together in obvious anticipation.

"Just recently a wife and kid was the last thing you wanted. We had to toss a coin to decide which of us would give Mom the grandkid she wanted so badly. Now look at you. A husband and soon-to-be dad, and happy about both." Chase shook his head, amazed and pleased with the changes in his little brother. The kid was settled and happy, which made

Chase happy. He'd done his duty by his family.

Roman shrugged. "What can I say? That was before. Now I'm a changed man."

"Before you grew up, you mean?" Chase winked and his brother chuckled.

Both men knew Roman had fought long and hard until he concluded that marrying Charlotte wouldn't mean giving up his foreign-correspondent lifestyle, merely trading it in for something more fulfilling. Now he had a job with the *Washington Post* as an op-ed columnist, a wife, and a family.

"You have no idea what you're missing," Roman said, not missing a beat. "A woman to come home to, a warm body in bed, and someone who loves you unconditionally."

Like religious fanatics, both Roman and Rick, his middle sibling who'd also recently gotten hitched, had begun to preach the benefits of marriage. Chase wasn't buying it. "Trust me, I can live without it, thank you very much. If I get that lonely, I'll find myself a dog."

His dreams didn't include a wife and family. His brothers, as much as he loved them, had been a handful to raise. He didn't need little rugrats of his own. From the time he'd turned eighteen and his father had unexpectedly passed away, Chase had been the male parent and role model. He'd taken over as publisher of the *Yorkshire Falls Gazette* and helped his mother raise his brothers — both jobs he'd never resented. Chase was not one to look back. And now, at thirty-seven, he was free to move on with a life of his own and grasp the dreams he'd put on hold. Starting with this trip to Washington.

He walked around a slow-moving couple and headed for the sign marked PARKING GARAGE. He glanced at Roman. The dimwitted gaze hadn't dulled and Chase grinned. "I guess I can call Mom and tell her you're strutting around like a proud papa."

"Don't bother," Roman said, falling into step beside him. "When we're not in Yorkshire Falls, she checks in once a day with Charlotte by phone."

Chase nodded. That was his mother, Raina, meddling and proud of it. "Well, I couldn't be happier for you." He patted his brother on the back.

"And I'm glad you've left the paper in someone else's hands and decided to put yourself first for once."

Chase answered Roman with a grunt. After all, the kid was right. Not once in the years since he'd taken over had he abdicated responsibility for the *Gazette*.

"The car's parked in the lot." Roman gestured in the direction they needed to go and Chase followed, nearly tripping over a young kid who'd decided to play tag.

"Thanks for picking me up," Chase said, noticing that the wayward kid had been corralled by his parents. Roman and Rick had been eleven and fifteen, respectively, when their dad passed away. They'd been old enough to take care of themselves and Chase hadn't had to deal with their toddler years. Thank God. Their late teens had been tough enough.

"How's Mom?" Roman asked.

"What do you mean?"

"Her . . . ah . . . health."

"Stuttering for a reason?" he asked.

Roman picked up his pace but remained silent. Chase could almost see his brother's brain churning to come up with a reply. A few months ago, Chase had rushed his mother to the emergency room with chest pains. Later, she'd told her sons she'd been diagnosed with a serious heart condition. Though they'd spoken to the doctor, confidentiality had prevented them from finding out anything more than what Raina had told them. Her three sons had danced around her bedside, making sure she took care of herself. Since she'd curtailed all activity, Chase hadn't thought to question the diagnosis further, until he began to notice inconsistencies in his mother's behavior. Too much color in her cheeks for someone with a weak heart. Too much swigging of antacids. The more recent prescription drug to treat gastric reflux, which if left untreated could have severe consequences. And running up and down the stairs when she thought she wouldn't be caught.

As a newspaperman with damn good instincts, he began to suspect blatant manipulation. He also suspected his brothers, who seemed less concerned with their mother's health lately, knew something he didn't.

"Rick and I need to talk to you," Roman said.

"About Mom's fake heart condition?"

Roman stopped in his tracks, causing one woman to nearly bump into him and a man to dart around him, cursing as he passed. "You know?"

Chase nodded. "I do now."

"Shit," Roman met his gaze. "We were going to tell you."

Chase ran a hand through his hair and groaned. He didn't give a damn that they were in the middle of the airport blocking pedestrian traffic. He'd been itching to confront Roman on this and was damn glad to have it off his chest. "Any reason I was left out?"

"I discovered the truth just before Charlotte and I got together for good. Rick figured things out more recently. If he could've come to D.C., we'd have told you this weekend." He held his hands out in front of him. "What can I say?"

"You don't owe me an explanation. Mom does."

Roman raised an eyebrow. "You don't know why she faked being sick?"

"Explanation's the wrong word. I know she did it because she wanted grandkids. She wanted us to feel so bad we'd do her bidding. I get that. But she damn well owes us all an apology."

"If it makes you feel any better, her antics have seriously curtailed her social life. She and Eric haven't been able to go dancing, date, do any of the things she'd like to do."

"Small consolation." Chase rolled his shoulders to release the tension. "What do you say we forget about the family problems this weekend and just have fun?"

"Sounds good to me. We'll get you settled at the hotel, have dinner with Charlotte, and tomorrow you'll get your first taste of D.C. politics. Let's get the hell out of here."

"No argument from me."

Roman started for the elevators leading to the parking garage and Chase joined him. "I'm not surprised Senator Carlisle's going to run for vice president," Chase said of the story that brought him to town.

Roman nodded. "Me neither. The man's political perfection, even on a second marriage."

Fortunately for Chase, Jacqueline Carlisle, the senator's deceased wife, was born and raised in Yorkshire Falls, giving Chase the link to his hometown that led him to D.C. "With the current V.P. too old and unwilling to run again, our president needs a newer model. Someone with shine and polish."

"U.S. senator Michael Carlisle from New York," Roman said.

"Yep. I did research on the man. After Jacqueline, the first wife, died, Carlisle married her college roommate and best friend. Madeline Carlisle raised the senator's first daughter, Sloane, then later Madeline and the senator had twins, Eden and Dawne." Political perfection, as Roman had said.

"Ever see photos of the senator's oldest daughter?"

Chase shook his head. "Just a glimpse of the twins or a grainy background shot. Why?"

Roman laughed. "I just think you'll like what you see. Elevator's this way." He pointed left.

"From a professional standpoint, I like everything about the Carlisles." Because barring scandal or stupidity, the high-profile, good-looking senator was on his way to the presidency. And Chase intended to use his local connection to make one helluva journalistic splash.

Roman laughed. "You do realize that when I asked about Carlisle's daughter, I wasn't talking about work?" He rolled his eyes. "Of course not. You're always on top of things, always the professional." He sobered. "You know, I learned from you."

The pride in his voice made Chase feel like a fraud. Roman had accomplished more in his lifetime than Chase ever had.

"And you're right," Roman said, oblivious to Chase's inner thoughts. "This story gives you the perfect opportunity to break out of small-town coverage. With the right angle, you could

15

get picked up by one of the bigger papers."

At his brother's words, Chase's adrenaline began pumping in a way he couldn't remember experiencing, not since he'd stood at his father's funeral and buried his dreams. But patience and family loyalty had paid off. Chase's time had finally come.

The elevator doors slid open and they stepped inside. "It just so happens, I have that right angle. The one that'll put you ahead of the other guys following Carlisle's scent. Want to know what I didn't tell you on the phone?" Roman asked.

"Sure." Chase dropped his duffel to the floor and glanced at his brother, his body humming with anticipation.

"Charlotte is friendly with Madeline Carlisle. She was a customer in her lingerie store here in D.C., but they've become friends. Good friends. Madeline doesn't give many interviews, but I can get you an exclusive, one-on-one with the senator's wife."

Roman's eyes gleamed with excitement and Chase's anticipation heightened, the thrill of a big story tantalizing him, arousing and heightening all his instincts. "Roman?"

His brother glanced up. "Yeah?"

Chase wasn't a man comfortable or good at expressing his feelings. His brothers were used to his long silences. They understood him better than anyone. He inclined his head. "Thanks."

16

Roman studied him through hooded eyes. "I'd say I owe you this one, but you'd probably haul off and deck me. Let's just say you're damn good, you deserve it, and leave it at that."

Chase nodded. "Fine by me."

"Last thing," Roman said as the elevator door reopened and the dark parking garage appeared. "D.C. isn't just good for political intrigue. It's got its share of willing women as well."

Chase frowned. "I thought you were happily married."

"I am. But you, big brother, aren't."

Sloane Carlisle attempted to pair her beloved fuchsia minidress with a staid black jacket, then cringed at the result. A Betsey Johnson original was meant to be seen, not covered. With regret, she relegated the outfit to the back of her closet along with the rest of her retro wear. She couldn't possibly put on such an outrageous color, short skirt, or bared-back halter. Not tomorrow, the day her senator father would announce his decision to accept the presidential candidate's offer to be his running mate in the next election.

She sighed and pulled out a powder blue Chanel suit and laid it on her bed. Though not her preference, the conservative choice was much more appropriate for Senator Carlisle's oldest daughter. Although Sloane often felt like the odd sibling out in a political family that enjoyed the spotlight, she understood the necessity for thinking before she dressed, spoke, or acted, just in case the press was sniffing out a story. And Sloane always performed as her family expected.

Twenty minutes later and half an hour early, she stood outside her father's hotel suite. Her parents had set up temporary residence in the D.C. hotel, leaving their home in New York State behind. And now they planned one last intimate family gathering before the media frenzy began.

She was about to knock when the sound of angry whispers carried toward her.

"I will not stand by and see twenty years of hard work disintegrate before my eyes." She recognized the voice of Franklin Page, her father's campaign manager, right-hand man, and long-time friend.

Frank frequently overreacted in order to prevent a crisis, and his bellowing didn't frighten her now. She raised her hand to knock on the door, which had been left open a sliver, when Frank's assistant, Robert Stone, spoke, preventing her from intruding.

"You say this Samson man claims to be Sloane's father?" He snorted, his disbelief evident.

"He more than claims."

Sloane sucked in a startled breath and clenched her fists. His words couldn't possibly be true. Jacqueline and Michael Carlisle were her biological parents. She had no reason to believe otherwise. But her stomach rolled and nausea threatened.

"Does he have proof?" Robert asked in a voice so low Sloane had to strain to hear and she missed Frank's reply.

"Doesn't need any. Michael verified it." Frank spoke, this time loud enough for her to hear. "He just refuses to act in his own best interest and do anything about this Samson person." A brief pause followed. "Dammit, don't you know better than to leave the door open? Michael and Madeline will be back from shopping any minute. He can't hear what we have planned."

"Which is?"

"Give us some privacy and I'll explain everything. This man Samson is a threat to the campaign. And any threat has to be eliminated."

Frank bellowed, but he never made idle threats. Sloane swallowed hard just as the door slammed shut in her face, leaving her on the outside of her father's suite and, if Frank's words were true, on the outside of her own life.

By the time dinner finally ended, Chase had had more of his brother and sister-in-law's matrimonial happiness than he could stomach in one sitting. While Roman took a tired Charlotte home, Chase decided to check out the D.C. nightlife and the singles scene. After some asking around, he found the perfect hole-in-

19

the-wall bar around the corner from his hotel where he could kick back and relax.

He ordered a Miller Genuine Draft and took in the scenery, which consisted of a pool table, a small, scarred dance floor, varied beer signs hanging on old paneled walls, and not much else. Until the door opened and *she* walked inside, a vision in a dress so pink, so short, so bare, it ought to be illegal.

No matter what his brother thought, Chase wasn't a monk. He'd just kept his social life discreet in deference to his fatherlike status, and over the years, the habit stuck. Most recently he'd hooked up with Cindy Dixon, who lived in Hampshire, the next town over. They were friends who'd begun sleeping together when the whim struck, neither wanting to be indiscriminate in this day and age. The arrangement satisfied Chase physically, but no longer inspired him, so he wasn't surprised when this sexy siren captured his attention.

Russet-colored hair cascaded past her shoulders in thick waves, making him itch to run his fingers through the unruly strands. Chase tightened his grip around the bottle and let out a slow groan. One glance and he wanted to know her. All of her.

"She's a hot number, all right." The bartender swiped the counter down with his rag. "Don't think I've seen her in here before. I'd remember if I had."

Chase wouldn't be forgetting her anytime

soon. The combination of sultry sexiness in her appearance and the inherent vulnerability in her expression as she settled in beside him made one heck of an impression.

"What can I get you?" the bartender asked, leaning across the expanse of the bar, too close in Chase's biased opinion.

"Hmm." She pursed her lips as she thought. "Scotch straight up."

Chase cocked an eyebrow, surprised. He'd have voted for a cosmopolitan or a white-wine spritzer.

"You sure about that?" the bartender asked. "A big drink like that doesn't mix well with a little thing like you."

She squared her shoulders, clearly offended. "Last I heard, the customer was always right," she said in a haughty tone more due a blue blood or politician than the sprite she appeared to be.

Chase grinned. Obviously, he could add gumption to her list of attributes.

"It's your choice," the bartender replied. "Just don't say I didn't warn you when I have to confiscate your car keys."

"Then it's a good thing I took the Metro," she shot back.

"Point, to the lady." Chase laughed.

"Thank you," she said without bothering to look his way.

The bartender placed the glass filled with amber liquid in front of her. "Remember, I warned you." He headed for a new round of customers at the end of the bar.

She stared at the contents a moment before lifting the glass for an experimental sniff and wrinkled her nose. "Still smells as vile as the last time I tasted it," she said to herself.

Chase laughed. Again. Twice in a matter of minutes. A record for him. A testament to the staid life he lived and a tribute to this woman's effect on him. He was beyond intrigued. "Then why order it?" he asked her.

"Heavy-duty stuff for a heavy-duty night." She shrugged but didn't lift her stare from the glass.

Chase wasn't insulted. Her preoccupation was obvious and from her words, so was her pain.

"Bartender? Give me the same," Chase said when the other man glanced over.

"What are you doing?" she asked, surprised.

"Joining you. It's unhealthy to drink alone." She looked his way at last and a burst of raw sexual energy exploded inside him, knocking him off balance.

Apparently, he wasn't alone because gratitude and a helluva lot more flickered in her golden gaze. He thought he'd been prepared, but it had been too damn long since he'd felt anything beyond the ordinary for any woman or any thing. Since stepping off the plane in D.C. a few short hours ago, the world had opened up for him, offering myriad possibilities. He wanted her to be one of them.

"Here you go, buddy." The bartender slid the glass Chase's way. "She just became your responsibility," he said, and walked off to help the thickening crowd.

She flicked a long strand of copper hair back off her shoulder. "I can take care of myself."

"I'm sure you can." He raised his glass, waiting while she did the same. "Cheers."

She inclined her head. "Cheers. Wait. It's proper to toast before drinking, and I always do the proper thing. To . . ." She paused, nibbling on her full lower lip.

His mouth watered, since he wanted nothing more than to suck that luscious, full pout into his mouth and taste her. "To?" he prompted.

"Life's dirty secrets." She clinked her glass against his.

The sound echoed inside him as did the raw anguish he sensed inside her. "I'm a good listener," he said, then mentally kicked himself. He wasn't looking to be her friend, when he'd rather be her lover.

Instant attraction, instant lust. He'd never experienced the surge quite so strongly before. He wasn't about to walk away from it now. Not on the night that represented the beginning of his new life. To hell with his usual sense of caution. It was time to leave the noble Chase Chandler behind and act on his desires.

"Thanks, but . . . I'd rather not talk." The flickering in her gaze told him she desired something more. Something from him.

Something he was all too willing to give.

Sloane stared into the stranger's seductive blue eyes. A woman could get lost in that serious, intent gaze. The man had a hidden fire deep inside him, something akin to what burned inside her. Dying to escape. Tonight. And her stomach churned with possibilities.

She lifted the butterscotch-colored liquid to her lips, taking a sip, never breaking eye contact. Because she'd had scotch with her roommate at school, she was prepared for the distinctive taste and the burning sensation going down. Warmth flowed through her veins, due more to his stare than the fiery liquor.

He raised his glass and matched her drink, a sexy smile curving his lips. She'd said she didn't want to talk. Obviously, he respected her wishes. She liked that about him.

His passionate stare held on to hers. She searched the blue depths as if they held the secrets to life. They didn't, of course. Those were held by the adults who withheld information from their children. She didn't doubt Michael Carlisle's motive. It was hard to think of him as her father now. It was just as hard not to.

As any parent does, he'd always claimed to act in his girls' best interests. But he'd screwed up this time because Sloane wasn't one of *his* girls. And the decision not to tell her about her parentage shouldn't have been his to make. She wondered what the media would think if they knew the perfect senator lived a lie.

She nearly laughed aloud. Sloane Carlisle lived a lie. Hell, Sloane *was* the lie. As a result, she didn't know who she was or where she fit in. She'd never known. At least now she understood why.

Why she wanted to run free, when her family was content with the restrictive boundaries imposed by the press and, by this time tomorrow, the Secret Service.

Why she hated being forced to conform in dress and personality, while her stepmother, sisters, and *father* reveled in formal attire and convention.

Sloane was different because she wasn't one of them. She didn't know who she was and, for tonight, she didn't care. There had always been a wanton woman inside her, and she wanted to set the long-repressed Sloane free.

"I've always thought talking's overrated," the stranger said at last.

"Me too." Tomorrow she wouldn't agree. But tonight she wanted to forget.

She deliberately brushed her arm against his. The electricity was scorching, reaching into the pit of her stomach while arousing vibrations beckoned. He leaned close. A whisper breath away. Within kissing distance, making her want to let go of her inhibitions.

Sloane Carlisle had never so much as stepped outside the bounds of propriety. She dated men she knew, men her family approved of, and she didn't sleep with strangers.

But she'd always wanted to test the unknown waters. Stay out past curfew. Approach this sexy man and take her chances.

And since *his* rough, gravelly voice set off white-hot arrows of fire inside her, she intended to take advantage of the desire licking at her veins. She was primed for this adventure.

She inhaled deeply. His musky male scent mixed intoxicatingly with the hint of liquor on his breath and she licked her lips, imagining she was tasting his.

His eyes darkened with banked arousal. "So we're on the same page?" he asked.

She couldn't mistake his meaning. Didn't want to. She placed her hand over his, lacing her fingertips through his strong, lean fingers, feeling his roughened skin.

"Word for word," she promised, barely recognizing the rough timbre of her voice.

He rose, reached into his pocket, peeled off a single bill, and left a twenty on the bar to cover their drinks. "My hotel's around the corner."

So he was a tourist. Even better. She wouldn't have to risk running into him again after tonight. She rose, leaving her drink behind.

She didn't need the alcohol for courage. Sloane Whatever-Her-Last-Name-Really-Was was 100 percent behind this decision. It was about time she acted on true instinct and rebelled against all the things in her life that had constrained her.

She placed her hand inside his. Tomorrow she'd return to the real world. Tonight was about indulging in the fantasies she'd only dreamed of when she thought she was Senator Carlisle's firstborn daughter.

Chapter Two

Sloane had plenty of time to back out on the walk to the hotel, but she hadn't come this far to change her mind now. His hand held hers tight, and as they made their way into the lobby, she realized no one was looking their way. Without her famous parents by her side, no one in D.C. ever gave her a second glance.

He paused, turning toward her. In his eyes, she saw the same desire pulsing inside her. "I need to stop by the front desk." He left her for a moment to speak to the clerk, then joined her once more.

Her heart pounded hard in her chest as they entered the elevator and the doors closed behind them.

His intense gaze met hers. "I didn't go out tonight looking for this, but" — he shrugged as if unsure how to continue — "I'm glad I ran into you."

She smiled, understanding what he meant. She hadn't come to the bar looking for a one-night stand, merely to forget her troubles or at least drown them for a little while. But one look into his eyes and she'd been captivated.

For her, the night could have had no other ending. "I wasn't on any kind of manhunt myself." She let out a self-conscious laugh. "But I'm glad I found you too."

He braced one hand against the wall above her shoulder. He was tall, his presence over-powering, and yet his calm demeanor and slow, easy manner made her feel comfortable. Safe. And mesmerized by those gorgeous blue eyes, she was able to forget everything but him. And that, Sloane realized, was her main objective.

"I think it's about time we exchange first names." A persuasive smile tilted his lips.

First names. She could handle that, she thought, until she realized Sloane was too distinctive, too recognizable in Washington, since her father was planning to put his hat in the proverbial ring. "Faith," she said, using her middle name.

"Pretty," he said in a gruff voice. He twirled a strand of hair around his finger, the light tug against her scalp curiously arousing. "I'm Chase."

She grinned. "It suits you. Don't ask me why."

Laughing, he wrapped an arm around her waist and pulled her close. His masculine scent surrounded her, a potent aphrodisiac. His head dipped lower, but before he could make a move, the elevator doors glided open, leaving her lips tingling, waiting for the touch of the unknown.

Grasping her hand, he led her to his room, and after pulling out his card key, he let them into a suite. The bedroom was obviously beyond the open door in the corner. Although the living area smelled and looked like an impersonal hotel room, when he stepped toward her, he dispelled the cold. He pulled her into his arms. With his molten gaze and overpowering physical presence, he cradled her in intense heat.

His eyes held hers as he lowered his head and kissed her for the first time. His lips were gentle yet firm, no hesitancy or insecurity in this man's touch. Though a stranger, he acted as an anchor during this storm in her life. He enabled her to relax and feel safe, let her grab onto him and accept everything he offered. She kissed him back, giving herself in return.

His hands came to rest on her cheeks, holding her head so he could devour her lips. He nibbled, drawing her lower lip into his mouth and deepening the kiss with broad sweeps of his tongue. With each successive stroke, fire burned stronger in her belly and the urge to touch him grew. She pulled his shirt from the waistband of his jeans and rested her hands against his heated skin.

He exhaled on a low groan, sliding his hands through her hair and trailing moist, damp kisses down her cheek, lingering against her throat. He was blocking out everything, all the disbelief, the pain, the hurt, and the anguish of today, until she could think of nothing but him. Her nipples puckered and her breasts grew heavy, while between her legs, slick moisture dampened her panties.

She tilted her head back to give him greater access to her throat and he sucked harder on her sensitive flesh, drawing a direct connection to more aroused body parts. A wash of sensation rushed over her and she gripped his waist harder in response.

"Oh yes." As if from a distance, she heard her voice, raw, hoarse, and full of desire.

"You like?" he asked.

She forced her heavy eyelids open to meet his hot stare. "Rhetorical question, right?"

A seductive grin lifted his lips and he dipped his head once more, this time to soothe the sensitive flesh of her neck with his tongue.

"Mmm." The man definitely had a way about him, Sloane thought.

"Faith."

It took her a moment to register that he was talking to her. "Yes?"

"Nothing. I just like the sound of your name."

She smiled, wishing he were calling her by her real name; wishing his rough voice would call out *Sloane* as he came inside her. Emboldened by the byplay between them, she raked her fingernails higher, rasping against his chest and hair-roughened skin. "I hope you like that too."

Before he could reply, a loud knock interrupted them. "I've got it." He strode to the door like the confident male he was, heedless of his untucked shirt or disheveled hair. He opened it a crack, and Sloane realized he was looking out for her privacy.

She appreciated his chivalry, considering this didn't mean anything more to him than a one-night stand.

"I'll take it," she heard him say. Then he turned back toward her, pushing a room service tray into the room, and kicked the door closed behind him.

"What's that?" she asked, taking in the two glasses and the champagne bottle in an ice bucket.

"You didn't strike me as the type of woman who indulges in one-night stands very often. So I wanted to make this . . . more special." To her surprise, a red flush rose to his cheeks.

Embarrassment. He'd gone out of his way to make this nice for her and he was embarrassed by the gesture. She stepped forward, more confident in her stride. "What makes you think this isn't my normal MO?" she asked, truly curious.

"It's a hunch and I'm usually accurate. Because despite the sexy dress, your speech is refined, your expression was sometimes hesitant, and by the look in those eyes, you're running from some deep, dark secret. It could be a lousy day, a lost job, but you're looking to get away from it all. You just don't jump into bed with strange men every day. I'd stake my life on it," he said with all the confidence of a cocky male.

"All this from one look?"

He grinned. "I'm a journalist. Observation is my specialty. What's yours?"

"Interior design," she said on autopilot, unable to think about anything except this revelation.

A reporter of any kind could wreak havoc with her father's presidential plans, and despite the hurt and betrayal lingering inside her, she loved the man. All the more reason to keep her real name from Chase.

She inched forward on her high heels. "You must be very good at your job because you're right. This isn't an everyday occurrence," she admitted. One trick she'd learned from her parents was to feed reporters as much truth as possible so as not to make them more wary.

"I like being right."

She laughed. "Which makes you a typical man."

"Right now I'd settle for being your man. Drink?" He gestured to the champagne with a sweep of his hand.

His thoughtfulness still pleased her. "I'd rather pick up where we left off and save the champagne till later." More honesty, Sloane thought. She wanted him as much now if not more than before.

Grabbing her hand, he walked to the oversize chair in the corner and sat down. "Join me." He tugged on her hand, his meaning clear.

She drew a deep breath and settled one knee

on either side of his thighs as she lowered herself to sit on his lap. The bulge in his jeans was obvious, pulsing deliciously between her legs, and his eyes were dilated with restrained need. Sloane didn't want or need the restraint.

She locked her arms around his neck. "Kiss me, Chase. Make me forget," she murmured.

"Make you forget what?"

She didn't want to answer. She wanted him to kiss her instead, so she leaned forward and locked her lips solidly against his.

But when she shifted in his lap and her pelvis came into intimate contact with his groin, kissing became secondary to overwhelming desire. He stood with her in his arms, his mouth never leaving hers, and he strode into the bedroom. Her heart thudded hard, waves rushing over and around her, as anticipation and need grew.

He placed her on the bed and she came to her knees. They worked together, first unbuttoning his shirt and tossing it aside, letting her revel in his muscular chest. Reaching behind her, he pulled the tie on her halter top, letting it fall forward, revealing her bare breasts. She should have been embarrassed, but his hungry gaze devoured her, and a low growl of appreciation rose in his throat, leaving no doubt he liked what he saw. Then his hands cupped her breasts, her nipples pressing deeply into his palms.

Heated sensations rippled through her and

she exhaled a low groan. He reached for the waistband of her skirt at the same time she grabbed for the button on his jeans; between them, they shed their clothing along with their inhibitions.

Sloane found her back propped against the pillows, Chase straddling her waist, one hand holding hers above her head. While he locked her in an erotic position, his touch was gentle and his grip was loose enough that she could break his hold if she wanted to. She didn't.

Her position aroused her too much and she liked the way he studied her, as if he could read her mind and provide every intimate touch she desired.

"I want to be inside you." His hard length rubbing against her stomach proved his words.

"Go for it," she said, and her hips jerked upward of their own volition as moisture slickened her thighs and a tide of arousal rose inside her.

"Not until I protect you."

That took her off guard. "Something I need protection from?" she asked lightly. She'd been so caught up in wanting to block out the painful truth she'd learned today, she hadn't been thinking clearly. "I'm on the pill, but . . ."

"Hell, honey, with the life I've lived, you have nothing to worry about. I just believe in safety first and kids never." He slid off the bed and strode toward the bathroom.

The knot in her stomach eased. She didn't

know why, had no reason to trust, but she believed him. And once again, she appreciated his gallantry during a one-night stand. After all, many guys wouldn't care what they left behind. Chase did. There was something different about this man. Something caring and uniquely special, she thought.

He returned as quickly as he'd left, and she couldn't help but admire his physique, the broad shoulders, narrow waist, and the other impressive parts of him standing at attention. No longer distracted by her thoughts, she was now completely focused once more. How could she not be with such a gorgeous man standing over her?

No guy had ever incited such overwhelming, instant lust. Then again, no man had ever looked at her as if he couldn't get enough. Chase did.

He held the foil packet in his hand and quickly took care of protection; then he came over to her and grinned, that sexy, intense smile causing her to catch her breath.

"Enough waiting, don't you think?"

She laughed, even as her body burned, on fire with wanting him. "More than enough," she agreed.

With a low growl, he kissed her. His mouth was hot and greedy and his hands were busy as he nudged her legs apart and poised himself intimately against her. Entry and fulfillment were so very close, but instead of thrusting, he reached down with his hands.

His long fingers dipped inside her, arousing her with his talented touch. She moaned, arching her hips and drawing him in deeper, forcing her muscles to contract around his finger, but it wasn't enough. She wanted something more.

He must have understood because he withdrew, and then he finally spread her thighs and drove himself deep with one long, satiny stroke. He filled her and immediately brought her close to the edge of climaxing.

So hard, so fast, and he felt so right. She closed her eyes as he withdrew, letting her feel every hard and slick ridge of him before pumping inside her again. She matched his rhythm quickly, the synchronization between them amazing, almost as if they'd been together like this before.

"Sweet heaven," Chase muttered. No woman should feel this good. Especially not one he just met, one who didn't know his likes or his dislikes. Yet, *she* knew all the right moves to turn him on. He saw so much in those green eyes of hers. They'd connected and he felt it in her body, in every slick inch he stroked inside her.

She was feminine and warm where skin touched skin, her nipples hard and arousing against his chest. She met him thrust for thrust, bringing him higher each time their bodies met and he burned with the need to let go. But not alone. He wanted them to be together when they found that ultimate burst of raw sexual satisfaction. Reaching between them, he slid his finger between her moist folds to increase the pressure and make her come.

He was rewarded by a shuddering groan and she rolled her hips, seeking to deepen the stimulating tension. Her thighs were clenched, her muscles cushioning him in wet heat. With each successive thrust, he was on edge himself, holding back only by sheer force of will.

"Chase."

His name on her lips surprised him. For as intimate as they'd been, as close as he felt, talking had been minimal. He forced his heavy eyelids open.

Dilated green eyes met his. "Roll over."

His eyes opened wide. "What?"

"After today, I need to be in control," she explained as she nudged him with her body, and together they flipped positions until he was flat on his back while she straddled his thighs. A shudder racked her body as she took him deeper than he'd been before. "Oh, God."

He swallowed hard because he felt it too, but along with sensation came knowledge. For her, tonight was about so much more than easy sex. She was running from something and using him to forget. But his body wasn't about to give him time to ask questions.

And with her gorgeous face, and full breasts poised over him, he wasn't about to argue. "Whatever works for you," he told her.

A flash of gratitude flickered over her features, and then, thankfully, she started to move, rocking her hips and milking him with her inner muscles until the tidal wave started to rise once more. Without warning, she stretched over him, kissing him full on the lips while her hips continued a systematic, gyrating movement. One that kept up the tension and let it build higher as her feminine mound pressed intimately against him, working him in a way he'd never felt before.

With each thrust of her pelvis grinding downward, she let out a soft, arousing moan. She was close and so was he, and she kept up the insistent pressure, bringing him closer and closer until his world imploded. Now he had but one focus: this woman and the intense sensations she pulled from him as her body continued to milk him, long after he'd come.

Even as he finally started his slow descent back to reality, she continued to shudder above him in one long, continual climax. Minutes later, Chase's breathing returned to a slower, more manageable rhythm. So did his thoughts. He was thirty-seven years old and he'd never had that kind of mind-blowing sex with any woman ever before.

Never. And he needed a minute to absorb the feeling.

But before he could think, she rolled over and started to rise, taking him completely by surprise.

"Wait." He reached out, but his hand merely skimmed her bare back. "What's the rush?"

She turned, but he couldn't see more than her mass of tangled hair and elegant profile. "I thought you'd want me to go."

She let out a laugh that was so obviously forced, it touched something inside him.

"This way we could avoid the awkward morning after," she said by way of explanation.

He understood why she'd take the easy way, but he wasn't finished with her just yet. And he hoped she wasn't finished wanting him. "I'd rather you stay." He rose onto his elbow and ran a finger down her spine. "If that's what you want."

She pivoted back to him, shock and confusion evident in her eyes and her open expression. He understood since he felt it all too.

"This is crazy," she said.

"I agree." He ran a hand through his hair and waited.

"I'll stay," she said at last.

"Good." He excused himself for a quick trip to the bathroom, and when he returned, he pulled her into his arms.

"Sometimes crazy's good, I guess." She laughed and her body vibrated, warm and delicious, against him.

He rested his cheek against her long hair, inhaling the fragrant strands. "I needed crazy tonight. Up till now, my life has always been predictable." He thought about the same routine he'd followed for the last nineteen years. "Expected," he continued, recalling raising his siblings and providing the perfect example for them. "And mostly lived for others."

"Sounds pretty much like my life," she murmured.

He brushed her unruly hair off his face and let her snuggle deeper into him. He didn't want to think how bizarre it was that he wanted to spend the night holding on to this soft, willing female. For once, he only wanted to do what felt right for him. "I promised myself tonight was the start of a new life. One I'd live only for me."

She sighed. "That sounds wonderful."

"So why don't you live by my example?" he asked. Chase hadn't a clue what was bothering her or dragging her down, but like him, she'd obviously allowed herself to be free tonight. She shouldn't go back to a life of confinement, or one lived for others.

"I have people relying on me," she said drowsily. "Even if my entire life has been a lie, I'll still be expected to do the right thing." Her voice grew sleepier as she spoke.

His curiosity was aroused. Not just because he was a reporter and ambiguous statements led to questions, but because she intrigued him. Too much. He was just beginning his search for fulfillment. He didn't need someone else's problems or needs weighing on him. He'd had too much of that in his life and he was too prone to doing right by others. It seemed to be the Chandler way.

So it was a damn good thing they'd be going their separate ways come the morning, he thought, drifting off himself.

The soft sound of crying woke Chase from a deep, sated sleep. It took him a minute to get his bearings, and when he did, he realized he was in a dark hotel room in D.C. with a woman he'd met the night before. A woman who'd blown him away with an incredible sexual encounter. One he'd begged to stay when she'd tried to leave.

An uncomfortable feeling of guilt and unease tore at him. She'd rolled to the far end of the bed and he reached out to touch her shoulder. "Regrets?" he asked her. Because shockingly, he had none.

"About last night? No. About my life and the way I've lived it? Oh yes."

The vise clamping around his heart loosened. Regrets and recriminations were something he didn't want to deal with. "There's not much you can do about the past except put it behind you and go forward."

She exhaled hard. "Wise words."

"What can I say? I'm a wise guy."

"Funny, but you struck me as more of a straight shooter."

He caught her joke and chuckled. "Think you can get back to sleep?"

"If you rub my back, maybe."

She wiggled toward him and he did as she asked, massaging the tense muscles in her shoulders.

"Mmm."

He nuzzled the soft, fragrant skin at her neck. She smelled and tasted delicious. "I was about to say the same thing."

Pulling himself up, he lay over her, his stomach aligned with her back, his groin settled between her buttocks. She let out a purr of contentment mingled with satisfaction and he hardened in an instant.

"I know what would really help me sleep," she said, wriggling her hips beneath him, before clenching her legs, capturing his erection between them.

Her desire was obvious. "You want me to exhaust you, huh?"

"Oh yes."

Chase didn't need a second invitation. He reached for the condom he'd left on the nightstand earlier, just in case, and quickly sheathed himself before poising himself to enter her. "Like this, okay?" he asked, his face buried in the nape of her neck as he slowly entered her moist femininity.

"Oooh," she said on a slow moan. "This is perfect."

And it was. Chase didn't understand it, this inherent trust and understanding between them, nor did he question it. He figured it had everything to do with his decision to live life for himself, and her decision to do the same, if only for one night.

After they'd sated their desire once more, she fell asleep beside him, hair sprawled on the pillow, completely relaxed. He'd done that for her. Just as she'd done something for him. She'd helped him take his first step in setting himself free of responsibility and constraint.

Tomorrow they'd part ways, but not before he ordered them room service, shared breakfast, and feasted with her, and on her, one last time.

But when he awoke, courtesy of the sun streaming through the windows, bathing the room in light, his visitor was gone. Chase rubbed a hand over his eyes, wondering if he'd imagined the entire affair.

But her scent lingered in the air and he'd woken up aroused, ready to reach for her again. He hadn't imagined her or the incredible night they'd shared. She'd left him with a damn good memory to take with him as he went after his dreams and started his new life.

But a part of him was disappointed they didn't have more time. That same part of him wished they'd met at a different point in his life, under other circumstances. If he were a different person and hadn't had to raise his brothers, he wondered if they would have stood a chance. He pinched the bridge of his nose, lost in ridiculous thoughts.

"Snap out of it," he muttered. As he rose and headed for a hot shower, he couldn't shake her from his mind.

Recalling the first time she'd tried to slip out on him, Chase forced himself to laugh now. She'd managed to avoid the awkward morning after, after all.

Chapter Three

Sloane returned home to her apartment around seven a.m. A quick shower and change and she was on her way back to the hotel where her life had been altered so drastically. And not just because she'd discovered Michael Carlisle wasn't her father, but because she'd finally begun freeing herself from the constraints in her life. She'd allowed herself to act on her own impulse and desire. And in doing so, she'd found Chase.

A man with whom she'd spent just one night, but one she'd never forget. Sloane wasn't into one-night stands. She didn't have sex for sex's sake. And she hadn't planned to pick up a man at the bar last night, at least not until she'd looked into Chase's slumberous blue eyes. With a glance, he'd compelled her to disregard her usual reserve. By ordering the same drink she had, despite the fact that he had a full beer sitting in front of him, he'd intrigued her. By offering to listen, he'd won her over. Whether or not that had been his intent, she didn't care. He hadn't struck her as a guy on the make, and after spending the night in his arms, she knew her first impression had been right.

Not only was he gorgeous, but he had an innate understanding of her needs. How else could she explain the champagne they'd never drunk? The way he hadn't let her leave? And then there was the Karma involved. Fate had paired her with a man who, by his own admission, had always done the predictable thing. Lived his life for others. Like she had. Even not knowing more details, Sloane realized they had more in common than she'd have expected from a one-night stand.

But it *was* a one-night stand, and though she'd have her memories and fantasies to relive later, for now she had to put him behind her. More pressing family matters called to her now. But she wished Chase well on the start of his new life and knew she'd think of him often as she forged ahead, trying to decipher hers.

She paused at her parents' hotel room door, unsure how to handle this confrontation. Her father would be in last-minute meetings and reviewing his speech, but Madeline would be inside.

Her stepmother was a beautiful woman, both inside and out, and with her normally calm demeanor, she was the perfect politician's wife. She'd also been a wonderful mother, stepping in upon Jacqueline's death, when Sloane was eight. To Madeline's credit, she'd never treated Sloane any differently than her real daughters — Sloane's twin sisters, Eden and Dawn — and Sloane adored her in return.

Which made the lie even more difficult for

Sloane to understand. She shook her head and shored up her courage, knocking on the door, which swung open within seconds.

"Where have you been?" Madeline grabbed Sloane's hand and pulled her into a motherly hug. "When you didn't show up for dinner last night, your father and I were worried sick."

So much for her stepmother's calm demeanor, Sloane thought as she squeezed her back. Although Madeline was dressed for the press conference, looking very Jacqueline Kennedyesque with her dark bobbed hair and beautifully made-up face, her concern was etched in the lines around her eyes.

Despite having good reason for ditching last night's family dinner, Sloane felt guilty for making her worry. "I'm sorry." She twisted her fingers together, searching for the right words. "But I needed to be alone. To think."

"About?" Madeline brushed Sloane's hair off her shoulder, the way she used to do when Sloane was a little girl. "You can talk to me."

Sloane nodded. "I think we'd better sit." She followed her stepmother to the sofa in the outer area of the suite, the same room in which she'd heard Frank and Robert talking last night. "Are we alone?"

Madeline nodded. "Your father's meeting with Frank in his room and the twins went shopping."

"I hope you gave them a money limit," Sloane said, laughing. Typical seventeen-year-old girls, her sisters loved to shop, and when they were at home in upstate New York, they constantly grumbled about the lack of decent malls.

"I gave them cash and confiscated the credit cards." Madeline's eyes twinkled with laughter but sobered quickly. "Tell me what's wrong."

The facade of joking fell away. Butterflies rose in Sloane's stomach and she drew a deep breath. "I showed up for dinner last night. I was half an hour early and you and Dad weren't back from shopping yet." She clenched and unclenched her fists, fighting the nausea and the fear. "Frank was with Robert and they were arguing about a threat to Dad's campaign."

Madeline sat up straighter, her eyes wide and focused. "What kind of threat?"

"The worst kind. A personal one." Sloane bit down on the inside of her cheek. It was harder to repeat the words than she'd thought. "A man named Samson claims to be my biological father."

"Oh damn."

Sloane's eyes opened wide. Madeline Carlisle didn't curse. Sloane did. So did her dad, as did Eden and Dawne, but Madeline believed someone in the family had to set a proper example. Her cursing wasn't a good sign.

"So it's true?" Sloane asked in a small voice.

Madeline grasped onto Sloane's clenched hands and held on tight. "Yes, honey. It's true."

Sloane hadn't realized it, but in her heart, she'd held out hope that Madeline would deny the claim. Instead, she'd acknowledged her worst fears. She fought back the lump in her throat, determined to get through this without falling apart.

Madeline met her gaze, and despite everything, Sloane felt the love her stepmother had always shown her.

"You need an explanation." Madeline's voice cracked, but she didn't pause. "Your mother and I were best friends. I would have done anything for her. You know that. In fact, I did. I married your father so I could raise you the way your mother would have wanted."

Sloane squeezed her stepmother's hand. "You couldn't have done any more." Except tell her the truth, Sloane thought, but this conversation was difficult and even Madeline seemed to need reassurance. "You never made me feel like you loved me any less than Eden and Dawne. I love you for that."

Madeline blinked back tears. "I love you too. And I love your father. Although, I didn't fall in love with him until long after we'd married."

Sloane smiled. She already knew the story of Michael and Madeline's marriage. They often told people how they'd come to love one another as they jointly raised Sloane. But that didn't explain the rest of the missing pieces. "How was lying best for me?"

Madeline raised steepled fingers to her lips

and paused in thought. "Your mother was born and raised in Yorkshire Falls. It's about twenty minutes from our home in Newtonville. She had been in college and was home on summer break when she fell in love with a man named Samson Humphrey."

So that was his last name. Her head hurt and she inhaled slowly, trying to ease the pain with no success.

"What happened between my mother and . . . Samson?" She forced herself to say the name, as if speaking would help her accept the painful truth.

Madeline shook her head. "It's a long story. But Jacqueline's father, your grandfather, was a politician who thought his blood was bluer than it really was. He didn't think Samson was good enough for his daughter, and worried about him hindering his career."

"Because Grandfather Jack was a senator too." She didn't know the older man because he'd died when she was a child.

Madeline nodded. "Your grandfather did some digging and came up with some dirt on Samson's family and used it to bribe the man into staying away from your mother."

Sloane shook her head in disbelief, trying to absorb all this information that had been hidden from her for years.

"Presumably, Samson felt he had no choice."

"Or he was weak," Sloane muttered.

"Not if your mother loved him, honey. And

she did. So there must have been something good in him." Madeline met Sloane's gaze.

The older woman's eyes shimmered with tears and emotion. Sadness? Regret? Guilt? Sloane couldn't be certain.

"Of course he was a good man," Madeline insisted in a forceful tone. "After all, look at all the good in you."

Sloane swallowed hard. She wasn't about to think about herself now. If she did, she'd fall apart, and she wanted to hear the end of this story first.

"And another thing" — Madeline blotted her eyes with the back of her hand before continuing — "your mother was devastated when he broke things off. She loved him so much. And when she realized she was pregnant, she packed to go back to Samson."

Sloane leaned forward in her seat, the story playing out as if it were someone else's history being discussed, not her own. "What happened?"

"Your grandfather didn't care. He admitted he'd bribed Samson to get rid of him. Jacqueline believed in him enough to know Samson hadn't dumped her because he was greedy. When her father threatened to destroy Samson's family if she returned to him, she was defeated. Just as Samson had obviously been." Madeline raised her hands in the air, then dropped them again, her frustration evident.

"This is unreal."

"I know. And to this day, I don't know the secret he held over Samson. Your grandfather took it to his grave, but it was enough to make your mother stay. To protect your father. Your real father, I mean."

Sloane's head was spinning. Recognizing the dizziness and aura she associated with a migraine, she rose and walked to the courtesy bar set up in the corner and poured herself a diet Coke. "Can I get you anything?" she asked Madeline.

"No. I'd rather just get this all out. Though your father will kill me for doing it when he's not here."

Sloane understood the guilt in her stepmother's voice. She knew her parents never lied to one another. They'd set a great example for their children. Until now. "Did he ever plan on telling me?" She returned to the sofa, taking a huge sip of cola before sitting down.

"He wanted to. So did I. But he just didn't know how."

Madeline's urgent voice begged Sloane to believe, but the evidence was too damning. "The man knows how to micromanage the smallest detail of a campaign, but he couldn't look me in the eye and tell me he's not my father?"

Madeline stared down at her hands. "He loves you. He didn't want to lose you or your trust, and neither did I. Do you want to know how Michael came into the picture?"

Apparently, Madeline was smart enough not

to ask how much of Sloane they'd lost now that she'd learned the truth. A good thing, since Sloane wouldn't know how to answer. "Tell me," she forced out.

"Michael, your father — and he thinks of himself that way — was in love with your mother. They were family friends, friends bred through politics. Michael's father and your grandfather were colleagues. It wasn't a hardship when the two senators arranged a marriage between him and your mother. You would have a name and Michael would have your grandfather's influential backing during his start in politics."

"A political bargain," Sloane said in disgust.

"But *you* were never thought of that way. Your mother loved you, your father — Michael — loved you both. He would have married your mother without the bargaining chip. That was your grandfather's doing." Madeline sighed. "I know this sounds sordid —"

"Because it *is* sordid." Sloane placed her glass on the table and rose to pace the room. "I can't believe this."

"Which is why we could never bring ourselves to tell you."

Sloane sighed, then turned to her stepmother, but Madeline spoke first.

"What else did Robert say?" A hint of fear crept into her voice.

Sloane's right temple throbbed. She paused to take an Advil she kept in her bag. Then she rubbed her forehead and focused on last night's overheard conversation. "Robert asked if Samson had proof and Frank said he didn't need any. That Michael verified his claim."

Madeline sighed. "What else?"

Sloane closed her eyes and tried to remember more. Frank had said Samson was a threat to Michael's campaign, but her father refused to act in his own best interest and do something about Samson. And Frank hadn't wanted Michael to hear what they had planned.

Because they obviously intended to eliminate the threat.

Sloane sat up in her seat, her heart pounding hard in her chest. Frank wanted to eliminate Samson. Before he went public with the news of her parentage? Sloane wondered. Was that what Frank meant by Samson being a threat to the campaign? He didn't want the public to know that Senator Michael Carlisle had lied to his daughter for almost thirty years. Because then they would think the senator would be capable of lying to them. It was the only thing that made sense.

"What is it?" Madeline asked, obviously sensing Sloane's distress.

"Nothing. I just . . . I need a minute to think." Sloane gripped the glass once more, trying to remain calm.

Frank had threatened Samson, the man she'd just discovered was her biological father, which presented her with an emotional minefield and imminent danger. And Sloane had no doubt Frank didn't issue idle threats, especially if his life's work was at stake, and he considered Michael Carlisle's bid for the vice presidency, and eventually the presidency, his mission.

It was the Carlisle family mission as well. All of them had worked hard for this moment. Even knowing the huge lie he'd told her, Sloane wouldn't allow anyone or anything to prevent her father from achieving his dreams.

But someone had to warn Samson that he was in danger, and there was no one else to do it but Sloane. She rolled the glass between her hands, the cool condensation dampening her skin. She had no choice but to find her biological father. Acknowledge their connection. She shivered at the thought, both unnerved and intrigued at the same time.

What would she do when she met him? Sloane wondered. Extend her hand and introduce herself, for one thing. Ask him what he wanted from her father, for another. Find out what kind of threat he posed. And hopefully be the one to diffuse any potential problem between him and her father's men.

But she couldn't reveal Frank's threat now or Madeline would never let Sloane go see the man. Not without the Secret Service following her, which would alert Frank and defeat her main purpose.

She sat forward to ease the cramping in her stomach, nerves threatening to overwhelm her.

She met her stepmother's silent stare. "I want to meet him." Sloane couldn't bring herself to call the man her father. She could barely bring herself to speak, let alone carry out her plan. One step at a time, she'd find the courage.

"You want to meet Samson?" Madeline asked, obviously taken off guard.

Sloane nodded.

Madeline inclined her head, taking time to think. "Okay."

"What?" Sloane had expected an argument.

"I've always known, even if your father didn't, that this day would come. And your mother, bless her heart, left a letter for you. She had no way of knowing she wouldn't live to see you grow up, but she was pragmatic and she planned ahead just in case." Madeline rose and walked over to where Sloane stood. "It's home. In the safe. And as soon as we're back there —"

"I can't wait. I want to meet him now."

"Now?" Madeline asked, startled. "Don't you want to take time and absorb the news? Talk to your father first?"

"No!" She wasn't ready to face Michael today. Not until she'd met her biological parent. Not until she warned him of any potential danger. And not until she'd secured the safety of her father's campaign. She had too much on her mind to deal with the emotions that would surely erupt if she had to confront him about his lie. "Is Samson still in Yorkshire Falls? Do you know?"

Frank would know, but Sloane couldn't tell

him anything. And Michael might know, but the same emotional considerations were involved. She just couldn't face her father now.

"Yorkshire Falls is as good a guess as any," Madeline said, resignation in her voice. "I'll explain things to your father. In the meantime, take my car," she said, reaching for her purse.

"I'll rent one." *Under an assumed name,* she thought, but Sloane didn't mention that. She couldn't afford anyone tracing her whereabouts. She pressed a hand against her stomach, but she couldn't still her raging case of nerves. "What about Dad's press conference?"

Madeline pulled her close and kissed her forehead. "If anyone asks, I'll say you're sick. Holed up in your room. Your father will cover for you too. What about your business?"

Sloane hadn't thought about her interior-design business since she'd fled this hotel last night. "I already took a long weekend off to be around for your visit. I guess I can put my clients off for a few more days." She didn't think it would take that long to find the man who was her real father.

"Okay, but I want you protected."

"No. No Secret Service. No detectives. No one. I need to do this alone." She folded her arms across her chest. She wasn't budging on this one. Not an inch.

"You have that look." Madeline's damp eyes twinkled.

"What look?"

"The one you'd get as a kid. *I'm not eating broccoli and you can't make me.* That look."

Sloane laughed. The memories she had with both Michael and Madeline were wonderful. She just wished they weren't based on one huge life-altering lie. "I didn't eat it, as I recall."

Her stepmother sighed. "So no Secret Service either. But you will check in? Often?"

"I promise."

They shared another hug and Sloane headed out the back elevator, avoiding the press that had begun to gather out front. She'd pack and be on her way.

To meet and warn Samson Humphrey.

At this moment, she didn't know which was more important.

After the press conference, where Senator Carlisle's oldest daughter was conspicuously absent, Chase followed Roman to meet Madeline Carlisle, who was busy shaking hands with her husband's supporters.

She took one look at Roman and a genuine smile replaced the one she'd obviously pasted on for the masses and she excused herself. "A family friend is here and I can't disappoint family," she said.

Roman laughed and pulled her aside. "You mean you've had enough handshaking for the day? You'd better get used to it."

"Don't I know it." Her warmth was unmistakable. "Who's this handsome devil next to you?" She turned to Chase and, without waiting for an introduction, said, "I'm Madeline Carlisle."

"Chase Chandler." He stepped forward and shook the woman's hand. "Congratulations."

"Thank you." Madeline looked him over, approval in her gaze. "Your mother is one lucky woman. Is the third brother as handsome?"

"Not if you ask us," Roman said wryly.

Chase laughed at his brother's dry sense of humor. "You're also fortunate. I saw your daughters and they're beautiful," he said of the twins.

Madeline beamed. "He's a charmer, just like you, Roman."

"Of course he is." Roman chuckled, then glanced around, seemingly searching for someone. "Where's Sloane?"

The smile on Madeline's face dimmed. "She's . . . not quite herself."

"Well, I hope she's feeling better soon." Roman took her hand. "Madeline, I've told you Chase publishes the *Yorkshire Falls Gazette*," he said, his concern turning to business matters. "It's Jacqueline's hometown and I told him I could persuade you to do an interview. Since you haven't done many to date, I was hoping you'd give my brother an exclusive."

"I'd be more than happy to follow any guidelines you set out," Chase explained. "I'm just looking for something extra. You have to know the public is interested in you. Your family is so politically perfect, the world would benefit from an inside look. And you'd get the opportunity to introduce the private side of your husband as seen from your perspective."

She narrowed her gaze, eyes focused on Chase. If she was waiting for him to blink or squirm, she'd be here a long time, but he understood her need to scrutinize him. Madeline Carlisle was known to protect her family and went overboard to guard the private parts of their lives despite the fishbowl in which they lived. No matter what politics dictated, she wouldn't give up an interview to just anyone.

"Are you as honorable as your brother and sister-in-law?" Madeline asked.

"More so." Roman grinned. "Not only did Chase raise me to be the outstanding gentleman I've become, but he followed the same rules himself." He slapped Chase on the back. "Honorable is Chase's middle name."

Ribbing aside, Roman had a point. Chase was known as the upstanding Chandler, the dutiful oldest brother. The honorable one. If he didn't count last night, Chase thought wryly. Taking the beautiful Faith to his hotel room and into his bed had been a departure from his normal upstanding moral code.

But she'd been different, just as their connection had been. Even now, he couldn't shake those beautiful green eyes from his mind or the sounds she made while he was deep inside her body. For a one-nighter, she'd made one hell of an impression.

Madeline grasped Chase by the elbow. "I'd like to speak to you and Roman alone. Away from prying eyes." She tipped her elegant head toward the people and reporters milling around, many waiting for her to extricate herself from them and make herself available once more.

Minutes later, they were in the Carlisles' suite, the door shut and locked behind them.

Chase waited until Madeline settled herself on the sofa before doing the same. He liked to study a person, take their measure, and he planned to do that to Madeline Carlisle now.

But Roman, his antsy younger brother, could never sit still and he paced around the room, picking up odds and ends before putting them down again and moving on. "What's going on?" he asked at last.

Madeline laced her hands together on her lap. Apparently, like Chase, she preferred to do business calmly. "I called Charlotte this morning."

"At the shop?" Roman asked from the other side of the room.

She nodded. "I wondered if either of you would be going home anytime soon. To Yorkshire Falls."

Chase didn't know the woman, but even to him, her question seemed odd. Roman and Charlotte commuted between their hometown and D.C., Roman's home base for work. Charlotte had her lingerie shop, Charlotte's Attic, in both towns. But why would Madeline Carlisle care?

"Unfortunately, we're in D.C. for the next week," Roman said. "Barring anything unexpected, work's got me busy here."

"That's what I thought Charlotte told me. What about you?" Her gaze strayed to Chase, and this time, she did the studying and her curiosity was evident. "Is that true for you too?" she asked.

"I'll be home tomorrow." Chase felt like he was being led someplace, but he hadn't any idea where. He pinched the bridge of his nose in thought but couldn't come up with any answers.

"Is there something I can do for you?" he asked, hoping she'd end the suspense.

She dug through her purse and pulled out an insert of pictures but didn't turn them over. "I need someone to watch out for my daughter."

"Sloane?" Roman asked before Chase could.

Madeline slid her finger back and forth over the top photo. "When I said she wasn't quite herself, I was serious. She's had some . . . disrupting personal news and she needs time alone." She raised her gaze to eye Chase once more and chewed on her bottom lip. "This has to be off the record."

"Of course." He wished he could see the picture, but she was keeping her cards close.

Madeline exhaled, obviously relieved. "Because I adore Charlotte and Roman, and because I consider myself a good judge of character, I'm trusting you with this information."

"You won't be sorry," he assured her. But he wondered if he would be. He stretched his hand over the back of the sofa and waited for her to continue.

She offered him a strained smile. "I hope not. You see, Sloane took off to regroup. She went to her mother's hometown. To *your* hometown," she said to Chase.

"Why?" Roman asked, jumping back into the conversation.

"Good question," Chase said.

"One with an easy answer. Yorkshire Falls is as quiet a place as you can get. Sloane thought she'd see where her mother grew up and maybe learn a few things about herself in the process."

Enigmatic, Chase thought. Senator Carlisle's daughter was searching for some R&R in his little small town? When all the family action was in D.C.? Didn't seem entirely plausible to him. "Where do I come in?"

"How do you feel about a quid pro quo?" Madeline asked.

Chase shrugged. "Depends on what's being exchanged."

"I do like your style." She tucked her hair behind one ear. "Here's the deal. You go home early and look out for my daughter. In return you'll get an exclusive interview with me when

64

this is all over. I'm not certain how long she'll be there, but I need you to make sure she doesn't get into trouble and doesn't call too much attention to herself. The last thing she needs is the press following her around."

Chase leaned forward in his chair and braced his arms on his knees. "What am I in all this?"

"When it comes to Sloane, you won't be a reporter, you'll be a friend." Madeline's eyes warmed to her idea. "And any information you want to use on our family, you'll get from me in our interview. We agreed this was all off the record, remember?"

He remembered, all right. He just felt extremely set up and cornered and didn't like it one bit. But Roman stood behind him, not objecting to Madeline's deal. Which meant Roman thought this idea had merit.

Chase scrubbed a hand over his face. "What about protection?" Chase was trained to take in every detail and he'd noticed the Secret Service agents in place around the room where the senator spoke. They had to be protecting Sloane as well.

But Madeline's next words killed that notion. "She slipped out alone. That's why she needs you."

He groaned. "I'm not a bodyguard. And forgive me for prying, but isn't Sloane a grown woman? Why does she need anyone to look out for her?" The more he thought about it, the more uncomfortable he became with the idea of getting involved with this woman's daughter in any way. He was a journalist, not a baby-sitter.

"She doesn't think she needs anyone. It's me. *I* need to know she's okay and has someone to lean on if it comes to that." Madeline backed up her emotional words by reaching for his hand and holding on tight.

But Chase still felt manipulated. "There's obviously a lot you aren't telling me."

"That's true. But if you want the exclusive interview, you won't ask too many questions. You'll just go home a day early, find Sloane, and look after her."

Chase frowned. "Whether she wants me to or not."

"Exactly. You're good-looking, charming. I'm sure it won't be too difficult to win her over." She patted his cheek. "Make use of those Chandler genes."

From her confident tone, Chase saw the woman behind the senator for the first time. He understood now she was a crucial partner in the man's climb to power. Yet, like his brother, he both liked and respected her. She obviously loved her children and would do anything for them — something Chase could relate to.

Family loyalty ran strong in the Chandler clan. Relating to her made it harder for Chase to say no.

Besides, the exclusive interview beckoned.

"When her time in Yorkshire Falls is over, you'll talk to me?"

Madeline nodded. "And if anything happens in the meantime . . . If any information needs to come from my husband's camp, you'll be given it first." She held out her hand to seal the bargain.

Chase had hoped to talk with Madeline this week, but obviously that wasn't her plan. He'd also hoped that by coming to D.C., he'd dig up something more on Senator Carlisle. If Sloane's disappearance was any indication, Chase was close to something huge. Something that he might just find at home, in Yorkshire Falls, with the senator's oldest daughter.

"Do we have a deal?" Madeline asked.

Chase placed his hand in hers, certain he could use this situation to his advantage somehow. "We have a deal."

She exhaled in pure unadulterated relief. "In case you haven't seen a close-up picture" — Madeline held out the photo she'd been zealously guarding — "this is Sloane."

Shock and disbelief rocked through his system as he glanced at the picture, and into the eyes of the woman he'd taken to bed the night before.

Chapter Four

Yorkshire Falls was the opposite of the nation's capital. Small-town USA was an apt description, Sloane thought. Her own hometown was a wealthy community with stately mansions and equally formidable trees. But as she walked down First Street, she took in the small shops and the people who'd congregated to talk, and she liked the homey, close-knit feel. And with each older man she passed, she wondered if she'd just seen Samson. Her father.

She'd left D.C. twenty-four hours ago, but it felt like a lifetime, thanks to the drastic change in scenery. With butterflies in her stomach, she entered a coffee shop named Norman's, located next to Charlotte's Attic, a store owned by the same woman her stepmother had befriended and wanted to introduce her to. A woman who crocheted handmade sexy bra-and-panty sets. If Sloane weren't in such a rush, she'd check the store out here. But she'd come on a mission to warn Samson he was in danger and she intended to accomplish her goal.

Inside Norman's, she was surrounded by a bird motif. Bird-houses, photos and paintings of bird species, all with a light, airy feel.

A large gray-haired woman walked up to her,

menu in hand. "Can I get you a table?"

"Actually, I'm looking for someone." Sloane smiled. "This seemed like a logical place to start."

"Honey, everyone who's anyone in this town comes into Norman's sooner or later. Who are you looking for?"

"A gentleman by the name of Samson Humphrey," Sloane said, the name still sounding foreign on her tongue.

To her surprise, the woman burst out laughing, covering her face with a menu and attempting to feign coughing.

"Is something amusing?" Sloane asked, affronted and uncomfortable.

"Oh no." The woman placed a hand on her shoulder as if they were old friends. "No, honey. Forgive me, please." She coughed for real this time, then wiped her eyes. "It's just that Samson's been called many things, but no one's ever referred to him as a gentleman before."

Unsure what to make of the comment, Sloane felt her insides clench hard. "Can you tell me where to find him?"

"First, come sit and have a soda. Then I'll fill you in on Samson. No one comes into Norman's and leaves with an empty stomach," she explained as she ushered Sloane to the swivel stools by the counter. "Drink's on me."

"Who's me?" Sloane asked.

The woman wiped down the place in front of Sloane. "Oh, forgive my manners. I'm just not used to many strangers coming through. I'm Izzy. My husband, Norman, owns this place. He makes the best burgers. Just ask those Chandler boys. They live on them."

Sloane laughed at the woman's rambling. She had a hunch this was just the beginning of the gossip and friendliness she'd find were she to stay in this small town. Recognizing that she might have to cozy up to Izzy before getting information, Sloane decided to accept her offer. "I'll have a diet Coke. Please."

Izzy placed her hands on her generous hips and tsked with her tongue. "A little thing like you could use some calories. Hey, Norman," she yelled to a graying man who stood in the kitchen, visible from a pass-through. "Get this lady a Coke."

So much for the customer always being right, Sloane thought wryly.

Only after she was seated with a Coke in front of her and Izzy beside her, did the woman get back to the reason for Sloane's visit. "So what do you want with Samson?"

It didn't escape Sloane's notice that she still hadn't told her where the older man lived. "We have personal business." She twirled the straw in her soda without meeting Izzy's gaze directly, glancing out of the corner of her eye.

The other woman propped her chin on her hand. "No one's ever had personal business with Samson that I can remember. How about you, Norman?"

"I think you should let the girl get to wherever she wants to go." He strode from the kitchen and came up to the counter. "Too bad you weren't here earlier. He was here mooching a chicken sandwich."

So far, Sloane didn't have a positive impression of Samson and no one had given her an actual description yet. "Does he live close by?"

"Everything's close by," Izzy explained. "Samson lives on the edge of town. When you get to the end of First, take Old Route Ten and keep going until you see the run-down place set back from the street."

"You can't miss it," Norman added. "And if you can't find him there, check out a place called Crazy Eights in Harrington."

"Crazy Eights?" she asked, making certain she heard correctly.

"It's a pool hall where Samson hangs out on nights he's got cash on hand," Norman said.

Izzy frowned. "Why'd you go and do that?" she chided her husband before turning to Sloane. "Don't you dare go to that sleazy pool hall alone. It's no place for a lady."

Sloane nodded, fear resurfacing at the thought of meeting this man who was related to her in the most fundamental way. For all the thinking she'd done over the last day, she hadn't dealt with the fact that this man was really her father. She wasn't ready to do it now.

And she didn't need any more caffeine hopping through her veins and making her more jittery. She took another sip to satisfy Izzy and reached into her purse, pulling out her wallet.

Izzy smacked her hand. "Didn't I say this was on me?"

Sloane laughed at her outrageous, frank demeanor. "Thank you."

"Consider it your welcome-to-town present. I'm sure I'll be seeing you back here."

Sloane wasn't as certain, since once she found Samson, she planned to return to D.C. During her long drive here and last night's stay at a small motel an hour outside of Yorkshire Falls, she'd had a lot of time to think. She didn't know what kind of threat Samson posed beyond his mere existence. But after twenty-eight years, he'd obviously decided he wanted something. Sloane had to find out what and diffuse that threat. She hoped that if he was just looking to meet his daughter, that by giving him that, he wouldn't go public and ruin Michael Carlisle's campaign.

Before Sloane could reply, Izzy continued. "Wait till the single men get a look at you." She whistled loud, so some of the patrons' heads whipped around. "Isn't that right Norman? A new face and one as pretty as this one will make heads turn."

But Norman had already disappeared back into the kitchen, thank goodness, sparing Sloane additional embarrassment.

As it was, heat rushed to her cheeks. "Thanks." She couldn't bring herself to tell the woman she might not be around a second time. "It was nice meeting you," she said to Izzy instead.

"Same here."

Good-byes exchanged, Sloane finally made it back to the street. She glanced around at the beautiful gardens across the way and the fountain drizzling water in the center. There was also a gazebo tailor-made for romance rising above the surrounding bushes. She experienced a brief twinge of regret that she wasn't here to visit and get to know the place where her mother had grown up.

She wondered if Jacqueline had liked it here. If she'd had many friends. Would Samson know? Have stories to share about the years her mother spent before leaving him?

She rested a hand over her jumping stomach. "Nothing to do but get into the car and head out of town," she said to herself.

Minutes later, Sloane turned onto Old Route 10, as Norman had instructed. Soon, clusters of homes gave way to a long stretch of trees lining either side of the road. Heavy fall foliage covered the perimeter in varying degrees of red, yellow, and brown, a sight that under other circumstances she'd love to take in and admire.

But a sense of urgency beckoned. One she hadn't felt earlier. When she'd walked into Norman's to ask about Samson, anxiety had filled her, but now fear accompanied the nervous energy that had propelled her so far. And it wasn't fear for herself or fear of the man who was her father. Rather, she was experiencing a more amorphous dread that bordered on panic, one she couldn't define but encompassed her anyway.

Without warning, the trees dissipated and an open field stretched in front of her. Sitting dead center, all alone on the empty land, was a pathetic-looking, dilapidated house. The closer she got, the more evident the disrepair. The roof was old and missing shingles, while the paint on the outside had cracked and peeled.

She'd never considered where or how Samson lived. And as she pulled the car to a stop in front of the house, an overwhelming sense of sadness filled her for what looked like a lonely, pathetic existence.

She walked up the graveled driveway. If blacktop had ever covered the long stretch, no remnants remained now. Halfway to the house, she was startled by a yipping sound. She glanced around as a small dog that resembled a pug came running toward her on short, chubby legs. Jumping up and down on his hind legs, he shamelessly begged for a pat on the head.

Sloane leaned down and ran a hand over his short fur. Grubby-looking, he needed a bath as much as he apparently needed attention, and despite her better judgment, she picked him up.

He was heavier than she'd anticipated. "You're a hefty one," she told him, and carried him to the house. She couldn't deny having her arms full gave her a more secure, comfortable feeling and she clutched the dog's warm body tighter against her chest.

At the front door, she paused, nerves overtaking her. Before she could back out and run to the car, she rang the bell. She wasn't surprised when no sound came out, and after trying once more, she started to bang loudly on the door. To her shock, the door pushed wide open. The dog squirmed and jumped out of her arms, running inside.

"Hello?" she called out, uncomfortable just walking in. But no one answered and so she cautiously stepped over the threshold. The jitters in her stomach were now uncontrollable, but so was her determination to find Samson, as she walked into a dark hallway.

The smell of rotten eggs hit her immediately. Though she lived in an apartment, she'd grown up in a house and Sloane knew a gas leak when she smelled one. The odor that assaulted her senses couldn't be anything else.

Wisdom dictated she get out and have someone call the gas and electric company, but what if Samson was inside? She called out once more. "Hello? Samson?"

No response.

She glanced around, but from the darkened rooms and obvious smell, the house had to be empty. Anyone home would have gotten out by now, though why they'd leave their pet was beyond her. And said pet had decided to act like a tough guy, running to the top of the basement stairs and yapping like crazy.

"Come on, pooch." She patted her thighs, calling him with enthusiasm.

He wasn't impressed.

And she wasn't leaving without him.

She walked slowly toward him. The closer she came, the more distinct the gas odor became. *Get out.* The mantra started to run through her head. She intended to heed it, but she had to get the dog first.

"Come on, Mr. Dog, let's go." She knelt down, and though his yapping didn't subside, he did run to her on his stubby legs.

Get out. The thought repeated itself as Sloane grabbed the still-barking dog and started for the exit. She made it outside, as far as the front lawn, when a loud explosion sounded, knocking her to the ground.

Chase figured he'd missed Sloane's visit to Norman's by a matter of minutes. Izzy couldn't stop raving about the new redhead in town, one gorgeous enough to stop traffic on First and one looking for the town loner and eccentric, Samson Humphrey.

This last bit of information took Chase by surprise. The town kids called Samson "the duckman," because he spent most of his days in the center gazebo talking to and feeding the ducks and geese. No one paid him any mind except for Chase's mother and Charlotte, both women with big hearts and soft spots for the sullen old man.

He couldn't imagine what the hell Sloane was doing looking for Samson, but he intended to find out. According to Izzy and Norman, they'd given her directions to the old man's run-down house on the edge of town. It wasn't a place any woman should venture alone. Not because Samson was dangerous. Heck, the older man was as harmless as he was nasty, but the area where he lived was a vacant place where bikers hung out. More than once, his cop brother, Rick, had arrested delinquents or bikers for vagrancy and loitering. The area was no place for a lady.

No place for Sloane.

Sloane, not Faith. Sloane, the woman he'd picked up in a bar and had hot, wild sex with all night long, before being asked by her step-mother, and wife of a vice presidential candidate, to look after her.

Damn.

When Chase Chandler gave up his quiet life, he did it in a big way. The hell of it was, he still had no regrets.

Plenty of questions, but not one regret. He had a hunch Sloane wouldn't want the word to get out that she'd picked up a stranger in a bar any more than he'd be publishing his memoirs in the morning's paper.

But he still had one helluva job ahead of him, making good on his promise to Madeline Carlisle. How he'd keep an eye on Sloane and keep his hands off her at the same time was something even a monk would have difficulty accomplishing.

"Damn," he muttered, this time out loud.

Pulling his truck in front of Samson's house, he immediately saw the rental car with out-of-state plates. At least she'd had the sense to cover her tracks the best she could.

Shoving the gear into Park, he stepped out, intending to get inside and see what Sloane Carlisle wanted with Samson Humphrey. He wasn't prepared to see Sloane running from the house or for the explosion that followed, knocking him briefly on his ass.

When the shock wore off he stood and glanced up. Flames erupted from what remained of Samson's place; at the same time, Sloane lifted herself from the ground a little ways in front of him on the front lawn.

Thank God she was okay. He exhaled hard, but his relief was short-lived. A little dog he hadn't noticed before jumped from her arms to the grass and bolted toward the burning building.

"No!" Sloane screamed, and started back to the flames.

No way could he let her run back inside, so he lunged for her at the same time she dived for the pooch, and they both hit the ground hard.

Awareness came to Sloane more quickly than she'd imagined possible. A hard body covered hers while the whining sounds of the dog came from under her. She didn't trust the pooch not to dart back into the burning house, so she lifted an arm to let him breathe, while still holding on to his collar.

"Are you okay?" a masculine voice asked. A sexy, familiar masculine voice.

A shiver, having nothing to do with the ordeal, rushed through her. "I think I'm in one piece."

She had aches and bruises she'd need to assess, but for now she was alive and breathing, while the house she was just inside burned in the distance.

Without warning, she was pulled to a sitting position and came face-to-face with Chase.

Her one-night stand.

Impossible, she thought. "The house isn't burning and you aren't real." She was off balance and confused, a state not helped by the high-pitched sound of sirens wailing in the distance.

"Unfortunately, this isn't some damn dream."

No, that sexy voice and serious face were all too real.

"Let's get farther away from the house." Chase helped her to her feet.

One step, and pain seared through her. She'd obviously twisted her ankle during her blind run from the house. Limping, she let him lead her away from the blaze, not saying a word.

He was good at that, she remembered, doing

all the right things to her without asking permission. Despite the bruises and the adrenaline still pumping through her veins, she still remembered his touch vividly. Erotically. So much so, that this next tremor had everything to do with the man pulling her to safety.

But there was a huge difference between seducing her body with his hands, lips, and tongue — during a night out of time — and real-life demands. She had to get control of herself and the situation, but since his order made sense, she wasn't about to argue. She forced herself to walk on, ignoring the pain in her ankle that subsided by the time they reached an old willow tree.

She leaned against the cool bark and let herself slide to the ground. Chills racked her body and trembling kicked in. She wrapped her arms around herself, but the shaking grew worse. "So much for control," she muttered.

Chase shot her a sideways, curious glance, but she wasn't up to any kind of explanation.

"I need your belt." Without asking, he unhooked her buckle and pulled the leather belt from the loops of her jeans.

She glanced down at his strong, competent hands. "I hardly think now's the time or place for a quickie," she said through chattering teeth. "And besides, I didn't know you were into bondage."

He paused, glanced up, and laughed.

The sexy light that she remembered in his eyes had returned.

"I knew you'd have a good sense of humor out of the bedroom," Chase said, then refocused on his task. He had to get the dog taken care of and out of the way. "Trust me," he told Sloane. "Fooling around's the last thing I have in mind."

Fooling around was exactly what he wanted to do. With Sloane, now, beneath the shade of the old tree. Unfortunately, he didn't have that luxury. Quickly he finished looping the belt to a short, stubby bush near the tree, secured it, then managed to tie the old bandanna that had been used for the dog's collar to the belt buckle. "There. He's not going anywhere and he's safe."

She glanced down at the dog, who stared daggers at Chase for tying him up. Then Sloane met his gaze once more. "I'm impressed. I thought only Boy Scouts could tie knots like that."

He met her liquid gaze. A combination of surprise, fear, confusion, as well as a hint of remembrance, flickered across her face.

At least that was how he read her expression. "You of all people should know I'm no Boy Scout."

"I don't know anything about you. Except that you picked me up in a bar in D.C. and followed me here."

"You've got it wrong, but I don't have time to explain." He pulled his cell phone from his pocket and dialed and spoke to his brother

Rick. The fire department might have pulled up to the house and the police wouldn't be far behind, but Chase wanted his cop brother here now, apprised of who Sloane was and taking care of this mess.

He inhaled and glanced her way. Right now she was too stunned to ask how he'd found her and why, but she would. Soon. He knew this because he had questions too. Like why she'd been in that old house to begin with. Why would she search out an old eccentric like Samson?

He took in her shivering form and realized how close she'd come to dying. How close he'd come to losing her. Without thinking, he pulled her into his arms to give her warmth. When his lips touched hers, he knew that once again he had lied. He wanted her.

She tasted familiar. Sweet, welcoming, and all too eager to lose herself in him the way he needed to immerse himself in her. His tongue made broad, greedy sweeps around her mouth and she reciprocated with a soft moan, then tangled her tongue with his.

His body heated instantly and his surroundings disappeared. Everything came down to this one moment with this one woman.

He threaded his hands through her hair, pulling her close at the same time he heard a deliberate cough. "Excuse me, but did someone call the police?"

Sloane jumped out of Chase's grasp and his surroundings returned.

Chase forced his gaze away from Sloane, who'd taken to kicking at the dirt on the ground. He met his middle brother's curious stare. "Thanks for coming so quickly," he said, and now that he'd come to his senses, he meant it.

"I'm part of Yorkshire Falls' finest." He grinned and tipped his head. "We aim to please." He extended his hand toward Sloane. "Officer Rick Chandler," he said, introducing himself.

She stopped grinding her toe in the dirt and looked up. "I'm Sloane —" She cut herself off. "I mean, I'm Faith. I . . ." She hesitated as if unsure which persona to use.

"Sloane Carlisle," Chase supplied, and didn't miss her shock upon realizing he knew her real identity. He had no option but the truth.

Rick needed to know about Sloane if he was going to help Chase figure out how to keep an eye on her while she was in Yorkshire Falls. And now that Samson's house had blown up with her nearly in it, keeping a low profile would be even more difficult. Chase would do his best, starting with a news blackout on Sloane's presence at the scene of the explosion.

His brother didn't register any obvious recognition at hearing Sloane's name, which wasn't surprising. Even though he was covering Carlisle's story, Chase hadn't figured out her identity that night in the bar. The vice presidential candidate's daughter wasn't that much of a public figure. Yet.

Sloane breathed a sigh of relief, obviously coming to the same conclusion Chase just had. Then she planted her hands firmly on her hips and glared at Chase, something the dog took as a sign to begin his barking once more.

"How do you know who I really am?" she asked as she bent down to pick up the mutt and calm him down with smooth pets over his head. "Come to think of it, why did you follow me all the way from D.C.?"

Confusion and shock crossed her features, and he realized he was really seeing her for the first time. Smudges of dirt stained her cheeks from their fall to the ground.

"It just so happens I live here." Not much of an explanation, but then he didn't know how much detail to give just yet.

"You live here. In that inferno?" She pointed toward Samson's old home, or what was left of it.

"I live in Yorkshire Falls." He ran a hand through his hair, frustration filling him. He wanted to explain, but he needed answers from her.

Rick remained suspiciously silent, while Sloane shifted the dog to her other hip and narrowed her gaze, studying Chase. "You being from Yorkshire Falls is quite a coincidence, and one that doesn't explain how you found me at this house."

He glanced over his shoulder, gratified to see the fire department had surrounded the place and hopefully would have things under control soon.

He wished he'd have this situation with Sloane under control nearly as fast. Turning back to her, he said, "It's a small town. No one can go anywhere without someone passing along the news. And a new face is definitely news."

"Especially such a pretty one." Rick spoke at last. He stood, hands on his hips, a wry grin on his face. "I hate to interrupt this very interesting conversation, especially when you two seem to have a lot to catch up on. But in case you haven't noticed, there's a fire going on over there, and Chase told me on the phone that you witnessed the start."

A group of firemen and the large chief of police headed toward them, causing Sloane to back up, her fear obvious.

"I'm going to need some answers," Rick said.

Chase nodded. "I agree."

She started pulling at the dog's collar, trying to detach him from the tree. "I can't talk here," she said, working at the knot. "I can't . . . We need to go somewhere private, okay?" She glanced up from her kneeling position and focused pleading eyes on Chase.

She seemed on edge, still in shock. Damned if he didn't plan on taking care of her and not because Madeline Carlisle had asked. He squeezed her shoulder in the only gesture of re-assurance he could offer.

Rick pulled out his notepad. "I'm sorry, but I'm going to need answers before you go any-where," he said to Sloane.

Chase caught the dismay on her face at Rick's insistence. She wasn't ready to answer prying questions here. Chase weighed his brother's dedication to his job against his loy-alty to family. Nothing ran stronger or deeper than Chandler family duty. He hated taking his brother's loyalties for granted, but another glance at Sloane and he knew he would do it anyway.

He grabbed Sloane's hand. "We're leaving. Rick, you can come by my place and she'll talk to you later." His tone brooked no argument.

When Rick snapped shut his pad and slid it back into his pocket, Chase let out a slow ex-hale. For the first time ever, Chase Chandler had chosen a woman over family.

Chapter Five

Sloane eased back into a comfortable recliner chair in Chase's living room of his old but well-kept Victorian house. It felt strange to be here with him now after she'd never expected to see him again.

The downstairs of his house held the *Yorkshire Falls Gazette* offices, while upstairs was his private domain. She looked around his home as a woman, not a decorator, seeing the private lair of the man with whom she'd slept. Despite its dark wood and lack of frills, she couldn't miss the homey touches: the Oriental rugs over the hardwood floors, the pictures of family that were placed in a way that highlighted their importance to him, and the clutter so typical of a man living alone.

And he was very much a man. As he stood talking to his brother by the window, she sensed his contained energy, the same energy he'd used when he'd made love to her. Sloane studied him now and realized her memory had failed her. He was even better-looking than she'd remembered. And as he gestured around, his grass-stained jeans stretched tight over his incredible behind.

She shivered and this time shock wasn't the

reason. Lord, the things the man did to her with a single glance. When he'd dived on top of her earlier, she'd recognized his familiar scent, and despite the danger, she'd become instantly aroused. They had an already-established connection, one that made this whole scene even more surreal. How *had* they come to meet up again? She'd given Officer Rick Chandler answers, but she had yet to receive some from Chase.

She stretched out her feet and her pummeled body felt the pain inflicted when she'd thrown herself to the ground to save Dog. That, she'd learned, was Samson's pet's name. The name was yet another sad commentary on the life this man named Samson lived. At least the fire department had confirmed that no one was in the home at the time of the explosion, relieving her fears about Samson being hurt, or worse.

After leaving the scene, she and Chase had dropped Dog at Dr. Sterling's, the town vet, so he could be checked out and cared for until Samson returned. No one had addressed the issue of what would happen to Dog if Samson failed to come home. Sloane shivered and wrapped her arms around herself to ward off the chill.

"Are you okay?" Chase walked over and laid a hand on the cushion behind her head, so close to touching her she automatically became distracted.

"Of course I'm okay. Why wouldn't I be?

Houses blow up around me every day." She let out a shrill laugh, knowing she was still on the edge of hysteria despite the fact that a good two hours had passed since the explosion.

Rick strode to her side, but Chase placed himself between Sloane and his brother. "She's had enough, Rick. Give her the night to rest and I can bring her by the station in the morning to sign any official statement."

He acted as a protective barrier between her and the police and she appreciated his chivalry. But no matter how tight she was strung, she could deal with Rick and answer whatever questions Yorkshire Falls' finest had. After all, she was Senator Michael Carlisle's daughter, or at least he'd raised her. And one lesson her *parents* had taught her: The more forthcoming she was, the less she evaded, the more satisfied her interviewer would be.

"If the officer has more questions, I'm more than happy to answer them," she said, glancing around Chase so she could see Rick.

He shot her an appreciative glance and she really saw him for the first time. Although both Rick and Chase were good-looking men, the similarities ended there. With chocolate brown hair and hazel eyes, Rick would attract any female's attention. But Chase, with his intense expression, incredible blue eyes, and that inky hair — he was the one she found all too sexy.

"Well?" Chase asked his brother, arms folded over his chest.

To her surprise, Rick shook his head at her offer to talk some more. "I think I have enough. For now." He shoved his pad into his pocket and stepped to the side so he had an unobstructed view of her. "I just want to clarify one thing, if it's okay with you?"

She curled her legs beneath her, ignoring the protest of her aching muscles. A hot bath would be heaven right now. "You said you came to Yorkshire Falls to visit your birth mother's hometown?" Rick asked.

"That's right." She chewed on her lower lip, hating the fabrication she'd woven for the officer, but knowing she had no choice. "I wanted to visit some of her old friends and stomping grounds."

"And Samson was an old friend?"

Here Sloane tread lightly. "My stepmother mentioned him briefly as someone who'd made an impact in Jacqueline's life. He seemed worth looking up." She raised her gaze and tried for her most honest look. As someone who'd snuck out a time or two past curfew, she'd perfected the expression.

"Which is how she came to Samson's old house," Chase concluded. "Case closed, Rick. Time for you to go." He slapped his brother on the back as a blatant excuse to prod him toward the door.

Rick tipped his head toward her. "Talk to you tomorrow, Sloane."

"Is that a polite expression for *don't leave town?*" she asked wryly.

"Yes, ma'am." He shot her a boyish grin and she wondered how many hearts he'd broken on the road to matrimony. She'd caught sight of the ring on his left hand, telling her some lucky woman had snagged the good-looking cop.

Which made her wonder about Chase. Was he involved with anyone prior to their interlude? Someone he'd continue to see now? She was surprised at how badly the thought bothered her.

As Chase escorted his brother to the door, Rick didn't seem insulted. Based on the rest of the interaction she'd witnessed between the men, there was a genuine caring that underscored everything they said or did. A family bond. One Sloane could well understand, since she shared the same connection with her parents and sisters. She had no idea what kind of reception she'd find with her one family member here in Yorkshire Falls, and she shivered at the thought.

How long before she'd find out? Sloane wondered. She'd failed in her mission to find Samson, and in lying to Rick and Chase about why she was here, she'd probably made her search more difficult. These men just might be able to help her locate Samson. Diffuse whatever threat Michael's men posed.

But to be truthful with them would entail a level of trust she didn't yet possess. Not for the police officer or the journalist. Rick's profession made him a wild card, and Chase was an enigma who could blow this story wide open.

She yawned, exhaustion threatening to overwhelm her. She couldn't believe what she'd been through in the past couple of hours, but after being forced by Rick Chandler to relive the explosion, she was certain it hadn't been a bad dream.

The door slammed shut and Chase reentered the room, his gaze keenly centered on hers. "We're alone. Now tell me the real reason you're searching for Samson, because I don't believe that cock-and-bull story you told my brother."

Sloane swallowed hard, gripping the fabric on the sofa with her hands. She hadn't expected him to see through her charade. "I already told you. Twice, as I recall."

He stalked toward her, braced his hands on the arm of her chair and leaned down so their faces were millimeters apart. She already knew what those lips tasted like. Her heartbeat sped up, and if he promised her a kiss, she'd probably cave into his demand for her to talk.

"I don't buy your excuse, honey. During that night we spent together, you told me other things too. Personal, intimate things."

"Such as?" Because at this moment, she could barely remember her own name. She licked her dry lips, gratified when his eyes followed the movement and dilated with desire. At least she wasn't the only one teetering on the brink of sanity.

"You said your life was based on a lie, but you'd still be expected to do the right thing. Is Samson a part of that lie?" he asked, his serious yet oh-so-sexy gaze never leaving hers.

She wanted to confide in him more than she wanted her next breath. Maybe even more than she wanted him to kiss her, and that was saying a lot. But the working part of her brain, small as it had to be right now, prevailed. "Do you really expect me to answer your questions while most of mine go unanswered?"

"Honey, I'm an open book." He rose, spreading his hands before him in a gesture of giving.

One she didn't buy, not for an instant. The man was as big an enigma as when she'd met him in the bar. Still, if he was offering answers, she wanted them. "Did you know I'd be in town, and if so, how?" Because she and her stepmother had carefully covered her tracks as best they could.

"I'm going to opt for honesty here." His blue eyes twinkled with a hint of mirth, but mostly with caution.

Whatever his secret, he was wary of revealing it. *Join the club,* she thought. "Honesty would be nice."

"I met your stepmother at your father's press conference."

"That's why you were in Washington? To cover the story?"

He nodded.

She shouldn't be surprised, nor should she be disappointed he wanted news coverage about her father. Possibly about her family as well. She could see the headlines now: SMALL TOWN JOURNALIST LEAPS TO NATIONAL PROMINENCE BY EXPOSING SENATOR CARLISLE'S DEEPEST SECRETS. *Thanks but no thanks,* she thought. She wasn't about to contribute to Chase's career coup.

"So then you came home." She stretched her legs out, feeling the pull of muscle as she settled in for a continued series of questions. "Did you know I was in town?" She couldn't imagine Madeline revealing such private, possibly dangerous information to a stranger, let alone a reporter.

He sat on the couch beside her chair, leaning close. So close she smelled the remnants of smoke mixed with the masculine aftershave she associated with Chase. It was a familiar, comforting scent in a time of complete chaos, and she found it difficult to maintain the distance she knew was necessary between them.

"I knew you were here. It seems that your stepmother and my sister-in-law Charlotte are good friends."

She blinked, surprised at a family connection. "The Charlotte who owns the lingerie store here and in D.C.?"

He nodded. "She's married to my brother Roman."

"Good Lord, there's another one of you?"

He chuckled, showing a flash of white teeth. "You got it, babe. Around here we're known as 'the Chandler boys.' The three of us are grouped together. We always were."

"Izzy mentioned you," she recalled. "But you and I hadn't exchanged last names, so I had no way of putting two and two together." She felt the heat rise to her cheeks at the memory of how she'd come on to him in the bar. A stranger whom she'd let take her to bed. But he hadn't felt like a stranger then, any more than he felt like one now.

Without warning, his hand came up to stroke her cheek. "Don't go getting embarrassed on me. I have no regrets and I refuse to let you have any either."

Soft yet callused, his fingertips caused an erotic tingling throughout her body and she felt the distinct puckering of her nipples beneath her shirt. "I can't say I have any regrets either," she admitted. Not even now, knowing who and what he was.

His reporter status hit her like a painful punch in the stomach. He might have saved her life, but he probably had an agenda. She forced herself to relax against the chair, sad at the reminder that he couldn't be her Prince Charming, after all. "But even with no regrets, we have a lot more to deal with than a one-night stand that's over."

He flinched and *now* she had regrets. She hadn't meant to hurt him. She only sought to put up a barrier that would keep her family safe.

She sighed and forced her mind to deal with the still-unanswered questions. "So you met my stepmother, and she told you . . . what?" Sloane asked, not convinced Madeline would set a reporter on her tail.

"She told me that you were dealing with some difficult issues, needed time alone, and came home to find your mother's roots." He spoke matter-of-factly, no emotion, no caring, the wall she'd erected firmly in place.

If her heart hurt a little, she reminded herself it was for the best. "In other words, she asked you to look out for me," Sloane guessed. That would be a typical response for Madeline, who'd given in too easily to Sloane's request to travel here alone, without protection. She'd been planning a countermission of her own.

"In a nutshell, yes. And believe me, honey, once I put the pieces together of who you really were, it wasn't a hardship to see you again." Yet Chase didn't even crack a smile. With the way she'd dismissed their one night, he obviously hated admitting he'd wanted to see her again. "But Madeline didn't mention Samson at all," he continued. "And considering his house blew up and you were almost in it, I have a lot more questions. Starting with, what's your connection to Samson Humphrey?"

She wished she could crawl into his arms and reveal all. Of course she couldn't. The only one she could trust was herself. Unless . . . "Is this Chase the journalist asking or Chase the man?" she asked.

A muscle ticked in his jaw and he ran a frustrated hand through his hair. "Fair enough," he muttered.

Her question acted like the proverbial last straw, shutting him down completely and cementing the wall between them. That had been her intent *if* he was asking from a journalistic need to know as opposed to asking from the heart.

Either he was unsure how to answer, or he didn't want to admit that the reporter in him wanted answers that could make his career. She was disappointed but she had to play her cards close.

"Rick had an officer bring your car and he dropped the suitcase off downstairs. Why don't you shower and freshen up. We can pick this questioning up again later."

Since she reeked of smoke and felt like hell, she agreed. "Thanks. A shower sounds wonderful." As for them talking again, Sloane didn't have time for exchanges of information.

Norman and Izzy had mentioned a place called Crazy Eights, a pool hall where Samson hung out when he had money in his pocket. Sloane recalled Izzy's warning, and though she was more afraid of meeting her real father than she was of the pool joint, she had to find Samson regardless.

97

The sound of footsteps distracted her. Chase returned with her suitcase in hand. In his gaze, she caught a hint of warmth, which in turn made her pulse race and her heart beat faster. Thank goodness he quickly masked it or she'd have done something stupid, like kiss him.

After her shower and a quick meal, she was out of here. Off to find her real father. Without this reporter's help or prying eyes.

Living in Yorkshire Falls, a single man could either eat at Norman's, bring in from Norman's, or learn how to cook. Chase mostly relied on take-out food from Norman's. He opened his freezer, searching for something he could defrost and serve to his guest. Not much looked appealing.

He ran a hand through his hair, feeling filthy from soot and dirt. He needed a shower, but he'd have to wait his turn. From his post in the kitchen, he heard the shower running in the other room. Or maybe he just imagined that he could hear Sloane in his bathroom, letting the water pour over her soft skin. Only one hallway and a door separated them. The thought was enough to nearly kill a man.

So was the way she'd dismissed that night between them as a one-night stand. So that's all it had been. It wasn't like he'd expected to see her again, let alone get embroiled in her life. But with her words, she'd sure as hell hurt his ego. In truth, she'd damaged more than his pride.

He cared about what she thought far too much for someone who'd been a brief fling. And those kind of feelings could prevent him from achieving his goals — a huge story picked up by the big papers and a shot at big-time fame. A scoop on vice presidential candidate Michael Carlisle.

Chase could practically *smell* that story right beneath his nose. And the fact that Sloane wanted to distinguish between Chase the man and Chase the reporter told him he might be even closer than he thought. But closer to what? What was she hiding?

He doubted he'd get those details from Sloane. Hopefully, Madeline Carlisle would be more forthcoming with her information once she realized he'd already done as she asked and saved her daughter's behind. And what a delectable behind it was, round and tight in her faded jeans.

He clenched his jaw and slammed the freezer door shut, unable to find anything edible. The easiest thing would be to call Izzy and ask her to deliver.

He picked up the phone at the same time the doorbell rang. Chase had done some renovations in the old Victorian house after moving in, and though he could reach the downstairs office from a private indoor staircase, he also had a separate entrance installed for his own personal visitors. He headed to the door and immediately caught sight through the window of his mother's honey blond hair.

"Shit." Knowing there was no putting it off, he opened the door and let her inside.

Before he could speak, she pulled him into her arms and held on tight. "Oh, my God, are you all right? I heard what happened at Samson's place and I've been sick with worry." She stepped back, and sure enough, concern etched her beautiful face as she ran her hands down his arms, presumably to make sure he was in one piece.

"Gossip mill ran that fast, huh?" he asked, trying to make light of a very serious situation. Raina might not have a real heart condition, but she was getting older and she adored her children. He didn't want her worrying about him unnecessarily.

"Since when is anything in this town secret?" She perched a hand on her hip and wagged the other finger in front of his face, lightly chiding him, yet her eyes were filled with tears, her expression one of stark relief. "Now help me inside with these bags." She gestured behind her with a grand sweep of her hand.

For the first time, Chase saw the large brown bags, all filled to the top. "What's this?" he asked as he gathered the packages together.

"Why, dinner, of course. You need your energy after such a stressful day. Norman cooked your favorite, the wonderful man." She followed him inside, chatting the entire way.

He managed to get the bags into the kitchen

before one handle broke and the contents fell to the floor. He glanced down but everything seemed intact. Still, the bags had been heavy, and for a woman with a so-called weak heart, she shouldn't be lifting them.

He was angry as hell at her for the charade, but with Sloane due to walk out of that bathroom any minute, now wasn't the time for a confrontation. In fact, now would be an excellent time to get rid of Raina before she got an eyeful of Sloane and came up with any more harebrained, matchmaking ideas. Heaven help him if she discovered he and Sloane had a past or that he actually liked the woman.

"Did you carry these bags yourself?" he asked, putting heavy disapproval in his tone.

"No, she had her chauffeur do it for her." From the open door, Chase recognized Dr. Eric Fallon's voice.

"Come on in, Eric," Chase called to the town practitioner, and his mother's *boyfriend*. What else could he call the male half of a late-in-life couple?

Chase appreciated the older man for the happiness he'd brought into his mother's life and for the voice of reason he presented in the midst of the chaos that was Raina. Eric kept her busy, made her laugh, and took charge when her ideas seemed to get out of control.

"This is the last of the bags," Eric said, placing them on the counter. Two bottles peeked out from the top of the bag.

"Wine?" Chase asked.

"Champagne," Raina countered. "To celebrate life."

So now they were having a party. He glanced toward the hallway and wondered what Sloane would think when she walked out of the bathroom to find she had an audience.

Raina lifted the expensive bottle of Dom Pérignon and eyed it longingly. She didn't drink often, but when it came time to celebrate, she loved a glass of bubbly with her family. Too bad Chase was about to kill her fun. It was the only solution he could think of as payback for her babymaking scheming.

He put an arm around her shoulders and squeezed lovingly. "You shouldn't drink, Mom. It's not good for your heart."

"The boy's right, Raina." Eric eased the champagne out of her grasp and placed the bottle on the counter.

"Killjoy," she muttered without meeting his gaze.

Chase met his gaze and Eric winked.

Two men, with Raina as a common bond. With his salt-and-pepper hair, the doctor was distinguished-looking and a nice complement to his mother's fairer looks. They made an attractive couple, Chase thought.

He glanced around the now-messy and chaotic-looking kitchen. Though he no longer had to worry about what to feed Sloane for dinner, he'd rather not do it with an audience. "Thanks so much for bringing over food." He stopped short of adding, *You can go now.*

"You're welcome." She bent down for one of the lighter bags, and after placing it on the counter, she began unpacking the contents. "I figured that a bachelor like you has nothing in the fridge to feed a houseguest, let alone a beautiful houseguest."

So she knew about Sloane. He glanced at the overloaded shopping bags filled with food and champagne. He should have realized she had an agenda. The only upside to the situation was that hopefully, if she was matchmaking, she wouldn't be staying for dinner. A mother's presence didn't make for romantic settings, he thought wryly.

Not that Sloane would be interested in romance tonight. She'd made it clear their one night had passed. "Beauty has nothing to do with what someone eats," he said, focusing on conversation with his mother. "Besides, who told you I had company?"

Eric chuckled. "Your mother has a direct line to Gossip Central. Not five minutes after the pretty redhead left Norman's, Izzy was on the horn with Raina."

Raina clucked her tongue, chiding him. "Don't make it sound sordid, Eric. The young woman's been through a lot today. So has my oldest boy. I just wanted to make sure they were well fed."

"And we needed champagne because . . . ?" Chase asked.

Raina rolled her eyes. "To enhance the atmosphere, of course."

Chase clenched his fists, hating being manipulated. "You don't even know if Sloane and I have chemistry. You don't even know if I'm interested, yet here you are with a gourmet dinner and a bottle of expensive champagne."

"Norman's is hardly gourmet," Raina countered. "And it's not like you to be surly."

"When you're meddling, it sure as hell is," he muttered.

"Shh." Raina placed a finger over her lips. "Maybe she doesn't like foulmouthed men." She glanced around, finally looking for his guest. "Where is she, anyway?"

"Cleaning up." He gestured toward the bathroom in the back hall. "And she's had a rough day. I doubt she's in the mood for company."

Eric's deep laugh echoed in the room. "I think he's asking you to leave, Raina dear." He grasped her elbow gently.

"Us," Raina said. "He's asking us to leave."

"He knows I have one foot out the door already, while you're angling to stay."

His mother pouted, but from the resignation in her eyes, she accepted that she'd been effectively shut down. "I'm not finished putting away groceries."

Chase laughed, steering her to the door with Eric following close behind. "I don't mind handling things. Besides, you need your rest."

"So do you after the day you've had. You and

that poor girl. And Samson!" She said the old man's name as if his situation had just registered.

Considering all she had on her mind — her son's safety and a new woman in town to attack — Chase understood her mental lapse. His mother was the most gentle, caring soul around, and despite Samson's often belligerent attitude, Raina liked him. She even brought him sandwiches for lunch when he hung out in the gazebo across from Norman's. Not that the old man seemed to appreciate her, but Raina treated him like a friend.

She stopped midway to the door and turned to Chase. "How is poor Samson? Any word?" Her eyes were huge, her concern so obvious and genuine it nearly broke his heart.

"I'd like to know that myself," Sloane said, walking out of the bathroom.

She wore a pair of dark denim jeans combined with a cropped long-sleeved white shirt emblazoned with a pair of shimmering glitter-covered gold lips on the front. Her burnished hair curled around her shoulders. He hadn't realized how curly her hair really was or how sexy she'd look fresh from a shower.

From his mother's eager and excited expression, she'd found a new female face with which she hoped to entice Chase. Unfortunately for him, he didn't need his mother's prodding on this one.

Sloane already interested him plenty.

Chapter Six

"I'm sorry, but there's been no news on Samson," Chase said to Sloane. "If there had been, Rick would have called."

"Oh."

Raina Chandler stared at the beautiful girl who'd just walked out of her son's bathroom. Disappointment flickered over her face at Chase's news, making Raina wonder what her connection was to the reclusive and often elusive Samson. "Are you and Samson —"

Chase stepped forward in a protective stance. "Do not ask her questions, Mother," he said, warning her with his tone.

And upon hearing those unexpected words, Raina decided to heed his request and back off. At least for now. A protective streak was a common trait for all her sons. But Chase only exhibited it toward Raina and, more lately, his sisters-in-law. That he'd step in for a woman he'd just met spoke volumes, and Raina's heart began to soar with the knowledge that she'd hit the jackpot and her last son might finally be falling in love.

Actually, from the expression on Chase's face when he gazed at the girl, he was the one who'd hit the jackpot. "I think introductions are in order," Raina said, changing the subject to please her son.

His shoulders eased, the tension gone from his stance. "Sloane, I'd like you to meet my mother, Raina Chandler. Unfortunately, she was just leaving. Weren't you, Mom?"

Aah, so he wants to be alone with Sloane. This afternoon, which had started out with a scare thanks to the explosion and had caused genuine heart palpitations for Raina, had taken an unexpected sunny turn.

Before Raina could greet Sloane properly, Chase continued. "And this is her friend, the town's best doctor, Eric Fallon."

"It's nice to meet you, Dr. Fallon." Sloane shook Eric's hand, then turned her attention to Raina. "And you, Mrs. Chandler." With a genuine smile, she grasped Raina's hand next for a brief shake.

As Sloane pulled a strand of hair off her cheek, Raina noticed her damp curls fell to her shoulders, while shorter pieces touched her face. For a brief minute, Raina had a flash of déjà vu. The girl looked familiar, but she couldn't figure out why.

"A pleasure to meet you too." Raina stared into Sloane's wide green eyes, taking in the obvious intelligence there.

Good. Chase would need a woman capable of smart breakfast conversation, something more solid than *How does this eyeshadow look, dear?* Sloane could most definitely provide that.

Her gaze darted between Raina and Chase. "I don't see a strong family resemblance," Sloane mused.

"That's because Chase looks like his father." Raina smiled, appreciating the chance to recall her beloved husband.

"While Rick looks like you." Sloane crossed her arms over her chest and nodded, sure of her conclusion. "Well, regardless of who they favor, your sons are handsome men, Mrs. Chandler."

"Thank you. Would it be too presumptuous of me to say I agree?" Raina laughed.

"Of course not." Eric placed an arm around her shoulders and she welcomed the warm, secure feeling he provided. "Raina wouldn't be Raina if she wasn't extolling the virtues of her sons. Especially her last unmarried one," Eric said wryly.

"You have to admit, he knows you well, Mother." Chase raised an eyebrow, daring her to disagree.

"Oh pooh. Both of you need to back off. I'm old and frail."

At that, Chase and Eric burst into disbelieving laughter. Raina wished she were joking, but lately, she was growing short of breath while doing activities she used to enjoy. She'd even cut back on her sneaky treadmill runs. She wondered if it was God's way of telling her that her charade had gone on too long. But since after a brief rest, she'd return to feeling normal, she ignored the problem. Surely it would pass.

Those around her continued to laugh and Eric squeezed her tight. Chase was correct. Eric knew her too darned well. He was aware of her charade and vehemently disapproved, yet he understood her reasons and accepted her without reservation. Though she adored Eric and he'd given her a future, she'd never completely forget the past. How could she, when John had blessed her with three handsome, wonderful sons?

Something Sloane had obviously noticed too. But Raina felt certain she had eyes only for Chase. In fact, she kept meeting his gaze frequently, and each time she did, the heat in the room would soar another notch.

Oh, to be young. Raina stifled a happy laugh. "You do realize that by complimenting my sons, you've found the right way to charm me?"

Chase shot Raina an annoyed look. "Mother, leave her alone. She isn't working her wiles on you. She's just being polite." He placed his hand on the doorknob. "You have to understand," he said to Sloane. "She's been trying to marry off all three of her sons and now that I'm the only one left, she's turned shameless."

Sloane chuckled. "That's okay. Your mother's assuming a few things. The first is that I'm interested in you." She raised one finger in the air. "The second is that even if I were interested, that I'd need her approval." A second finger went up. "She's right on the last one.

Any woman who is interested in a man should make nice with his mother."

"She's a smart woman," Raina said, enjoying the girl's forthrightness.

"It's just that in this case, we're simply friends, Mrs. Chandler." Sloane put a hand on Raina's arm. "But I'd still like your approval."

She tilted her head to the side, waiting for a reply, and with Sloane's chin at an angle, Raina felt that sense of familiarity again. "You have my approval. In spades."

Pink stained Sloane's cheeks, while Chase's gaze zeroed in and didn't let go. Oh, Raina liked this girl. She was exquisite and her son was obviously enthralled. Raina didn't buy for a minute that Sloane didn't reciprocate that interest. She was just being coy, completely appropriate so early in the game.

If Raina was reading the signs right, Sloane and Chase could possibly end up together. If so, the end of Raina's "heart trouble" was in sight. She'd be able to slip Eric's engagement ring, now settled in a bank's safe-deposit box, on her finger, get married, and dance at her own wedding. *After* she danced at her eldest son's wedding, of course.

Not that she'd figured out how she'd wrangle her miraculous recuperation, but she'd manage. She'd finessed the marriage of her two youngest sons, and once Chase was settled, managing to bounce back would be a welcome piece of cake. The first two hadn't quite forgiven her, but they obviously hadn't yet told Chase. And with Sloane here, Raina would milk the situation for all she could.

"We have to be going now," Eric said. "Your mother needs to get off her feet." He squeezed Raina's hand, silently urging her to go. Eric tended to pull her out of the fray and prevent her from meddling further.

She appreciated his concern and since she *was* unusually tired, she nodded. "I would like to lie down."

Chase narrowed his gaze as he stared at her. "Are you okay? You look a little pale, and with your heart problems and all, you shouldn't be running around town."

"I'm fine." She mentally crossed her fingers. Not even the mild pain she'd experienced recently eased her guilt over lying. The charade was awful, but she couldn't deny it made her boys soften toward women and the idea of marriage. Even if it was an imperceptible softening at first, in the end, it had led her first two sons down the aisle.

Surely Chase had to be next.

Eric glanced at her and his lips turned downward in a frown. "Chase is right. You *do* look a little wiped out." He glanced at Chase. "Don't worry, son. I'll take care of your mother."

Chase opened the door to let them through. "I know you will. She couldn't be in better hands." He smiled at Eric.

"The way you're both talking about me, I feel

like I'm not even in the room," Raina grumbled.

"And now you aren't," Eric said, pulling her over the threshold and into the outdoors. "Good-bye, Chase. Nice to meet you, Sloane."

Raina had but a moment to wave and then Chase shut the door, leaving them on the street. Eric was laughing so hard, Raina thought he'd fall onto the grass. "I'm not amused," she said, knowing she was pouting like an unhappy child.

"Only because you're on the outside looking in. Don't worry. Chase is old enough to take care of himself." He patted her hand, but she knew he wasn't placating her, rather trying to alleviate her distress. "Meanwhile, I'd like to take care of you. Are you feeling okay?"

His gaze told her he was truly worried, just as Chase had seemed to be earlier. An odd reaction for a man who knew about her charade, Raina thought. She debated telling him about her recent bouts with shortness of breath and slight pain, but she'd just been checked by his new partner and given a clean bill of health. There was nothing to be concerned about, so why mention it?

She nodded in reply. "I'm fine." But she'd be even better once she knew Chase was settled and happy. "Sloane is a beautiful girl. That red hair and those curls. I kept thinking she reminded me of someone, but I couldn't figure out who." And then realization dawned, the fragments she'd been grasping for falling into place.

"Who?" Eric asked.

"Do you remember Jacqueline Ford from high school?" She and Eric had been born and raised in Yorkshire Falls.

He narrowed his gaze, obviously trying to remember. "Pretty redhead, lots of curls?"

"That's her," Raina said excitedly. "She kept to herself because her parents were such snobs, but she and I were very good summer friends. We'd hang out in the tree house in her backyard when she was home from college. It's still there, on the McKeever property."

Then one hot summer day, Jacqueline's family moved with no warning. The house went on the market and no one except servants returned to pack up their belongings. Jacqueline didn't keep in touch. In fact, she never returned. Her death was town lore, if only because her father was a senator who made news, as was the man she eventually married, Michael Carlisle, who was now running for vice president. Raina had seen clippings of the press conference on the late-night news.

She didn't recall details of his family, but then she hadn't been paying much attention. Not with Eric sitting by her side and nuzzling her neck. She glanced over, not forgetting for a moment how lucky she was to have been given this second chance with a wonderful man.

Jacqueline, whose life had been cut short,

hadn't been given that kind of opportunity. And Raina hadn't thought of her old friend in too many years. Not even seeing Michael Carlisle on television had reminded her. Too much time had passed.

But then she'd seen flashes of Jacqueline in Chase's female guest. Enough to strengthen her hunch. Raina grasped Eric's hand tighter. "I'd bet anything that Sloane is Jacqueline's daughter. In fact, I'm going inside to —"

"No, you are not." Eric rarely took a stand, but his dark eyes flashed determination. If that, along with his stern voice, wasn't enough to halt her, his firm grip on her hand was. "Those two want to be alone. It's not only obvious, but Chase threw you out."

"He threw *us* out," she countered, then bit the inside of her cheek, knowing good and well Eric was right. Raina was the only one who'd lingered.

He shook his head, a smile tilting his lips despite it all. "What am I going to do with you?" He pulled her close, then brushed a light kiss over her mouth.

A delicious tingling took hold of her body and Raina inhaled deep. The scent of the outdoors, cut grass, and late fall lingered in the air, making her jubilant and happy. Just when she thought age would catch up with her, Eric had come along, causing her to feel young, vibrant, and alive.

"Whatever you're doing is working wonderfully." She brushed her hand over his cheek. "And you're a dear for postponing announcing our engagement until Chase is settled."

"I agreed to wait until Rick and Kendall got themselves settled. They have. Now all I'm waiting for is to have all three of your sons in town at the same time."

"Roman's in D.C., but he'll be back soon," she reassured him.

He frowned, rubbing a hand down his face in a weary gesture she'd come to recognize. "Still —"

"What's wrong?" she asked, not liking when he seemed upset.

He groaned. "It just seems that now's not the right time anyway. Even if Roman and Charlotte were here, Chase has his hands full with Sloane's problems. Whatever her relation to Samson, with that house burning down, it's insensitive to start planning a wedding."

She'd thought the same thing but feared bringing up the issue. She didn't want him to think she was finding an excuse to stall.

He was such a sweet, understanding, caring man. "I'll make it up to you." Raina grasped his face in her hands. "I know I've been a handful for you lately, but when this settles, I promise everyone will know and we'll get married as soon as possible." She kissed his cheek, inhaling the masculine scent of musky aftershave that never failed to warm her senses. "I'm lucky to have you," she murmured.

"And that's what makes it all worthwhile, Raina."

She looked into his eyes and smiled. "Now let's go home and let me take care of you for a change."

"I'd like nothing better." He guided her toward the car, unlocking and holding open the door for her to sit inside.

"You know," she said before he walked around to the driver's side, "you've successfully managed to distract me from bothering Chase and Sloane."

Eric chuckled. "But not for long, I imagine." He winked and slammed the door shut tight.

On the ride home, he left her to her thoughts, which was a good thing since her mind swam with memories and possibilities. Who was the girl inside Chase's house?

He hadn't offered any useful information. In fact, he'd failed to mention Sloane's last name during their introduction and Raina knew her son and his manners too well to believe it was an accidental omission. Sloane could very well be Jacqueline's daughter. But why would she be looking for Samson? Raina didn't recall them knowing each other back then.

Samson had been just a solitary young man with an unhappy family life. Now he was a loner, and a recluse who grew more bitter with each passing year. If Jacqueline's daughter was here looking him up, there was a connection Raina hadn't been aware of.

And the young woman deserved to be fore-warned about the kind of man she'd find.

No sooner had Chase gotten rid of his mother, when he turned his devouring gaze Sloane's way. "So you aren't interested in me, huh?" He started across the hardwood floor.

She licked her dry lips. "I had a feeling you'd pick up on that line." That was why she'd tossed it out in the first place. More to convince herself that she didn't find the exhausted, disheveled, still-sooty-looking man too appealing. She'd failed in her attempt.

"Say it again, and this time, look me in the eye when you do." He drew closer.

Instinctively, she backed up, not because she feared Chase, but because she feared herself and the certainty that she'd betray her instincts and common sense in favor of the desire and heated feelings he evoked. She stopped only when she reached the back wall.

"Say it." He leaned an arm overhead, much as he had in the elevator that first night. "Say you're not interested."

"And then?" she asked, buying time.

"And then we'll see if I believe you."

Sloane swallowed hard. She needed to get out of here and find Samson. She figured she'd start with Crazy Eights. But first she'd have to ditch Chase, whom she felt certain wouldn't let her go there alone. Which meant she had to be convincing in her rejection, when every fiber of her being screamed how much she wanted him.

She leaned against the hard wall for support and met his sexy blue gaze. "I'm not interested."

To her surprise, a wry smile tilted his lips. "Oh yeah?"

"Yeah." Her palms grew damp and only sheer force of will prevented her from wiping them on his shirt. Any excuse to touch him would do; then she could curl her fingers around the soft cotton and pull him closer, until the heat of their bodies singed the clothes they wore. A soft, little moan escaped the back of her throat and his eyes dilated with need.

"You don't want me." With his thumb, he began to stroke the sensitive flesh on her neck, pausing at her rapidly beating pulse. "Is that why you just made that little noise in the back of your throat? The same sound you made when I came inside you?"

She sucked in a startled breath. Even his words had an erotic, almost hypnotic effect on her. One she couldn't afford right now. "What's your point?" she asked, hoping to break that spell he wove.

He leaned forward and brushed his lips lightly over hers in reply, a soft touch that sent shivery tendrils of desire shimmering through her system. Just when she expected him to deepen the kiss, he raised his head and met her gaze.

"We'll finish this after I shower." His mouth

lifted in a knowing grin and she realized he'd just made his point without speaking. She desired him and protesting was ridiculous.

His cocky retreat toward the bedroom came as a welcome respite. She needed space and time to think.

They were working backward, she and Chase. Having slept together first, she already knew the man was a master with his hands and could turn her on in an instant. All he had to do was look at her and her body temperature soared. Lord, but she was *hot* now.

But she wasn't into one-nighters, wouldn't have slept with Chase had she not been reeling from the revelation of her parentage. She'd done so because she'd also felt something special that first time she'd looked into his eyes. And having made love with him, she was already emotionally bonded with him in some inexplicable way.

Her only hope of keeping her distance would have been if he'd turned out to be someone she couldn't like or respect. She mentally recounted what she'd learned so far: He tried to act tough but had an obvious soft spot for his mother; he'd stepped in to save Sloane; he'd thought of protection their one night together. With those attributes in the pros column, how could she not like him?

But he was a journalist, Sloane reminded herself. Starting over in life and seeking a story. That much she'd pieced together on her own.

And if that fact weren't enough to tip the scales against trusting or falling any harder than she already had, there was her future. Once she settled this mess she was in now, Sloane very much wanted a husband and children and the designing career she'd temporarily left behind. In his own words, Chase Chandler believed in protection always and children never.

Words she couldn't ever let herself forget.

Somewhere out there, Samson awaited her. With the list of cons against Chase firmly in mind, and his shower running in the other room, she slipped out the door.

Chase considered his options, strangling Sloane among them, as he pulled up in front of Crazy Eights, a pool and beer hall on the seedy side of Harrington, the next town over from Yorkshire Falls. With its bright neon lights and motorcycles parked out front, the bar didn't attract the best crowd and was no place for a lady, let alone Senator Carlisle's daughter.

When he'd walked out of the shower and into deafening silence, he knew she'd slipped out on him and cursed himself for being taken off guard. He'd pushed too hard when it came to *them* and she'd bolted. She had an agenda where Samson was concerned and Chase had a hunch she'd gone off to find him. Not knowing where to start his search, he'd called on Izzy and Norman, the only two people he knew of who'd had contact with Sloane today besides himself, his brother Rick, his mother, and Eric.

Sure enough, Norman had told her of Samson's favored hangout, something Chase hadn't been privy to. As he entered the dive bar, inhaling the smell of stale beer and heavy smoke, and bypassing the tattooed men and their biker-chick girlfriends, he wished he didn't know now.

He squinted to see through the thick smoke and even thicker crowd, looking for Sloane's white shirt in the sea of black leather jackets, or a hint of her red hair. He finally found her in the back along with the locals. Sloane had gotten herself into a pool game with a couple of old men who appeared to be teaching her the ropes. Considering the dangerous-looking bikers in the bar, these men seemed harmless enough and Chase decided to observe first before interrupting.

Letting her mingle with these guys without him stepping in went against every instinct he possessed and he locked his hand around the cool chrome railing to make sure he stayed put. He told himself he was here because he'd promised Madeline he'd look out for Sloane, but he knew that was a lie. He was possessive and protective and not just because of a promise made to her stepmother, or those erotic sounds she made when he touched her.

Something about this woman set off his most primal male instincts. He desired her, he wanted to protect her, and he needed to know her secrets. Not always in that order and not because she was the subject of a dicey story.

She shifted with the cue and leaned over the table. Her shirt rose, revealing an expanse of her bare back and an enticing hint of lace peeked out from the low-slung waistband of her jeans. At least the old men teaching her were too aged to notice or care. They appeared happy to have a new pool buddy and didn't give her femininity a second look. Chase wished he could say the same. Hell, he wished the bikers who surrounded the pool table to watch her could say the same. Even dressed down, she stood out among the women here. He shook his head, gritting his teeth so he'd feel pain and focus on something other than getting her the hell away from every other man looking at what he considered his. A completely foreign, utterly cavemanlike notion.

Hell, he thought, running a hand over his eyes. He didn't want to deal with these new and unnerving feelings. Not now, not ever. And considering he had a job to do here, namely watching Sloane, he didn't have to. Besides, he wouldn't learn anything about her agenda in Yorkshire Falls if he made a scene and dragged her home. As a reporter, he needed to be on the lookout for whatever story she was trying to hide. Chase relegated all possessive thoughts of Sloane to the farthest recesses of his mind and settled in to watch.

She made her next shot, a difficult one no

novice could make, and he realized she didn't need the lessons the old geezers were too happy to provide. Whistles of approval echoed around the room. Chase wondered if they were caused by her prowess at pool or the way her top pulled tight over her breasts, the gold lips taking a neon purple cast under the lights.

"Hey, Earl. It looks to me like she's a real quick learner." The call and accompanying laughter came from the sidelines.

Earl shook his head and pushed back his shoulders, certain of his abilities. "No, I'm just the best teacher this place has ever seen." He grinned and Chase realized he was missing one front tooth.

"You're a moron. She's snookered you good. No man should play for cash with a lady or put up with one besting him," a man dressed in black leather with a bandanna tied around his head said. "Samson's a pro at working these assholes for money. Looks like you're just like him," he said to Sloane. "How did you say you knew him anyway?"

Chase leaned closer, knowing he'd like an answer to that too.

"I didn't say. But he's an old friend of the family, if you have to know." But she didn't glance back toward the sound of the man's voice or otherwise acknowledge him in any way as she lined up her next play. This time, she missed a too-easy ball and gestured for Earl to take his turn.

He sunk the ball and the next two after, finishing the game. She raised her hands in defeat. "You win."

Earl let out a whoop and accepted a pat on the back from another old guy with less teeth than Earl had. Meanwhile, Sloane dug into her pocket and pulled out a handful of wrinkled bills, tossing them onto the green velvet. "Good game, Earl. Thanks for showing me the ropes. I wasn't taking anyone for a ride," she called over her shoulder.

"The lady's calling you a fool, Dice," another biker chimed in, laughing at his friend.

Chase winced. Starting with these guys wasn't a smart move.

But toothless Earl grinned, preening at being complimented. It probably didn't happen too often. Chase had to hand it to Sloane, she acted as if she were in her element, as comfortable here as she'd be with her senator father. She impressed him with her bravado, but he knew, even if she didn't, the biker wasn't going to let her just walk away. He liked what he saw for one thing, and she'd embarrassed him in front of his friends for another.

She propped the cue on the floor and leaned against it, focusing on Earl. "You said Samson would probably be here Friday night?"

He nodded. "He comes in 'round eight."

"That's assuming he has cash in his pocket," someone added.

All of which sounded like Samson, Chase thought.

"I'll make sure you're here to greet him on Friday," Dice said, finally stepping out of the shadows and he wasn't an impressive sight. He wore the standard black leather jacket, possessed too much facial hair, and sported an oversize beer belly. And he was bigger than Sloane and could snap her in two with one hand.

Chase groaned. His time to observe was over. He straightened and strode up to the table. "The lady's already got a date Friday night."

"I do?" she asked, her surprise obvious. But from the flicker of relief in her eyes, she wasn't unhappy to see him.

Dice grabbed the cue from her hand and threw it across the room. "Doesn't sound like she wants to be with you, loverboy." He edged closer, his big body taking up a hell of a lot of space. His friends huddled in, acknowledging their intent to back up their pal.

"How'd you find me?" Sloane asked Chase in a small voice.

"I don't think you want to waste time talking or your buddy here is going to stake his claim."

"The way you just staked yours?" She glanced down, taking in the arm that he'd wrapped possessively around her shoulders. She'd started to tremble.

Good, Chase thought. She'd finally realized she was in over her head and that realization, coupled with fear, might help him keep her from doing anything this stupid again.

"I'm with him," Sloane said, pointing to Chase but speaking to Dice.

He folded his big arms over his chest and nodded. "We're fair here." He ignored Sloane, looking into Chase's eyes and staring him down. "If she's yours, I'll back off, but seeing as how possession's two-tenths of the law and I found her here alone, I'm gonna need some proof."

Chase hadn't thought the guy had any more room, but Dice stepped into their personal space. He reeked to high hell of beer and smoke, and heaven only knew what else.

"Is she your property or isn't she?" Dice asked.

Sloane's muscles tensed beneath his fingertips. "*She* has a mind of her own and can speak for herself."

Shit.

Dice scowled. "Five minutes on her back with me and she won't have the energy to talk back." He still didn't speak directly to Sloane, addressing Chase as if he had the decision-making rights over Sloane, mind and body.

From behind him, Dice's friends laughed, a menacing sound that assured the biker of backup should he need it.

Chase dug his fingers into her shoulders and spoke. "She doesn't usually have such a big mouth. Damn woman slipped out on me while I was taking a leak. Now that I found her, you can bet I'm going to teach her a lesson." He wondered how *that* sounded for taking possession.

Dice nodded in approval, but beside him, Sloane squirmed, obviously eager to add her two cents. He leaned in close, catching the fragrant scent of shampoo in her hair. Arousal hit him hot and hard despite their circumstances.

His timing sucked, Chase thought, and swallowed a laugh. Still, he had to admit Sloane brought adventure to his life at a time when he'd been looking for a change. "Play nice," he whispered so only she could hear. "Or else we're not getting out of here without a brawl." And he liked his body parts just fine where they were.

"Okay," she hissed, and he knew he'd pay later. In the meantime, she was probably grateful enough for his intervention that she'd keep quiet.

"I hear a lot of yapping and excuses, but I ain't seen no proof of possession." Dice leaned a hand on the pool table. "And like I said, that's our rule round here." He nodded at Chase. "Prove she's yours and me and my boys'll make way for you."

Chase glanced at Sloane, who stared at him wide-eyed, obviously uncertain of what came next. He might not make places like this his main hangout, but he knew what Dice expected. He slipped his hand from Sloane's shoulder to grab her hand, then swung her around so her back was against the pool table.

He braced his hands on the scarred wooden edge, encircling her with his body. He smelled her scent and felt her heat. They had an audience, and damned if it didn't arouse him even more. For the first time, she felt small and scared, backing away instead of huddling close. But he wasn't going to hurt her, far from it. He was going to mark his territory, then get her to safety, if she considered being alone with him safe. At this point, he was so damned angry she'd put herself in this position, he barely trusted himself. But before he could worry about killing her, he had to make her his.

He met her gaze, and when she looked into his eyes, she obviously realized his intent because fear dissolved, replaced by trust. And damn it, a hint of excitement. Desire. Lust.

"A man's gotta do what a man's gotta do," Chase muttered; then he sucked in a breath and lowered his mouth to hers.

Chapter Seven

Chase's mouth felt slick and hot, and Sloane moaned at the intimate assault. She knew he was only trying to get them out of the bar without a fight, yet she'd seen the flicker of heat burning in the blue depths. He desired her and he was showing her now. He was showing the entire bar, but Sloane didn't care.

How could she care about anything when he took charge with complete mastery? His lips slanted over hers, first one direction, then another, his tongue making broad sweeps inside her eager mouth.

Sloane was a woman who'd always dated men who were eager to do as she pleased and behaved with utmost decorum and respect. She was smart enough to know her father's status had everything to do with their actions, but she'd grown used to being in charge. No man had ever dared to treat her as his property. Chase did. He took over, his movements greedy and possessive, and darned if she didn't like this new attitude of his, enough for her to wrap her arms around his neck and kiss him back, nearly to the point of losing control herself. So much so, she was taken off guard when he broke the hot connection.

"How's that for proof?" he asked Dice without tearing his fiery gaze from hers.

"Hell, man, even I could kiss her and make her melt."

"More like pass out," Sloane muttered. She was sick of this disgusting man's macho attitude.

"I'm done taking orders from you," Chase told the biker. "We're out of here." Chase grabbed Sloane's hand, obviously intending to pull her across the bar.

"You ain't going anywhere. At least not with the lady." From the menacing look in Dice's eyes and the way his gang began to circle around him, Sloane knew they were serious.

Her stomach clenched in pure fear. And then she looked at Chase's harsh profile. The man might be a newspaper reporter with a soft spot for his family, but she was discovering that he wasn't a man to mess with. Despite the danger surrounding them, Sloane felt ridiculously safe with him by her side.

"Leave her here and I'll show you the door myself." Dice snickered, but Sloane didn't find him funny.

"I'm sick of this shit." Chase squared his shoulders and kicked a pool cue across the floor, its rattling sound echoing in the sudden silence. "Nobody tells me when and where to mess with my girlfriend. I'm not going to kiss her again unless I'm in the mood and you're killing mine. So get the hell out of my way." He stepped forward with determination.

She spared a quick glance his way. His facial expression looked as if it'd been chiseled out of hard granite. Now Sloane was scared. She didn't want Chase getting his gorgeous face kicked in or his body hurt, thanks to Dice. Or rather, thanks to her since she'd gotten him into this bar, and this mess.

Dice wanted proof of possession? It was time Chase gave it to him, something he'd just made clear he'd only do on his terms. Sloane intended to make sure those terms were met.

She sidled closer to him, then slid her hands over his shoulders, feeling the hard muscle beneath his shirt. "Come on," she whispered. "I like having an audience. It's so . . . hot."

She nipped his earlobe and his body shook. She wasn't exactly lying, since being with Chase anywhere was *hot*. It's just that she'd rather be in the comfort of his home at this moment. No Dice, no threats.

"You want hot? I'll give you hot," Dice said, obviously showing off for his friends.

Chase's hands clenched into fists at his side as he realized the big biker hung on Sloane's every word and action, ready to pounce. On her.

Showing patience and restraint, Chase glared, obviously debating his next move. Sloane wasn't as content to hide her emotions. Trailing her fingers up his neck, she thread her hands in his hair, massaging his scalp with the palm of her hands. "Don't you want me?" she asked, when she really meant, *Don't you want to get the hell out of here?*

Desperation tinged Sloane's voice and her fingers dug into Chase's scalp. He couldn't react to her fear or he'd lose the upper hand with Dice.

He met her gaze. "I want you, all right." He spoke the truth. Chase was on the edge. On the edge of pulling Sloane away from this crowd and on the edge of taking her right here on the damn pool table.

She had a point about the audience. Kissing her and staking his claim had a carnal, caveman sort of appeal. He'd been holding back out of respect for her, but they weren't getting out of here unless he marked her as his.

Something she obviously understood and was angling for, something she apparently wanted despite her fear — that is, if the excited gleam in her eyes or husky voice was any indication. And the way her fingers tugged against his scalp heightened his awareness and aroused his senses. So did the surrounding danger.

"Then what are you waiting for?" she asked.

He sensed Dice's approach from behind, felt his time running out. "Good question." He lifted her by the waist, turned back, and seated her on the edge of the pool table; then he settled himself between her legs. Even with the denim barrier, warm heat enveloped him. He recalled exactly what the moist place between her legs felt like and broke into a sweat.

Behind him, Dice called for him to make his move, but Chase planned to go at his own pace. Lowering his head, he took his first taste of her neck. She smelled sweet and felt warm as his tongue gently lapped at her soft skin. She let out one of those moans that he loved to hear. She might kill him, but at least he'd die a happy man.

Still, he couldn't put things off much longer. He pulled her long, tangled hair farther away from her flesh and blew on the moistened spot on her neck. The clapping, whistles, and cat-calls surrounding them grew louder, yet for all Chase cared, they might as well have been alone. But they weren't, and in order to get there, he had one more move to make.

Once again, he slid his tongue over her tender flesh — once, twice — then lingered, long enough to let Dice think he was marking her in the most visible, primal way. He raised his head and pulled a dazed Sloane to her feet. Then he shrugged off his jacket and wrapped it around her shoulders, the collar and her hair covering her neck. Let Dice think what he wanted.

"We're out of here." He squeezed her hand tighter and started past the biker, noticing his friends were awaiting the man's okay before letting them through.

A nod from Dice and the group parted, revealing a path toward the rest of the bar and the exit beyond. Chase's relief lasted for two seconds, long enough for him to lead Sloane past the crowd. Then she paused. She jerked on his hand, causing him to stop in his tracks.

She looked back to Dice, his buddies, and to the old men who'd resumed their game of pool as if nothing had happened to disrupt them.

"Hey, Earl," Sloane called out.

Chase tensed, gripping her hand in a death-lock, knowing what was coming and powerless to stop her.

"See you Friday." She waved with her free hand. "And if you see Samson, tell him to be here."

Chase had had enough. He stormed for the front door, pulling Sloane behind him. Once safely in the vestibule, he grabbed her by the forearms. "You are insane," he said, shaking her and letting out his frustration. "No way in hell am I letting you come back here Friday night. Not after what I had to go through to save your pretty behind this time."

She glanced at him, those wide eyes too big and innocent for his liking. "Thank you for the compliment." She patted her behind, and though she tried, she couldn't hold back a grin.

"That wasn't what I meant."

She laughed this time, a light, airy sound that lifted his angry spirits.

"I know. And thank you for saving me. Truly." She reached up and touched his cheek.

"No one's ever gone to such extremes for me or my —"

"Pretty ass?" He wasn't about to let her off the hook completely.

"Not my choice of words, but they'll do." She pulled the jacket tighter around her.

"I'm sorry I had to make such a ridiculous scene," he told her.

"I'm not." She grinned as a blush stained her cheeks.

He shook his head, amazed and awed. Who was this woman named Sloane Carlisle, daughter of a prominent politician, who looked like fine china but had more backbone than any man he'd ever met, and who, from all appearances, liked what they'd just been through?

So had he, but he was a guy and he knew he'd had the situation under control. Sort of. She'd known no such thing.

"You didn't have to come looking for me, but you did. And don't tell me it was because you promised my stepmother you would," she said.

He groaned. She had him cornered. No one had put a gun to his head or forced him to go searching out Sloane. He'd done that on his own. Because he was worried about her.

All these emotions pushing to the surface had him edgy and off balance. And he knew just one way around it — get back to doing his job, the one thing that grounded him and kept him sane. "Let's go home."

She nodded. "I can't argue with you there."

"As soon as we get there, you can tell me exactly why it's so important that you find Samson."

Panic flared in her eyes. "But —"

"No argument. I didn't nearly get my ass kicked by a bunch of bikers only to be kept in the dark now."

She lowered her head a notch. "It's personal, Chase. Deeply personal."

The plea in her voice tore at him, but along with that need to give her anything she wanted, there came a stronger resolve to get answers. "Do you want to come back here Friday night?" he asked.

She nodded. "You know I do."

"Then unless you want me to borrow Rick's handcuffs and keep you shackled at home, you're going to have to explain. Otherwise, there's no way in hell I'm putting my ass or yours in danger again." He pushed the door open as he spoke.

"I planned to stay in a hotel."

"No." He wasn't letting her out of his sight.

"You're not responsible for me, despite what Madeline made you promise."

He held her hand tighter. "There's no hotel in Yorkshire Falls and you aren't coming into Harrington again unless you're with me. Subject closed."

"Okay." She shrugged, knowing how to pick her battles. Instead of arguing, Sloane figured giving in now would benefit her later. "Thanks."

He grunted in reply.

Sloane clenched her jaw as they walked to Chase's truck. Another argument ensued about her driving home. Once again, she agreed with him and he'd promised they'd pick her car up in the morning. Given his current mood and the fact that she was the cause, not to mention that he had saved her behind, she figured she owed him the little things.

Like staying at his home instead of a hotel. She wondered if he had a guest room or if he expected them to sleep together after her performance in the bar. If that's what he desired, she knew he'd be impossible to resist.

A cold wind whipped up around her, fall quickly turning to an early winter. The wind seemed to penetrate her skin, seeping straight through to her bones. Sort of like what Chase had done earlier tonight. She trembled at the memory of him standing between her legs, looking down at her with a predatory gleam in his eyes. Dice might have commanded the performance, but when Chase came over her, they were all alone.

Without warning, he lifted the jacket off her shoulders and held it out so she could slip her arms through the sleeves. "Your teeth are chattering."

"And you're a nice guy."

He scowled at that.

"Don't worry. I haven't figured out how nice." Nor had she figured out what to tell him about her relationship to Samson. On one hand, he'd helped her out and answers weren't too much to ask. On the other, this was the most private, painful moment of her life.

Then why did sharing it with Chase, an almost stranger, a journalist of all things, feel so right?

"Truck's right here." He pointed two parking spots ahead on the street and she nearly ran, happy to get out of the cold.

"Chase!"

A woman's voice took Sloane by surprise and she followed his lead, pausing by a pretty brunette who greeted him with enthusiasm and a surprising kiss on the lips.

Sloane bit the inside of her cheek, hating that another woman knew Chase well enough for any kind of kiss. Which was ridiculous. The man had a life and she'd been a one-night stand.

"I saw your truck. I recognized the plates," the woman said. "Then I went into the supermarket. I just came out. I'm shopping late tonight, as you can see." She shifted the package in her arms. "And here you are." She looked at him with pure pleasure.

And Sloane's stomach cramped as she waited for Chase's reply.

"Hello, Cindy."

Sloane couldn't read his tone of voice. Was he happy to see this woman or not?

"I haven't heard from you in a while." She

spoke matter-of-factly, not petulant or whiny, but a hint of disappointment was evident in her voice.

"I've been busy. Here, let me help you with your bags." Chase grabbed for her packages.

"Aren't you going to introduce me to your friend?" Cindy asked, taking in Sloane, who'd opted to pull Chase's jacket tighter around her and watch the scene unfold.

He exhaled a long sigh. "Cindy, meet Sloane. Sloane, this is my . . ." He paused long enough for Sloane to narrow her gaze. "This is my friend Cindy." Chase finished the introductions, clenching his jaw, obviously not happy.

Sloane wasn't thrilled either. Apparently, these two had a relationship of some sort. What sort was the question and he wasn't being forthcoming.

After the awkward greetings, Chase helped Cindy put her packages in her trunk and sent her on her way. But not before giving her a quick kiss on the cheek, which made Sloane's stomach burn with jealousy.

When was the last time any man had evoked that kind of emotion? Never. She gnawed on her lower lip, settling herself into the passenger seat of Chase's truck, wondering what to do or say next.

"I'll make you a deal." She heard the words escape before she'd completely thought them through.

"What sort of deal?" he asked, turning the ignition, pulling onto the road, and heading for home, before glancing at her from the corner of his eye.

"You tell me about your relationship with Cindy and I'll answer your questions about Samson."

On the way home, Chase stopped at Burger King, and because they were starving, they ate in the truck. Sloane knew he expected answers, but she had an important phone call to make as soon as they reached the house, and he understood her need to check in with Madeline first.

Their conversation eased Madeline's mind, since she'd been frantic. Thanks to Roman, who'd already spoken with Rick, her stepmom had heard about the explosion. Sloane promised to keep in touch more often from now on, although she had little information on the explosion to report. Chase had called Rick from his cell phone on the way home from the pool hall, and though the fire department was still investigating, preliminarily they were calling the situation an accident.

If she were running on pure emotion, Sloane would be inclined to agree. She'd grown up with both Frank and Robert and she had a hard time believing they'd knowingly — physically — hurt another human being. Yet when she thought with her head and remembered Frank's threats, she had to allow room for doubt. She refused, though, to burden Madeline with that kind of worry.

As for Michael, according to Madeline, he was frantic because Sloane knew the truth about her parentage and hadn't spoken with him yet. She promised she'd talk with him soon and would even have had a short phone conversation except he was in a meeting planning strategy with Robert and Frank. According to her stepmother, both seemed unconcerned about Sloane's "illness" or her absence from campaign events, and as agreed, Madeline hadn't enlightened anyone but Michael.

Sloane hung up, opting not to mention Chase or the fact that her stepmother had assigned him to look out for her. She figured Madeline deserved some motherly liberties. With matters at home as settled as they could be, Sloane changed clothes and headed back to the living room.

She was exhausted from the day's events. If not for the subjects that still needed discussing, she could easily fall asleep and rest easy with the knowledge that her secret was still safe.

But she still had to deal with Chase.

Exhausted and wired at the same time, Chase stretched his feet out on the table in front of the sofa. Glancing over at the telephone, he noticed the red light flicker off. Sloane had gotten off the phone.

Seconds later, she walked out of the guest

room, the smaller bedroom Chase had given her for the time she stayed with him. "Still waters run deep, huh?" she asked.

"What's that supposed to mean?"

"Just that nothing's apparent with you. You shocked me back in the bar, with your dominant attitude." She curled into a corner of the couch, across from him, bringing with her the fragrant scent of vanilla. Now that they'd agreed she'd be staying here, she'd unpacked a few things in his one and only bathroom.

She'd asked him if he minded. He'd said no. He lied. Already she was making herself impossible to forget.

She'd changed out of her bar clothes and now wore a comfortable pair of gray sweats, which covered her legs, while an old pink T-shirt pulled tight over her breasts. And she wore no bra.

He tried to swallow, but his mouth had grown dry. "Would you prefer that I'd have let Dice have his way with you?"

"No." She managed a laugh. "But now I know there are many sides to Chase Chandler."

"I could say the same about you, Sloane Carlisle." Which was why he couldn't risk taking her into his room, into his bed. Not again.

Though she'd sent out all the right signals earlier tonight, he wasn't about to take her up on her silent invitation. He was so drawn to every aspect of her personality, even the parts he didn't yet know, she presented a real risk to his future.

Which brought him back to her secrets. "I think it's time you told me why you were in Crazy Eights to begin with and why we have to go back Friday night."

"We?" She wrinkled her nose, questioning his choice of words.

He frowned at her obvious attempt to change the subject. "You already know I'm not letting you go alone. So just fill me in on why we need to go back there at all."

She leaned against the cushion and shut her eyes. Her hair fell in soft curls over her shoulder and the intoxicating burnished hue stood out in contrast to his bland gray couch. She brought such color and light into an otherwise drab existence. He wanted to stretch her out on the couch and take that light inside of him in the only way he could.

Not now Chandler. Tread lightly, he warned himself.

"Before I tell you about Samson," she said, her voice startling him back to reality, "I need to know I can trust you." She rolled her head to the side and met his gaze.

"Not that I believe in calling in a debt, but I did save your life today. Twice," he reminded her. "And you're still questioning whether you can trust me?"

The hurt in his voice took him by surprise. He was a journalist. His interest in her was supposed to be about the facts. Not feelings. But for some reason, his interest was anything but dry and factual.

She bit down on her glossed lips, thinking before she spoke. "I'm trained to be wary of reporters." She nervously twisted her fingers together.

As a barrier, she was putting up a bigger one than he could have come up with on his own. "We can't change who we are."

"True. And I can't forget things you've said." She drew a deep breath. "Anything I tell you that can help your career, it can also hurt people I love. So forgive me if I need to know and question how much I can trust you, Chase."

He wished he could offer assurances at the same time his instincts and adrenaline began pumping hard. "Are you asking for my silence?" Because if her secret was as big as she implied, he wondered how and if he could keep such a huge promise.

"I'm hoping that once you hear what I have to say, you'll understand why you need to keep it quiet. But at some point, I'm guessing the time will seem right for you to expose the story." She squeezed the armrest on the couch, her fingers turning white. "And that scares me."

He was frustrated, clueless and completely in the dark. "You're not giving me a straight answer."

"I know." She shifted to her knees and came up beside him.

Her scent knocked him off balance.

She inched closer. "That's because I haven't gotten what I want from you yet."

"Information on my personal life." He treated her to a wry grin, but he felt anything but sarcastic and light.

"It seems like a fair trade."

When she faced him, lips inches away, teasing him with their glistening moisture, nothing seemed fair. Especially divulging information on a life he'd always kept private, even from his brothers. And they were his best friends.

But sitting with Sloane in his home, a place where he'd never brought another woman, seemed comfortable and right. "You can't really want to hear about me, not after the long day we had."

"Stalling?" she asked him.

He laughed. "No."

"Then talk."

"Okay."

At his agreement, she curled in beside him, letting her body lean against his. He felt the moment her muscles relaxed and she yawned, sighing with what sounded like contentment. Ironic. She was obviously hesitating about revealing too much information to him, yet with this subtle body language, she'd given him trust in a completely different way. Did she realize that?

He did, and it scared him to death. Even talking, divulging his personal secrets, seemed a less painful exercise than thinking about his feelings for Sloane. "My father died when I was eighteen," he said at last.

He'd never had this conversation with a woman, not even Cindy, whom he'd been intimate with for far longer than any other woman in his past.

"I'm sorry," Sloane murmured.

He shrugged. "It happened; I dealt with it. I withdrew from college, took over the paper, and helped Mom raise my brothers. There was no other way." He recalled those days, the pain and difficulties a dim memory, yet one that still drove him now.

As Sloane listened to his words, she finally understood what had shaped him. "You're a good man, Chase Chandler." And she knew now what he meant when he spoke of living life for others. How much he was willing to compromise his own life for his family was humbling.

He merely grunted, and she guessed accepting compliments wasn't easy for him. "It must have been tough."

"At times. And setting a good example for Rick and Roman was a pain in the ass." His laugh rumbled through her. "It didn't leave any room for a social life. Not while they were young and living at home."

She tensed as she asked, "And what happened to your social life after they moved out?"

"Discretion had become a habit. Besides, living in a small town, if you don't want your social life broadcast the next morning, you don't do anything you might regret. Either that or you spend time in the neighboring town." His fingers ran over her hair, tangling in the strands as he tugged on her scalp.

"Where does Cindy fit in?" She forced herself to ask him, even as she focused on the sensual feelings he created inside her by the simple act of touching her hair.

"What if I said we had a relationship? Would you leave it at that?"

"If I said I have a relationship with Samson, would you leave it at that? Would you let it go?" she shot back.

He chuckled. "Touché."

"What kind of relationship?" Sloane had no choice but to push. She wanted answers too badly.

A long period of silence followed and she wondered if he was annoyed.

"We're lovers," he said at last.

The pain in her stomach was worse than she'd anticipated. "Present tense?" Sloane was amazed she could speak.

He let out a long breath. "We have an understanding. Neither of us wanted a relationship or anything that would require commitment. We get together when it's convenient," he explained.

"You still haven't answered the original question. Are you still involved?"

"It's not that simple. You heard her say she hasn't heard from me in a while." She felt him shrug, and his fingers began to massage her neck. "With Cindy, the allure has been gone for a long time now. It's just that she's . . ."

"Convenient?" Sloane asked hopefully.

"And safe. It kept life simple for me. No worries about my brothers, and with my meddling mother, privacy had its privileges."

Having met Raina, Sloane managed a laugh. "And what did Cindy have invested in you?" His fingers kept up a steady rhythm and pressure against her skin. His touch reassured her in some small way. "Because somehow I don't think she was counting on you picking up a strange woman in a bar."

"To be honest, I wasn't counting on it either. But I never made Cindy any kind of promise."

Sloane wasn't certain how to feel. He obviously cared about this woman, Cindy, since he'd been in a relationship with her for a long time. But he wasn't committed to her. He didn't want to be committed to anyone, Sloane reminded herself.

This wasn't the first time he'd made such a comment and she'd better make sure she did more than listen. She'd better believe and protect herself because she could fall for him way too easily.

He held Sloane tighter. "I'm a man of my

word, and if I make a promise, you can be certain I'll keep it."

"Was that your backhanded way of telling me you'll keep my secret about Samson?" she asked.

"For as long as you need me to keep it quiet. But I guess it's up to you whether or not to believe me." He pulled her away from him and she met his steady gaze.

The time had come for her to confide in return. And she would. But first she wanted to seal their agreement with their bodies. She needed that emotional connection, to feel him inside her again and to know that he wanted only her for now.

He inclined his head, waiting for her to reveal her secrets. But instead of talking, she leaned forward, sealing her words with a kiss.

Chapter Eight

Chase wanted answers, but when Sloane's arms came around his neck and her lips brushed across his, his body came alive. When she touched him like this, he found answers of a different sort — and damned if he didn't like it — but still, he pried her arms apart and held them at her side.

"Samson?" he reminded her.

"I'll tell you later." She looked at him with wide, imploring eyes. "After." She nuzzled his neck with her mouth, her lips warm and soft against his skin. "You have my word," she assured him. "Just make me feel alive first and I promise to tell you everything you want to know after."

"Wait." Her gaze held not just desire but honesty, and since Chase prided himself on reading people, he accepted her answer at face value. But he wasn't ready to jump into bed. "Needing answers about Samson isn't all that's holding me back." He couldn't be anything but honest with her.

A slow smile tilted her lips. "I'm sure I know what is. It's commitment, right? You're worried I'll want more than you can give," she said, reading his mind.

He nodded. Even if she didn't want more, she deserved more than he could promise or give. "Last time, we knew the rules going in."

She stroked his cheek, her gaze never leaving his. "And this time we'd know them too. I'm not staying in Yorkshire Falls beyond finding my . . . beyond finding Samson."

She'd just given a clue. She'd also given him the reply he thought he needed — the one that would give him permission to release the pent-up passion that had been building all day. Without worrying about commitment. If that were true, why the uncomfortable feeling burning in his gut at the thought of her leaving him a second time?

"Chase?" She licked her finger, then traced his lips, leaving his mouth damp, his body yearning.

He'd be a fool to deny his burning need. In one smooth move, he laid her down on the couch.

"I'm going to have to assume we're in agreement again." She giggled, a light, infectious sound that wiped out all the worries and concerns and left him smiling and happy.

Happy. An alien state for him, he acknowledged. "I'd say you're right."

He kissed her, hot and deep, thrusting with his tongue, mimicking the movement with his lower body. His erection was thick and heavy between his legs, and he needed the friction of coming inside her with a desperation he'd never felt before.

Taking her hand, he pulled her to her feet and led her into his bedroom, a place he'd always considered his sanctuary. A place he'd come to get away from *Gazette* business, family pressure, and life in general. His haven. And now that she'd set foot inside, he'd never look at this room the same way again.

"Chase?"

He blinked and realized she'd beaten him to the bed and was sitting cross-legged in the center of the mattress. Her hands slid to the hem of her shirt and she pulled the top over her head. Damned if he hadn't been right. No bra.

He took a step forward, but she held him off with one hand. "Not yet." A sexy grin took hold of her lips as she reached for the drawstring on her sweats.

Coming up to her knees, she pulled the bow and released the knot, letting her pants fall below her waist. She wriggled and kicked them off before returning to a kneeling position, giving him a clear view of what she wore beneath her pants. A sheer scrap of material covered her feminine mound, so transparent, it teased him with darkened shadows.

He let out a long, tortuous groan. She was baiting him bit by bit, making him wait, increasing his desire. He didn't know how long he could play by her rules, looking and not touching, wanting and not being able to satisfy his need. He leaned against the high chest of drawers near the wall, welcoming the support, because this woman could bring him to his knees if he let her.

He met her sparkling green gaze. "You're killing me."

"That's not in the plans." She hooked her fingertips in the waistband of her panties. "Because if I kill you, you'll miss the best part."

He laughed, folding his arms over his chest. "It's just an expression, babe." He shot her a wry grin. "I'm up for anything you have to offer."

"I can see that." She lowered her gaze to the bulge in his jeans and shimmied her hips, giving him a real show as she pulled the panties down and off, tossing them his way.

Now she was naked on his bed, leaning against his pillows, and beckoning to him with a crook of one finger. "Come and get me, Chase."

Between the come-hither look in her eyes and the seductive way her body called out to him, his restraint fled. He undressed in seconds, meeting her on the bed, making sure that his body met hers in the most intimate way on first contact. His groin pressed against her flesh, feeling her moist, damp heat. Chase wasn't sure whose groan sounded louder in the otherwise silent room, but the noise was damn arousing.

Especially for a man who'd been on the edge all day. He closed his eyes and saw the moment Samson's house went up in flames. When he opened them again, Sloane stared back at him, wide-eyed and waiting.

"When that house exploded, I thought you were inside," he said gruffly. "I thought I'd lost you." He brushed her hair off her face and tried to memorize each and every feature. "You took twenty years off my life."

"And when I saw you standing outside the house, you added twenty years to mine."

At her words, every part of him swelled — his heart, his body, his mind. Nothing mattered except doing as she said, joining with her and making them both feel alive.

The time for foreplay was over. He covered her mouth with his and, at the same time, thrusted hard and deep inside her.

Sloane inhaled and took all of him. She couldn't believe she'd been so bold, so brazen. But with Chase, she not only had no problem asking for what she wanted, but she also felt safe and secure in doing so. He pulled back slowly, only to rear forward again, and her body registered every slick inch, every hard movement. She clenched her thighs tighter and sensation rocked through her, taking her higher and higher, closer to climax, someplace she didn't want to go alone.

Still feeling bold, she reached down to where their bodies met. For a brief moment, she savored the thrusting motion, letting the texture of their joined bodies arouse her mind too.

"God, you do something to me," he murmured.

She opened her eyes. "Yeah, you're doing something pretty incredible to me." Her hips arched upward as if to back up her claim.

Tipping his head down, he licked at her breast, then suckled one nipple into his warm mouth. Her body shuddered at the erotic sensation, and when his teeth lightly grazed the distended tip, she arched off the mattress, pulling his penis all the way inside her needy body. He plunged deep and deeper still, until she felt him filling not just her femininity but something more, something she dare not name.

Apparently, he felt the same sensational waves, because he let out a low growl, one coming from deep in his throat as he began a steady pumping motion that brought them both to the edge fast and quick. Sloane knew she was losing control, yet she wanted to feel more. She discovered that if she held her breath, the waves spiraled higher and surrounded her in complete ecstasy. She inhaled once more, catching her breath. A cascade of bright light and amazing, exquisite pleasure took over, until the world seemed to explode. At the same moment, he found his release, his hips grinding in a circular motion, his big body trembling, shaking around hers.

By the time she came back to earth, her breathing wasn't just shallow, she was gasping for air. She leaned her head back and sighed. "Wow."

"Yeah." His voice sounded gruff and not all that steady either.

She grinned. She hadn't been kidding earlier when she spoke of still waters. He was a man of few words, something she was coming to appreciate about him. She laid her head on his chest, listening to the quiet sound of his heartbeat, and marveled at the calming effect he had on her in the midst of a life crisis.

His big hands smoothed the back of her hair and she reveled in the luxurious feeling of being cared for. "Mmm," she purred, but she wasn't oblivious to her promise. "About Samson . . ." she said, ready to talk.

"Shh. It's late and you've had a long day."

His words surprised her. "But I know you're wondering."

"Are you going anywhere?" he asked.

"No."

"Then go to sleep and we'll talk in the morning. Unless driving to Yorkshire Falls, nearly being in an explosion, and wrestling with bikers is your idea of a normal, relaxing day." Behind his wry tone, she sensed his concern. Beyond that, she sensed his innate belief that she would indeed be beside him in the morning, ready and willing to answer his questions.

"Thank you," she murmured, appreciating his understanding more than he could possibly know. She'd had too little trust given to her lately, especially by the people closest to her.

"You're more than welcome. Now sleep," he said in a rough voice. Pushing her hair aside, he kissed her neck and held her close.

His strength and emotional understanding let her relax, and she yawned, curling against his warm skin, waiting for sleep to come. As he said, tomorrow would be soon enough for answers.

Sloane awoke to find Chase's arms still tight around her. She couldn't remember the last time she'd slept so soundly and knew she had the man beside her to thank. She turned in his arms to find his blue eyes studying her.

A smile tilted her lips as she traced his profile with one finger.

"You're awfully quiet," he said at last, pulling her until her body was aligned with his.

"Used to chattering women, are you?" She bit the inside of her cheek, wishing she could withdraw the dumb, blithe joke. Nothing was funny about Chase and other women.

"Actually, I'm not used to women at all. Discretion, remember? No one came here and I never stayed over."

But he'd let her stay last night. She arched toward him, her breasts crushing into his chest, his musky warmth cocooning her in delicious heat. "Sounds lonely."

Though she'd have hated to imagine him in an emotionally intense relationship, she didn't want him alone either. He deserved so much more out of life, considering how much he'd given in return.

"You get used to it." He placed a warm, lingering kiss on her lips. "But it's too damn easy to get used to this too."

Her heart leaped at his words, even as she cautioned herself against thinking he meant anything by it. Changing the subject was the smartest route. Ironically, the more dangerous subject of her real father seemed the safest topic.

One she was ready to share with him, and Sloane instinctively knew it was because he'd invaded a small part of her heart. "Chase?"

"Hmm?"

"Samson, whoever . . . whatever he is . . . He's my real father."

"What?" Obviously shocked by her admission, Chase slid out of her grasp, bolting to a sitting position.

Before she could explain, a loud knocking sounded from the far side of the apartment. "Chase? Are you up yet? We need you downstairs."

"Damn. It's Lucy." He stood and grabbed for his jeans. "She's my right hand at the paper," he said to Sloane. "Hang on, I'll be right out," he yelled over his shoulder. He snapped his jeans and explained while he dressed. "Technically, I'm still on vacation, but they know I'm back and apparently they need me." He glanced Sloane's way, obviously torn. How could he not be after the bombshell she'd just dropped on him?

"Go. I'll still be here when you get back," she promised.

His blue eyes met hers, deep and questioning. "And you'll finish explaining?"

She nodded and pulled the covers up over her. "I brought the subject up, didn't I? I'm not about to bail on you now."

He inclined his head in silent acceptance, then turned and headed out, shutting the bedroom door behind him and leaving her alone. Sloane leaned back against the still-warm sheets. All around her, she could feel Chase's presence, feel how much he wanted her.

Too bad he only wanted her for as long as she was in Yorkshire Falls. Because deep down, Sloane had a hunch that she'd give him much more, if only he'd ask.

Chase's *Gazette* staff was comprised of good people with exceptional abilities, but because he'd been so hands-on over the years, they'd never once gone to press without his okay. Many times the front-page story was as mundane as a town meeting or as huge as a national tragedy. Then there were special occasions when Yorkshire Falls news led the day. The panty thief had been the last prime example, when his brother Roman had been pegged as the town Lothario due to a childhood prank and ridiculous coincidence. The newest headlines had happened yesterday. The *Gazette* was a weekly, and this week, Samson's house explo-

159

sion would lead the news.

Samson — Sloane's father. Chase pinched the bridge of his nose, unable to process that bit of truth. And since they'd had no time to talk before being interrupted, he could only draw his own conclusions now.

Sloane was in Yorkshire Falls, looking for Samson Humphrey, a man she'd never met. His house had blown up, and Chase's staff wanted to know why the police department — Rick Chandler in particular — wasn't releasing the name of the woman who'd witnessed the explosion. Because Chase had asked Rick to put a lid on Sloane's identity. He didn't want the paper running the news that Senator Carlisle's daughter was at a potential crime scene, or any other scene that would bring the national press to Yorkshire Falls. Chase refused to create a scandal. At least not until he knew more facts.

The only additional points he knew involved Madeline Carlisle, who had asked Chase to look out for Sloane. She'd also promised him not just an interview, but a possible exclusive in return. "If any information needs to come from my husband's camp, you'll be given it first," she'd assured him. Then that damn explosion and Sloane's revelation. All connected somehow, he was sure.

And the answers lay with the woman upstairs in his bed.

She had his loyalty, for reasons he wasn't ready to dissect or name. "Lucy," he called.

She came running, spry despite her years, which was just one reason she and Raina got along so well. "Yes, boss?"

"Tell them, since the cops aren't talking, to only use the term *unidentified woman*. No speculation, no description. No matter what they think they know," he added pointedly.

She nodded. "Mind if I ask you a question?"

"Since when do you need my permission?" he asked with a grin.

Lucy had been at Chase's side since the day he'd taken over the paper, and at his father's side before that. She spoke her mind, didn't hold back, and had free access to his apartment in case he was needed. Something that would have to change with Sloane around.

She tucked a pencil behind her ear without disrupting her neatly bobbed hair. "This is a key issue."

He sighed in resignation. "What do you want to know, Luce?"

"Well, the staff's been taking bets." She rocked on her heels, not meeting his gaze. "Sort of like an office pool."

He raised one eyebrow. "What's the subject?" he asked, though he had a hunch he already knew.

"Seeing as how you never brought a lady home with you before, the boys are wondering if this is the one."

Chase had always kept his private life private.

Hell, in this town, if he'd brought a woman to sleep in his bed and stay over night, every citizen would know. He'd been involved with Cindy for so long, their affair confined to her place, he'd been able to keep his private life private, and people like Lucy and his meddling mother wondering.

Which was why he should have known better than to think he could let Sloane stay upstairs and not have anyone get wind of it. He shook his head and muttered, "Shit."

Lucy remained unfazed. "Meanwhile, I thought since you and I go way back, you could give me the inside scoop," she said in a hushed voice. "Remember now, I'm the one who actually heard her in your bedroom."

To his shock, Chase felt his cheeks burn. Discussing his sex life with Lucy was as bad as discussing it with his mother. And with Lucy's penchant for gossip and long-standing friendship with Raina, it was tantamount to the same thing. The news would be shared by morning.

"Lucy?" he said in a voice distinct with warning.

She caught his inflection and saluted. "Yes, boss. I'm getting right back to work." But he heard her laughter all the way down the hall.

Chase made sure Ty Turner, the man he'd left in charge, had things under control, knew to beep him with any questions on the explosion piece, but to handle everything else himself. A solid hour had passed by the time he

162

finally walked back into his bedroom, hoping for answers.

But Sloane wasn't there. She'd left a note saying she'd gone to pick up something to eat, since his refrigerator was bare of breakfast food. While he waited, he lay down in his clothes and let himself rest. He trusted that she'd be back and his questions *would* be answered.

Chase had done so much for Sloane in a short time, breakfast was a small way to thank him. And talking would come easier over food, enabling her to keep her hands busy while she admitted her secrets.

She walked into Norman's at nine a.m. sharp and was greeted at the door by Izzy, wearing the same white apron from yesterday, her hair pulled back in a bun.

"I knew you'd be back." The woman gave Sloane a hug as if they were old friends. "I'm glad you're in one piece. I never would have sent you over to that old coot Samson's if I'd known the house was going to blow up like that." Izzy squeezed her harder, her relief obvious.

"Don't blame yourself," Sloane said, trying to gasp for air.

"Don't you worry. Rick told me to keep my mouth shut about sending you there and I will." Finally Izzy let her go, stepping back to pull menus from beside the register. "But it's someone's fault. Dang Samson anyway. The man doesn't pay attention to his shoe size. It'd be asking too much for him to notice the smell of gas and call the proper authorities." She waved menus in her hand as she spoke. "So you need a table?"

"Actually, I'd like breakfast to go," Sloane said, grateful for the change of subject.

Izzy leaned closer. "For two?" she asked, and winked. "I've known Chase since he was a boy and the man's got a solid appetite."

Sloane sighed. Apparently, Chase wasn't kidding about word traveling fast in this town, at least about some things. "Well, I'd love a large coffee with milk and sugar and one of those delicious-looking blueberry muffins." She pointed to the mouthwatering display of cakes and pastries. And since Izzy already knew whom Sloane was staying with, she might as well go for broke. "And I'll also take whatever is Chase's favorite."

Izzy patted her face and treated her to another wink, and an immediate burn rose to Sloane's cheeks. "I'll take care of breakfast for you," Izzy promised.

Sloane wondered how long before the rest of the town knew she'd spent the night with Chase Chandler. She shifted back and forth on her feet, waiting for her order to be filled. Luckily, no one else approached her, and within minutes, she had paid, received a bag full of food, and was ready to leave.

"You take care and I'll be seeing you later." Izzy added a few extra napkins into the bag.

"Thanks, Izzy."

The older woman grinned. "My pleasure."

The lines around her eyes and on her friendly face were a testament to the years she'd lived and many smiles she'd given. If Izzy was an indication of the people in this town, Sloane figured her mother had probably stored some good memories here. At least Sloane hoped she had.

And for the time she was here, Sloane decided she'd like to get to know this place too. She'd start by visiting shops and meeting people and hopefully finding out more information about Samson at the same time. "What time does Charlotte's Attic open?" Sloane asked Izzy.

"Beth Hansen, the manager, usually gets the place open around ten. Unless she's had a late night with her boyfriend. Then it's closer to ten-fifteen." Izzy nodded knowingly.

Sloane immediately recognized the older woman's intention to impart more gossip, but she wouldn't have privacy if she didn't respect others'. "I'll try to stop by later."

"Make sure you do. They've got sexy stuff. Items that'd make a normal man drool, if you get my drift. Not that my Norman cares anymore." She wagged a finger back toward her husband, who was busy cooking in the kitchen.

That was more information than Sloane

needed to know, but Izzy was oblivious and continued without missing a beat. "Now, a virile young man like Chase" — she wiggled her eyebrows suggestively — "I'm sure I don't have to say more."

Definitely not, Sloane thought. But Izzy was friendly and meant well, so Sloane smiled. "I'll be sure to let Beth and Charlotte know you're a talking advertisement." She decided to get out before Izzy could share any more.

Turning, she started for the door and bumped into a blonde about the same age as herself. She grabbed her bag tighter so as not to drop breakfast. "I'm sorry."

"No problem." The other woman stepped back to make room for Sloane to pass. "You're new in town."

Not a question, Sloane mused. Apparently, a new face was something immediately recognized around here. Nothing like D.C., where she saw different people every day.

Sloane nodded. "I'm just passing through." She didn't want to be rude, but she could feel the minutes ticking by since she'd left the house. She didn't want Chase to wake up and have him think she'd slipped out on him to avoid talking.

The pretty blonde smiled. "I was just passing through too, when I came to Yorkshire Falls. Then I decided to make my stay permanent. Oh, I'm Kendall Sutton. I mean, I'm Kendall Chandler." She shook her head and laughed. "I guess I'm still not used to the new name. I'm a newlywed," she explained.

Recognition dawned. "You're Rick's wife."

Kendall nodded, smiling.

"I'm Sloane —"

"Carlisle," Kendall whispered. "I know. Rick told me about you. But unlike the rest of this town, you can trust my discretion."

Something about Kendall's warmth told Sloane she could believe her. That and the fact that she was married to Chase's brother. The Chandlers struck her as smart men, wise in their dealing with people. "I appreciate that," Sloane said.

Kendall held open the door for her. "I don't know how long you plan on staying, but if you ever need a friend or want company or whatever, call."

"I will." Sloane liked Rick's wife. As she walked to her car, she realized she liked an awful lot about this quaint upstate town, including the warm people who said hello to her as she passed, and the more leisurely pace compared to D.C.

And as she pulled into Chase's driveway and parked around back, she discovered she liked coming home to him most of all.

Chapter Nine

The car door slammed and the front door creaked on opening before shutting closed. Chase relaxed in bed, listening to the sound of Sloane's return. Opening his eyes, he saw two delicious sights, Sloane and a tray of his favorite breakfast, French toast and bacon.

He eyed the food and his guest with gratitude. "You didn't have to go to any trouble."

"I did if I wanted to eat." Laughing, she settled in across from him, curling her knees beneath her so the tray separated them. "Besides, it was no trouble. I wanted to do something nice for you."

It was a novelty he wasn't used to. Such a small gesture, yet one that had his heart opening toward Sloane.

She picked up a napkin and handed it to him, then pried the plastic lid off his coffee cup.

"And you wanted to keep busy while we talked?"

"You're too perceptive."

He recognized the nervousness in her voice. She was a combination of strength and vulnerability, caring and independence, and Chase was drawn to all facets. "Thank you for the food."

"You're welcome."

Reaching across the tray as if to breach a divide, he squeezed her hand. "Don't be nervous. I'm not out to hurt you."

She wrinkled her nose, obviously thinking about his words. "It's funny how much I trust you despite the fact that there's that reporter inside you."

His smile came without warning. "I'm glad."

She paused for a sip of her coffee and he did the same, but he didn't need the jolt the caffeine would give. Sloane provided enough of a jump start to his system. "Want to tell me why this sudden trust?"

She shrugged. "You saved my *pretty behind* as you so eloquently put it."

"That's gratitude, and a far cry from trust." And why did he need that trust so badly, when every journalistic fiber of his being screamed to him that her story would make his career. Translation — he shouldn't get any more personally involved.

"Why did I have to find a perceptive man?" She glanced down at the tray and pulled a fork into her hand. "There are other reasons too. For one thing, I already trusted you in a completely intimate way. I don't do that often or lightly as I said once before." She toyed with the uneaten muffin on her plate, mashing bits with her fork and not meeting his gaze. "And I wouldn't have repeated being with you if you hadn't come to mean something to me," she admitted.

His rapidly beating heart nearly stopped. "You mean something to me too," he said in a rough voice.

"Not even Madeline knows some of what I'm going to tell you, Chase. You *can't* report on this. At least not until it's safe," she added, and swallowed hard. "But at some point you'll have to decide what's right for you."

She looked at him with such hope and belief in him shining in her eyes, he wondered if she was doomed to disappointment. He couldn't believe fate could be so cruel as to make him choose between Sloane's approval and his own long-held desires.

But that time hadn't yet arrived. "Talk to me, Sloane. You said Samson's your *father?*" He still couldn't reconcile the news or put this beautiful woman together with the reclusive loner in any way.

"Believe it or not, yes." She dropped the fork.

Her muffin remained untouched, and because he hurt for her, he couldn't bring himself to eat either. "How did that happen?"

"I'd guess the old-fashioned way."

He laughed. "That's not what I meant."

"I know." She shifted positions, uncrossing and recrossing her legs beneath her. "Apparently before my father — I mean Michael — came into the picture, my mother was in love with Samson. From everything people have said about him around here, I take it he's not the most upstanding citizen?"

Chase hesitated, grappling for diplomatic words to describe the old man. "He's . . ."

"Don't sugarcoat it," she ordered. "Be as honest with me as I'm being with you."

He nodded, admiring her strength. "He's eccentric and antisocial. Those are the most usual words bandied around."

"Maybe he wasn't always that way?"

He shrugged. He really had no idea. "It's possible. I'm sure my mother would know, and considering she's always been kind to him, I'd guess you were right." But Chase had never thought to question the man's past or what made him into the odd creature he'd become. He didn't like realizing he'd been so negative and close-minded against a man who, it turned out, was Sloane's father.

Sloane met his gaze, a forced smile on her lips. "I just may ask her one day."

"Then be prepared to answer questions of your own," Chase said wryly.

She laughed. "I really liked your mother. She has spunk."

He rolled his eyes. "That's one word for it."

"Hey, don't knock it. It's obviously something my parents lacked."

"Why do you say that? You're full of spunk and fortitude and you had to have inherited those genes from them," he said, seeking to reassure her about an emotional and upsetting subject. One he still had many questions about.

"I don't know." Her eyes, wide and full of

hurt, shimmered with unshed tears. "What kind of people let themselves be bought off?"

He sat up straighter, every journalistic nerve ending on high alert. "What do you mean?"

"It seems that my grandfather, Jacqueline's father, threatened Samson with something strong enough to get him to leave my mother and he took money to do it."

Chase blinked, startled by the admission. Bribery? And did Senator Carlisle have anything to do with it, Chase wondered. He held back accusatory-sounding questions for now, in favor of keeping Sloane calm and rational. He was worried about her feelings and her bruised emotions.

He shook his head, knowing that wasn't the path any self-respecting journalist would take. But he'd never felt less like a reporter and more like a man than he did around this woman. "Let's go under the assumption that Samson had good reason to take the money. At least until we know otherwise, okay?" He wasn't sure if he believed his own words, but Sloane looked as if she needed hope. The least he could do was give it to her. "If it's any consolation, Samson never lived like he took money from anyone."

"I know. I saw the house before the explosion. I walked inside." She shivered and wrapped her arms around herself. "It was scary. And sad."

He nodded. "I can understand why you feel

that way." He pinched his nose, trying to assimilate his thoughts. "Why did you come looking for Samson now?" he asked, taking her back to the beginning. With her father's campaign under way, this had to be the least opportune time for her to seek out her real father.

"Because I just found out. The night we met, actually." She rose from the bed and began to pace. "I was supposed to have dinner with my parents and had arrived at the hotel room early." She twisted her hands together as she spoke, the rapid movements and perpetual motion obviously necessary for her to work up the nerve to continue.

"Go on."

She cleared her throat. "Michael and Madeline weren't there, but his campaign manager was, along with an assistant. Men I'd grown up knowing. They were talking in hushed, frenzied whispers about Michael not being my real father and needing to eliminate a threat to the campaign. Frank never makes idle statements or promises." Her shoulders straightened, her path clear. "And so after I stopped reeling from the news that Michael wasn't my real father, I realized I had to come here and warn this man I'd never met. The man who is my . . . father."

And the man whose house had just exploded, Chase thought. Either that fire was one hell of a coincidence or Michael Carlisle's men had carried through with their threats. He clenched his hands around the bedsheets, realizing how serious this situation really was. Apparently, Sloane wasn't as concerned about danger to herself as she was about finding Samson. Which meant he'd have to be concerned for her.

She was too busy focusing on other things and he had a hunch he knew why. The truth about Samson was still raw and fresh. "So you heard the news and you ran." He rose, coming up beside her and placing a comforting hand on her shoulder.

"Right into your arms."

She turned toward him and tipped her head upward.

He grinned. "Good thing I was there to catch you."

"Yeah." She smiled back. "Good thing."

"You said when you finished reeling, you decided to warn Samson. But I don't think you have."

"Have what?"

"Finished reeling." He curled his fingertips into her skin, brushing the pad of his thumb over her soft flesh. "Because it would be perfectly normal if you hadn't." And he wanted to help her through the conflicting, confusing feelings.

"I haven't had time to worry about myself. I'll deal with all these leftover feelings once I find Samson."

"I think you need to deal with your emotions,

Sloane. It's not like Samson's here now or you can do anything about finding him. At least not this minute." He caressed her cheek and her eyes sparkled with gratitude, and thankfully a helluva lot more. "Why don't you let me take care of you?"

"Because I bought you breakfast so I could do the same for you. Take care of the man who's always taking care of everyone else."

"Who told you that?"

"You did." She laughed, her gaze never leaving his. "I can take care of myself, but I appreciate the offer." Standing on her toes, she pressed a quick kiss on his lips, one not nearly long enough to suit him. "Your French toast must be cold. Let me warm it in the microwave."

She turned for the door, but he caught her hand in time. "I'm not hungry." He didn't want her running from her feelings. She'd already glossed over her emotions as unimportant, then changed the subject to food.

He wasn't buying her nonchalance. She was hurting and Chase didn't want her suffering in silence. "Even self-sufficient people need a shoulder every now and then."

She inclined her head, acknowledging his point. "And when we have time, maybe I'll take you up on your offer. Right now I need to talk to your mother. You said she knows Samson, so she might have some clues about where he'd go." She glanced down at her hand, still entwined with his.

"Either you let me go or I drag you with me into the shower." She shook her head. "I didn't mean that literally," she said, blushing at her words.

"Why not?" He lifted her hands to his lips and feathered soft kisses over her knuckles. "I can't think of anything more soothing than a hot shower." He let his tongue take over, tracing the soft slopes of her hand, tasting her salty skin. "Or anything more mutually satisfying." He blew on the moist patches he'd left behind.

She let out a low moan. "You do tempt me. But you were right the first time, when you said we weren't finished talking. I need to know you're not going to tell anyone about Michael Carlisle."

From her flushed face and dilated eyes, he knew ignoring the passion wasn't easy for her. He ought to know. Pushing aside the connection they'd found while she revealed her deepest pain was even harder to do. But her question was valid and couldn't be avoided.

Would he tell anyone? He couldn't print the news, not while Sloane's or Samson's life was at stake. He didn't want to turn her into a walking target. But how could he keep the truth from the police?

"Chase, please," she said in the wake of his silence, squeezing his hands tighter. "If the public found out the senator kept such a secret from me, it could destroy their trust in him and ruin not just this campaign but his career aspirations." She pinned him with her stare, waiting for an answer.

Chase was floored. Despite the senator's lies, Sloane supported him. "I admire your loyalty."

"He raised me as his own child and never treated me any different than my" — she hesitated — "than my sisters and they're his flesh and blood." She swallowed hard. "He loves me. I've never not felt that love. Whatever his reasons for keeping my parentage a secret, I won't let his life's work be destroyed. So promise me you'll keep quiet."

I trusted you, Chase. He heard the words she chose not to say and he was torn. "Rick can put out an APB for Samson. It's in his best interest to be found."

"No. That would make things public. Give us time to find him first."

"Us?" he asked, liking the sound of the word on her lips.

"You already said I'm not going to Harrington alone. I've come to consider you my partner in all this."

"And Rick can help us," he insisted. "That explosion might well be a warning we should heed."

She nodded. "If it turns out the explosion was more than an accident, I'll go with you to talk to Rick. How's that for compromise?" She clenched her hands in front of her. "In the meantime, we search for Samson ourselves.

Pretty please?" She shot him a blatant, disarming grin.

She was manipulating him and they both knew it. He couldn't help but laugh anyway. Besides, for now, his decision was easy. "I promise not to say or print a word. But if the accident classification changes, I'm holding you to your promise and our first stop is the police."

In the meantime, he didn't want the threats from her father's associates following her here. Hell, maybe they already had — something he wouldn't know until the fire department finished investigating and officially classified the explosion.

She grinned and saluted, obviously relieved. But she shouldn't be too complacent, he thought. He was a journalist who'd never shied away from reporting. After they found Samson and figured out how to handle the threat, her story would make damned good headlines. If he didn't print the news about the senator's lies and other reporters got wind of the scandal, they'd expose all. And the result wouldn't be pretty. At least debuting in his hands, Sloane had a chance of the story being told in a factual, nonbiased way.

But he had time before worrying. Time to get in deeper with Sloane.

Chase pulled his truck in front of his mother's house. The old Colonial he grew up in still looked fresh and new, thanks to a coat of paint and the constant care he and his brothers supplied.

He turned, placing his hand over her seat. "Are you sure you can handle my mother?" he asked Sloane.

"I'm certain I can hold my own." A long curl had escaped her ponytail and she tucked the strand behind her ear. "Raina seems harmless enough."

He cocked an eyebrow but didn't touch that comment. "I already called her this morning and discussed what you'd be talking to her about. She understands the need for secrecy."

"You didn't need to do that."

He heard the steely tone in Sloane's voice, the one that never ceased to remind him she'd indeed been raised by Senator Michael Carlisle, a master at getting what he wanted, and his wife, Madeline, the strong woman alongside the man.

"I wanted to."

"I could have explained things myself," Sloane said.

"But you don't want her spreading this rumor about Samson and inadvertently exposing the very story you're trying to hide."

Not that he was concerned about his mother being informed about Sloane's relationship to, or search for, Samson. Nobody would go further than Raina to protect someone they cared about. Once he'd explained their reasons for needing Raina's discretion, Chase trusted her promise to provide it. His mother only participated in town gossip out of boredom and to maintain a sense of community. She'd put Sloane and Samson's needs first now and remain silent.

Yet Sloane was still quiet. She still didn't seem pleased that he'd interfered and he felt compelled to explain. Which surprised him. He'd always made decisions first and explained himself to no one. As the head of the family and the paper, he'd never had to justify a decision.

But he didn't want this woman to think he'd steamrolled over her needs and desires. Her feelings were important to him. "I just felt better paving the way," he said, uncomfortable and gripping the steering wheel harder as he spoke.

Sloane nodded. "And now that you have, I can handle it," she said once more.

Her placating tone set his nerves on edge. He hated sounding like a worried parent, when all he really was, was a concerned lover. Besides, older habits died hard and he couldn't help wanting to look out for her. "And don't leave here until I get back," he added.

"Yes, sir." She saluted him again.

He winced. "Am I really that bad?" he asked.

She chuckled, her light laugh allowing him to release much of his emotional tension.

"Let's just say it's a good thing for you I like my men assertive." Her voice dropped, taking on a husky quality he couldn't misinterpret.

One hand on the wheel, he leaned closer. "We'll discuss your penchant for dominant men when we get home later."

"Promises, promises." She reached for the door handle, then turned back to brush a kiss over his lips before getting out of the truck.

She adjusted the turtleneck sweater she'd worn and walked up his mother's front lawn, her hips swaying, her mood good despite everything going on around her. He admired her spunk. Chase figured the two women would get along fine. He gripped the steering wheel harder, knowing that thought ought to worry him much more than it did.

Once Sloane safely entered his mother's house, Chase pulled back onto the street and turned around, heading out of town. Now that he knew the potential for danger, he'd promised himself he wouldn't leave Sloane alone. With both women together and not out looking for trouble, he could rest easy. Unless he counted Raina as trouble, he thought wryly. But he was certain Sloane could handle anything his mother tossed her way and would return question for question, giving as good as she got.

In the meantime, he planned to make good use of his time alone. He couldn't stop thinking of Cindy's expression after seeing him with Sloane and he intended to head into Harrington to officially end a relationship that was already

long over. Then he planned to do some journalistic digging on Sloane's grandfather, Senator Jack Ford, and his past with the elusive
Samson Humphrey.

Sloane waited in the family room while Raina
made them tea. She walked from bookshelf to
bookshelf, examining the photos of Chase and
his brothers as young boys, studying their pro-
gression to grown men. They'd been adorable
children and even more handsome adults. And
when Raina had her way, they'd have gorgeous
families of their own. In Roman and Charlotte's case, that day wasn't far off since Chase
had told her Roman's wife was pregnant, due
next month. Having met Rick's wife, Kendall,
Sloane had no doubt the good-looking couple
would also have beautiful babies.

But Chase's children could be the most incredible of all, and the vision was all too clear
in her mind. Blue-eyed, black-haired imps. But
reality intruded painfully. He'd already decided
against the notion. *Too bad,* she thought, her
stomach fluttering with warmth and an unexpected sorrow.

Her gaze drifted to the photos and that sadness inside her grew stronger each time she
caught sight of Chase. With each passing year,
his expression grew ever more serious. He'd
borne so much on his broad shoulders, more
than any teenager should have to bear. But he'd
held up well and his family had benefited from

his sense of duty and caring.

"Like what you see?" Raina asked, walking into the room with two white mugs filled with liquid. "Those photos are like a timeline. I can't tell you how often I look at them just because they make me smile." She held out one cup.

"Thanks." Sloane accepted her drink, the ceramic mug warm in her hands. "You have every reason to smile." She glanced at her hostess.

Sloane had met Raina only once, but she noticed that today her coloring seemed off, her pallor too gray beneath the makeup. Commenting would be rude, but Sloane was worried. "You raised three incredible boys," Sloane said, refocusing on their conversation.

"They're men now." Raina shook her head as if unable to believe. "Time does fly. Two of them are even married." She grinned, obviously pleased.

"I met your daughter-in-law Kendall," Sloane said.

"Isn't she wonderful? Her aunt Crystal was one of my closest friends."

"Really?"

Raina nodded. "Crystal passed away recently and Kendall moved back here to take care of her things. Her sister, Hannah, followed, and they're both living here now. Hannah's a handful to raise, but Kendall and Rick deal well with her." Raina's tone showed her pride.

"She's got fortitude and speaks her mind. Exactly what I want in a granddaughter."

"Because she's just like you." Sloane laughed.

"But of course." Raina crossed the room, walking over to the long couch. "I hope you don't mind but I'm a little tired, so let's sit." She settled herself onto the couch and motioned for Sloane to join her on the chair across from a large cocktail table.

She placed her glass on a waiting coaster and sat down. "I hope I get to meet Hannah while I'm here."

"Just how long are you planning to stay?" Raina asked with no amount of shame.

"Are you asking to be polite or because you want to know how long you have to matchmake?" Sloane asked, chuckling.

"Shame on Chase. Has he been telling tales about his mother?"

"None that aren't true," Sloane assured her. "Actually, I'm not sure how long I'll stay. I'm on a mission of sorts. I suppose it depends on how long it takes me to accomplish it." She took a sip of the tea while Raina did too.

"I love a good mystery, but in this case, let's just be honest with each other. Chase called this morning and as I'm sure you realize, I know your secret."

Sloane nodded. "And it really does make things easier on me, not having to explain." Though she'd given Chase a hard time for taking control, she appreciated him smoothing things over.

She'd had her reasons for being overly forceful with him. She couldn't let him push her around, even if she found his often domineering tendencies sexy and endearing, if only because they showed he cared.

But how much?

Oh, he cared enough to sleep with her, and Sloane definitely wasn't making him beg for sex. But to her, sleeping with Chase definitely fell into the *making love* category. She couldn't bear to think he'd just transferred his dependability to her and would move on easily once she found Samson. Although that was the inevitable outcome, she still wanted to know he cared and would miss her once she was gone.

"Sloane? Sloane?" Raina had come up beside her, knelt down, and snapped her fingers in front of her face.

"I'm sorry. I was just lost in thought," she explained.

"That's okay. I'm sure you have a lot on your mind." She rose quickly and gripped the arm of the chair hard enough that her knuckles turned white. "Raina?" Sloane put her hand over hers.

"I'm fine." She straightened and walked slowly back to her seat on the couch. "It's just this heart condition I've been diagnosed with." She didn't meet Sloane's gaze, her eyes darting to the photos she'd seen earlier.

"Chase didn't mention anything." Sloane was

concerned as well as confused.

"That's because he tries to act as if things are normal." Raina waved a hand in the air. "And they are. But your life has been turned upside down. Would you be surprised if I said I'd figured out your relationship to Jacqueline soon after our first meeting?"

"Very surprised!"

"I had no idea she'd been in a relationship with Samson, but as soon as I took a look at you, I knew you were related to her. You two look so much alike," Raina murmured.

Sloane leaned forward, overwhelmed by the excitement of meeting someone who knew her mother from way back. "How well did you know Jacqueline?"

"We used to spend summers together." Raina rubbed her hands together, warming to the subject.

"Then you knew her when she was younger?" The older woman nodded.

Sloane's heartbeat picked up. "Tell me about her? The only stories I know are from my — from Michael and Madeline and they knew her after she'd turned eighteen." She drew a steadying breath. "I just want to know what she was like. What we had in common."

Raina's gaze softened. Though Chase didn't share her hazel eyes, the shape and expression were similar, something more noticeable now, when Raina's were filled with warmth. "Your mom loved the summer. She loved fresh air and being free from school and the constraints around her. That's why she and I would spend time in a tree house behind her house."

"A tree house?" Sloane asked, surprised. "From all I heard about my grandfather, I can't imagine him building a tree house." She crinkled her nose at the thought.

"Smart girl." Raina smiled. "The tree house came with the property, and when your mother was late for dinner, your grandfather would threaten to cut the thing down."

The thought made Sloane sad. "Now, that makes more sense."

"The tree house wasn't big, but it was private and no one would bother us there. We could talk about boys, and about girl things. Jacqueline was a very sweet person, but she lived with parents who stifled her sense of self."

"I know what that's like," Sloane said, shocked she and her mother had something so fundamental in common. Having grown up with people who also expected certain etiquette and behavior, Sloane felt a sudden kinship with the mother she'd never really known. And suddenly she didn't feel so lonely or unusual, the outcast in a political family. She was her mother's daughter. And that knowledge filled her with an unexpected sense of belonging in this small town.

"So you can understand why the tree house was so important to her. It was a place she could go to get away." Raina shook her head, her eyes wide.

"Is it still there?"

Raina shrugged. "It sure is. Do you want the address so you can see for yourself?"

"I'd like that."

Grabbing a sheet of paper and a pen, Raina scribbled the house number and street and slid the paper across the table. "Don't go alone or you'll likely stir up questions you don't want to answer," Raina warned her.

She laughed at the older woman's protective tone, then slipped the address into her pocket. "Now you sound like Chase."

Raina leaned forward. "And is that a good thing?" she asked, obviously back in matchmaking mode.

"Tsk, tsk, Raina," Sloane chided. "You're too obvious."

"Oh pooh. And you're no fun."

"Chase tells me you know my father?" Sloane latched on to the next subject of importance. So far, she'd learned much more than she'd hoped from Raina Chandler.

"You mean Samson."

Sloane nodded. "He's just a name to me." She rose and began pacing the room. As she always did when discussing her unknown parent, she became restless and uncomfortable. "But since I came to town, I've got the distinct impression he's not going to be what I expected."

"Or hoped for?" Raina asked perceptively.

Sloane figured Chase got his intuition from his mother, who had nailed her feelings. "I never had the chance to form any sort of expectation," she admitted. "I found out that Michael Carlisle wasn't my father and came here almost right after. Next thing I knew, people in town are dropping odd comments about how no one's ever called Samson a gentleman, or how he mooches sandwiches from Norman's. Chase used the word *eccentric?*" She shook her head, confused and hoping Raina had more answers.

"Samson's odd," Raina allowed, as diplomatic as her son had been. "Surly would also describe him. But he's harmless and mostly misunderstood."

Sloane turned to face Raina. "How so?"

"People react to a person, but they tend to forget who they are or more accurately what they were."

"What do you mean?"

Raina stretched out on the couch, looking more weary than she had earlier. Sloane made a mental note to discuss his mother's health with Chase as soon as possible.

Pulling an afghan blanket over herself, Raina began to explain. "Samson's mother was a quiet woman. She worked as a cashier at the general store, bringing in barely enough to make ends meet. But his father was a gambler."

"Gambling?"

"It was very bad." Raina ran her hand over the back of the sofa, deep in thought. "He was always in debt and had even spent some time in jail for stealing money to pay back a debt. Luckily, the Coopers, who own the general store, took care of their food needs because his father too often would gamble away what little his mother earned. Awful, really."

Sloane agreed.

"Circumstances made Samson a loner," Raina continued. "But who can blame him? I mean, wouldn't any teenager withdraw if they were embarrassed to bring anyone home?"

A lump formed in Sloane's throat and she was unable to answer.

"But he was nice and kind and handsome in his day." Raina smiled, remembering. "And he turned his attention to studies. His goal was to get a college education and do better than his parents had."

Hope and admiration replaced Sloane's earlier despair and she hung on Raina's every word. "We can assume that at some point he had a relationship with my mother."

Raina sighed. "I suppose so. And I wish that Jacqueline had told me." She shook her head, her frustration obvious. "Now that the pieces are coming together, I remember her mentioning being in love that last summer she spent in Yorkshire Falls. She didn't want to use his name. She said she was afraid of jinxing the relationship, but I knew she meant she was afraid her father would find out. Jack Ford was a tough old bird."

Sloane recalled the details of how her grandfather had bribed Samson to stay away from her mother and Sloane knew Raina's description was way too kind. She had a hunch that Samson's father's gambling had something to do with the bribery and money that had exchanged hands. "Did Samson ever go to college?"

Raina shook her head. "He changed. Actually, it was around the time Jacqueline's family moved away. He started spending all his time at home instead of at the library. Eventually his mother passed away and his father took off one day, never to be seen again. Rumor had it he went to Las Vegas, though I always assumed that was the easy answer to where a gambler would go."

Sloane tried, but she couldn't even manage a laugh. "And then?"

Raina raised her hands and spread them wide. "Then nothing. Your mother had moved away long before and Samson became more and more withdrawn, more odd, reclusive. . . ." She dropped her hands, shaking her head. "I'm sorry. I just think you need to be prepared for the man you find."

"*If* I find him."

"Well, his house is gone, so you're going to have to try —"

"Friends?" Sloane asked wryly. "We both know he has none in town."

"None we know of. He has to be somewhere," Raina insisted. "In the meantime, I've answered your questions. Now humor an old lady and answer some of mine."

Sloane burst out laughing. "I admire you, Raina. I really do." In fact, she enjoyed the older woman way too much. She liked spending time with Chase's mother, and because Raina had known Jacqueline, Sloane felt an emotional bond she hadn't expected.

"Why is that?"

"You don't hedge, for one thing."

"Any reason why I should?" Raina grinned, and to Sloane's relief, the first hint of color returned to the older woman's cheeks. "Now for my most important question." She straightened her shoulders and tossed her best volley. "Are you and Chase a couple?"

Sloane wasn't too stunned to reply, she was just taken off guard. "I'm not sure how to answer that."

"Just tell her the truth." Chase strode into the room, handsome, sexy, and disarming, with that cocky grin he didn't use often enough. But its effect was devastating when turned her way.

"Which is?" Raina rubbed her hands together in anticipation.

Sloane met his heated gaze, wanting an answer to that question herself. "Go on, Chase. If you're so good at answers, *you* tell your mother the truth."

And then she held her breath while she waited to find out what that truth was.

Chapter Ten

Chase caught the anticipation on Sloane's face. She hadn't a clue what he was going to say, but she didn't have to worry. He had more class than to tell his mother they were lovers. He would, however, give Raina the answer to her prayers. "Sloane and I are an item, Mom." Something he'd confirmed with Cindy earlier.

They'd parted on amicable and understanding terms, but he hadn't told Cindy he and Sloane were temporary. It didn't seem appropriate or necessary.

"I knew it!" Raina clasped her hands together, her pleasure at Chase and Sloane's pairing obvious.

Apparently, the women had hit it off, and as Chase expected, she'd already okayed Sloane as daughter-in-law material. For that reason, he'd decided to use Raina's own needs against her.

If she thought Chase was seriously involved with Sloane, she'd leave them alone, freeing him from any unexpected visits and keeping his mother out of harm's way while they searched for Samson.

"Now that you have your answer, I've come to take Sloane to lunch." He walked to the living room and held out a hand, helping

Sloane rise from her seat. "I trust you ladies had a nice morning?"

"Wonderful," Sloane said. "Productive too. Your mother knew my mom much better than either one of us realized."

"I'd love it if you'd come back and visit," Raina said without getting up from her seat on the couch. "In the meantime, I'll see if I can remember anything else."

Sloane nodded. "I'd appreciate that. Maybe you'd like to join us for lunch?"

Damn, Chase thought. "Mom needs her rest." He shot a pointed glance at his mother. She wouldn't dare join them if she thought he wanted intimate time with Sloane.

Sure enough, she treated him to an almost imperceptible nod of understanding.

"You're sweet, Sloane, but Eric's taking me to a movie tonight, so I should take it easy now. I'll just watch the soaps this afternoon. How's that?"

"Sounds good to me." He'd have to explain about his mother's health later. Though he'd told her about Raina's matchmaking tendencies, he'd neglected to mention her fake heart condition — something he'd yet to come to terms with. And he hadn't yet decided how to deal with the situation.

He studied his mother for a quick moment. She still looked pale, but he wasn't worried. When she wanted to be convincing, Raina had appeared weak and frail, and Chase had bought the act. He wouldn't be so susceptible again.

"We should go." Chase tugged on Sloane's hand. "Rick would like to meet with us," he whispered, wanting her to realize this was more than a casual lunch. His brother had called, indicating he had information on the explosion he needed to share, and Chase had a hunch they'd be needing to open up with Rick in return.

He stepped toward Raina and gave her a kiss on the cheek, good-byes were exchanged, and ten minutes later, Chase found himself seated beside Sloane at Norman's while they waited for Rick.

She fiddled with a spoon, occasionally glancing into the reflection as if looking for answers.

"You've been quiet since we left my mother's."

She glanced up. "I have a lot to absorb. For starters, Samson's father was a heavy gambler and I'm guessing that habit had something to do with Samson taking a bribe to stay away from Jacqueline."

He nodded, sensing she had more to say and not wanting to interrupt.

"Raina said Jacqueline was in love that last summer before they moved away. But she didn't know with whom."

"That's one answer we're certain of," Chase said wryly, trying to lighten her mood.

"I know." She twisted the spoon handle between her palms.

Reaching over, he stopped her jittery movements and held her hand. "What else has you so bothered? Because you got the answers you were searching for and obviously there's more upsetting you than what you've said."

"It's about your mother," she said, meeting his gaze.

Chase couldn't imagine Raina doing anything to upset Sloane. Not when she clearly liked her and was pushing for romance. Then again, when it came to Raina, he knew to expect the unexpected. "What did she do?"

"She seemed tired today. And pale." Sloane furrowed her brows in thought. "And when she jumped up from her seat, she seemed to be in pain from the sudden movement. I don't want to upset you, or butt into something that's none of my business, but —"

"Raina was playing you," Chase interrupted, not surprised that Sloane had noticed his mother's distress. No doubt that was what Raina had intended.

"Playing me how?" Sloane crinkled her nose. "I don't understand. Raina wasn't feeling well. How was that playing me?"

At that moment, Rick strode up to the table and Chase saw his chance to kill two proverbial birds. "Why don't you explain to Sloane why Mom would pretend to be sick," Chase said, confronting his brother about their mother's charade.

"Shit." Rick slicked a hand through his

windblown hair. "Roman called and told me to be prepared."

"And I would have nailed your sorry ass days ago if I wasn't busy with other things," Chase muttered. "Just tell Sloane about Mom's pretend heart condition."

Her eyes opened wide. "Pretend heart condition?"

"Mom had an episode a while back. She figured if she told us it was serious, then played on our good natures, she could get us settled down with the *right* women and get herself some grandchildren in the process." Rick grimaced and Chase knew he was recalling the days leading up to his meeting Kendall.

"Mom set him up with all sorts of women before Kendall hit town," Chase explained.

"Anyway, she doesn't know that Chase knows the truth. Not yet. So if you saw anything today, it's because Mom wanted you to think that she was sick and report back to Chase."

"So he'd feel bad and start thinking I might be a good candidate?" Sloane guessed accurately.

Chase nodded. "Bingo. But she's got a grandchild coming from Roman and Charlotte, and with Kendall she's got Hannah. She's being ridiculous still trying to set me up."

"Is that why you told her we were an item?"

She glanced at him warily, trepidation in her eyes, and he couldn't bring himself to hurt her.

"I told her that so she'd back off, yes," he admitted, careful to be honest. But he also wanted Sloane to know she wasn't just a convenience for him. "I also told her that we're a couple because while you're here, it's the truth."

She licked her lips and his gaze followed the movement. "Yes, it's true. While I'm here, I mean. Nothing beyond."

She parroted his words, but coming from the mouth that he knew intimately, they sounded too hollow for his liking.

Rick cleared his throat. "Okay, folks. Now that we've established Mom's good health, let's move on and talk about Samson's."

Before Chase could ask questions or Rick could explain further, Kendall slipped into the open fourth chair. "Hi, guys."

Chase groaned at the interruption, but he figured it would be too much to expect Rick to ask his wife to leave.

Sloane turned her gorgeous smile toward Chase's sister-in-law. "Hi, Kendall. Nice to see you again."

"Hi, honey." Rick wrapped an arm around his wife's shoulder. "Can you give us a second? We're conducting business."

Chase raised an eyebrow. Apparently, he'd misjudged his sibling.

Kendall gave him an understanding smile. "Sure. I'll just go say hi to Pearl and Eldin. They're up front placing an order. A huge order, come to think of it."

"Pearl and Eldin?" Sloane asked, leaning forward, propping her chin in one hand. "Who are they?"

"My tenants," Kendall said.

"Hard to call them tenants when they're living in our guesthouse for free," Rick said wryly.

Chase laughed. "It's a long story," he said to Sloane.

Sloane's eyes lit up. "I'd like to hear it. I'm beginning to enjoy small-town life."

He wondered if she was serious or if Sloane Carlisle was just being polite.

"Tell you what. I'll bring them by after you finish talking, and I promise you, Pearl will sum up her life story in one minute flat." Kendall planted a kiss on Rick's lips and headed for the front of the restaurant.

"She's my dream wife," Rick said, laughing. "Never questions when I have to do business and disappears when I need her to."

"Something tells me she's your dream wife for more reasons than that," Sloane said indulgently.

Chase caught the hint of wistfulness in her voice and knew he wasn't imagining things. She'd been through so much recently, not the least of which was the betrayal of her parents. She was missing out on love, trust, and dependability, Chase knew. And she sensed the depth of which Kendall and Rick felt those things for each other. She wanted it for herself.

The notion brought a lump of pure fear to

his throat. Because he had a hunch that Sloane's vision of love, trust, and dependability included hearth, home, and stability, the very things he swore he was finished with.

"Earth to Chase." Rick tapped his fist on the table, jarring the silverware and Chase jumped. "What the hell's got you so distracted? Kendall's gone, so let's talk."

Chase blinked and realized his brother and Sloane were staring, waiting for him to focus. "I'm ready now," he muttered, offering no explanation for spacing out on them.

"Okay." Rick leaned forward, motioning for them to do the same. "First things first. Off the record, the explosion at Samson's was no accident. The boiler had been tampered with."

"What?" Sloane's voice raised to a high pitch and Chase lay his hand over hers to calm her down.

"I thought you should know." Rick splayed his hands in front of him.

"We appreciate that. And we have something we need to tell you too," Chase said.

Sloane tipped her head to the side and whispered in his ear. "No, please. Not yet."

"You promised if we found out that the explosion was deliberate, we'd go to Rick," he reminded her.

"What's going on?" his brother demanded. "If it has anything to do with the explosion, I don't want you holding out on me."

Chase met and held Sloane's gaze, knowing

he had to push her and hating it at the same time. "Do you want to fill Rick in or should I?"

Sloane grit her teeth. Chase's tone brooked no argument. Someone would be informing Rick that her father's men had threatened Samson and two days later, his house had exploded.

"It's my story to tell." She explained what she'd overheard between her father's men and how she and Chase planned to go back to Crazy Eights in Harrington in order to look for Samson. Tonight.

Rick pinched the bridge of his nose, and in that instant, the brothers who didn't look alike suddenly had an eerie resemblance. "You two don't do anything halfway, do you?" Rick asked, and motioned to his wife to rejoin them.

"She plans on going with or without me," Chase muttered. "So I'm in."

"And so am I. I'm off duty tonight, so I'll go along." Rick patted the gun in his holster. "Because you two might need backup."

Sloane was shocked to discover her eyes welling up with tears. The bond between the brothers, the lengths to which they would go to help one another, were all something she envied. Something she shared with her family, but since finding out that her life had been based on a lie — that her family wasn't really her family — she felt the enormous loss.

She cleared her throat, trying to push the emotion aside. "Thank you, Rick."

"He's the best," Chase assured her. He winked at his brother, and Sloane cleared her throat once more.

"We already have an APB out on Samson," Rick said, all business. "Carlisle's men can be questioned, but tipping them off without real evidence isn't smart. In the meantime, we're all going to Crazy Eights tonight," Rick said.

"That place is the epitome of slime," Kendall said, slipping back into her seat. "Why would we want to go there?"

Chase groaned, something he seemed to do often since sitting down at the table. Not that Sloane blamed him. Now they had Kendall to deal with and she obviously planned to accompany them. If Sloane were married to Rick, she'd plan to do the same thing.

"Why don't you explain everything," she said to Rick. If Kendall was going to go with them, she deserved to know details. "Kendall's coming with us can work in our favor. We'll seem more normal going out as two couples anyway."

"I don't believe this," Chase muttered.

Sloane grasped his hand beneath the table. "I'm sorry."

"For turning my life upside down?" He treated her to the lopsided grin she adored.

She opened her mouth to reply and he took advantage of the opportunity, kissing her into silence. As always, his touch was electric, fueling a desire that always simmered just below the surface, no matter what went on around them.

"What was that for?" she asked when he finally let her up for air. Rick and Kendall, she noticed, were deep in conversation.

He shrugged, looking sheepish. "Because I felt like it."

He wasn't normally an impulsive man, and though the change surprised her, she was careful not to read too much into it or attribute it to her influence. Though he cared about her, he'd also admitted that he had an agenda. Making this relationship public was a way to keep his mother off guard and avoid her matchmaking. And now the entire town was in on the act. The charade would continue while she stayed in Yorkshire Falls, not any longer.

Something she'd better remember and quit getting so attached to Chase or to his wonderful family.

"Okay, we're on for tonight." Kendall smiled, obviously pleased to be in on the action.

Rick frowned and Sloane recognized his stern cop face. "Only because she promised to behave herself and not get into any trouble."

"We won't stay long," Sloane promised. "Just long enough to see if Samson shows up."

"Sodas for everyone!" Izzy interrupted, placing drinks on the table. "I provided all your favorites. If you want to order lunch, just give me a wave."

"We're ready now, Izzy," Chase said. "If we

wait any longer, it'll be dinnertime. What are today's specials?"

"I love you Chandler boys and your appetites." She pulled her pad out and read from the back. "Today's specials are Norman's potpie —"

"Since when do you need to refer to a pad for specials, Iz?" Rick asked.

"Since they involve more than just food." She winked and continued. "In addition to the daily special, we've got a betting pool going. The more people who enter, the bigger the winnings, so I've been told to mention it to every table. But seeing as how two people here have the inside track, only Rick and Kendall are eligible."

Sloane narrowed her gaze. "What are you talking about?" She turned to Chase. "Do you know what she's talking about?"

"Unfortunately, yes." He actually envied Sloane her confusion. "Come on, Izzy. Why the hell are you bringing this up here?"

"Isn't it obvious?" She placed her hands on her generous hips. "The pot's bigger than the Super Bowl. I want to win and you two can give me the advantage."

Rick snickered. Damn fool obviously knew what was going on too.

Chase groaned. "Sloane, it seems we're the subject of a pool."

"I'll just put up some burgers on the house."

Rick chuckled. "Good idea, Iz."

"What kind of pool?" Sloane asked.

"They're laying odds on whether or not you're *it*. For me." Chase's cheeks burned and he could only imagine what shade of red he'd turned during this embarrassing conversation.

"*It?*" She bit down on her lower lip.

He itched to kiss that mouth and forget everything else.

"Everyone in town is betting on whether you're the one for Chase," Kendall piped in.

"The woman to finally make the heartbreaker part of a couple. A permanent couple," Rick added, and wagged his eyebrows in exaggeration. "Get it?"

"Got it," Sloane said, obviously shell-shocked and stunned.

"It started as a *Gazette* office pool and somehow became a town bet." Chase held his head in his hands. "Still enjoying small-town life?" he asked Sloane wryly.

Her eyes opened wide. He wondered what she was thinking and wouldn't blame her if she ran far and fast. Instead, she burst out laughing, obviously amused by it all. "I am. I really am enjoying this town and these people."

The truth was as much a revelation to Sloane as it obviously was to Chase. But sitting here, the subject of town speculation, watching Rick laugh at his brother's predicament and seeing Chase squirm, Sloane felt lighter than she had in years. She was happy despite her very personal, now very dangerous, circumstances.

Because she wasn't *on call*. Wasn't expected to perform.

Wasn't expected to be a Carlisle who fit the family mold. She was just a woman whom Chase Chandler seemed to enjoy, whom his family seemed to like and approved of.

Izzy returned with a bottle of ketchup and extra napkins. "So? Any inside tips?"

Sloane chuckled. "I'm not sure what to tell you. You know yourself, Chase is the ultimate heartbreaker and I'm only in town for a short time," she said over her shoulder.

"Oh pooh." Izzy waved her hand in the air. "That's what they all say. Just ask Kendall. You're here now and I'm laying odds on you going all the way." She snickered; then to the older woman's credit, she turned a beet-red shade. "Didn't mean that the way it came out."

Sloane grinned, laughter bubbling forth again.

"Hello, all." An older woman in a housecoat, her hair pulled into a gray bun, strode up to the table. "Say hello, Eldin." Packages filled her and her companion's arms, yet she managed to elbow him in the side anyway. "Who's this new woman in town?" She eyed Sloane curiously.

"I'm Sloane —"

"A friend of the family," Chase said before she could advertise her last name.

"I'm Pearl Robinson and this here's my significant other, Eldin Wingate."

"Hello." Eldin shuffled the bags. "Sorry. Can't shake with my hands full."

"That's okay." Sloane smiled. "Nice to meet you both. Kendall mentioned you earlier."

"Which means she told you we're living in sin," Pearl said, lowering her voice. "If Eldin didn't have a bad back, he'd carry me over the threshold and we'd get married. But until he can, we're living in sin." She nodded, pleased with her explanation.

"I see," Sloane murmured. Kendall had a point when she said the woman could sum things up quickly. "Kendall just said you rent out her guesthouse."

"When her aunt Crystal was alive, she used to let us live in the main house in exchange for upkeep, bless her soul." Pearl sniffed. "Then Kendall came to town and she fixed up what we couldn't and gave us an easier place to live. The guesthouse has no stairs, so it's easier on Eldin's back."

"Are you having a party?" Kendall pointed to the bags of food.

Pearl started to cough. "Heavens no. It's just hard for me to cook and so it's easier if I load up for the week."

"I understand," Sloane said, laughing.

"We've got to be going," Eldin said. "If I don't stop her, Pearl will talk all day."

"Eldin Wingate, if you don't have anything nice to say, don't say anything at all." Pearl shot him an annoyed glare. "Bye, Kendall. It was nice meeting you, Sloane. Boys, you say hello to Raina for me."

"We will," both Chase and Rick said at the same time.

The elderly couple took their leave, Pearl talking Eldin's ear off the entire way out of the restaurant.

"They seem nice." Too afraid she'd laugh again, Sloane bit the inside of her cheek and didn't meet anyone's gaze.

"You mean weird," Chase muttered.

"Odd," Rick added.

"They're just old and harmless." Kendall chuckled. "You guys better be careful because one day people will be talking about those old Chandler brothers and their strange habits."

Sloane sighed wistfully. "I'd think it would be nice to grow old in a place where everyone knows and accepts you for who you are."

The sound of her own voice startled her. Realizing she'd spoken aloud, she glanced at her companions, who were staring at her as if she'd lost her mind. Little did they realize, she was just starting to find her mind, and herself, in this small town called Yorkshire Falls.

Chase paused outside his guest room. The door was open and Sloane stood by the wooden dresser, adjusting her shirt, another tight long-sleeved number, this one emblazoned with USA on the front.

He knocked once. "Ready to deal with your biker friends?" he asked as he stepped into the room.

"Don't you mean, am I ready to find my father?" She turned his way and treated him to a warm smile, but he didn't miss the hint of nervousness in her voice or the fact that the smile didn't quite reach her eyes.

She was scared.

"I'll be there the whole time," he promised, walking up beside her. "But you realize we may end up no closer to finding Samson than we are right now?" He wanted her to be prepared for the worst.

She nodded. "I hope Earl's heard from him. If not, maybe he'll just be more willing to talk about where Samson might be." She drew a deep breath and exhaled hard. "I'll be ready in a minute." She picked up a scarf from the dresser and tied it around her neck.

"I brought you something." He showed her the shirt he'd taken from his closet.

"What's that?"

"My shirt." He held it open for her to slip on like a jacket. "In case our biker buddies are there."

She raised an eyebrow in surprise.

He shrugged. "It's safer not to take chances. This way we make the statement that you're mine before we walk in the door." He folded his arms across his chest, determined to get his way. And even more determined not to let her wide-eyed stare and full glossy pout get to him.

Fat chance, he thought as she willingly slipped one arm into a sleeve, then the other, wrapping the shirt around her, much the same way he'd like to wrap her in his arms and keep her safe. Accepting that he could protect her physically but not from the emotional upheaval that was sure to follow her search for Samson wasn't easy. And he hated the helpless way it made him feel. Hated the implications of his feelings even more.

She pivoted toward him and he instinctively grabbed the lapels, pulled her close, and sealed his mouth against hers. She parted her lips and his tongue slipped inside, finding her warm and welcoming. He hadn't realized how much he needed this. Since he'd been sitting with Sloane, watching her with his family, and seeing her enjoy his small-town life, his craving for her had grown. He was falling for this woman and it wasn't in his plans.

She stepped backward, breaking the kiss, a satisfied smile on her face. "I do like how you take possession."

"Does that mean you'll wear the shirt?"

She lowered her arms and the sleeves fell below her fingertips. "It's too big," she said, her eyes flashing playful sparks.

"Make do." He wasn't playing games, not with her safety. And not, he admitted to himself, with the chance another man might be interested enough to come between them.

She raised her arm, saluting him with a shirt-covered hand. "Yes, sir." Laughing, she turned back to the mirror. She picked up a tube of lip gloss and proceeded to fix her makeup.

Shaking his head, he returned to the living room to wait, trying to reconcile Sloane Carlisle, the senator's "daughter," with the woman who so obviously enjoyed the game. Not the game of chasing after Samson, but the role of playing Chase Chandler's woman.

And damned if Chase didn't like it too.

Chapter Eleven

Crazy Eights hadn't changed in the few days since Sloane's last visit — the smell of smoke still permeated the air and the drinks flowed fast around her. However, there was a difference, and it wasn't subtle. As she walked into the back poolroom, she had the support of Chase and his family behind her this time.

She couldn't lie to herself. Their presence meant a lot. No matter how much she loved her family and they loved her, she'd always felt the differences between them, enough for her to sense she was the odd woman out without knowing why. With Chase, Rick, and Kendall, she not only felt the unconditional support, just as she'd had growing up, but she was comfortable. She fit in.

She glanced around the smoky room. The bikers congregated around a back table, Dice making eye contact long enough to acknowledge their presence. He'd obviously seen Chase behind her and since *ownership* had been established that first night, he chose to leave her alone. Considering how Kendall had huddled up alongside Rick, Sloane decided her new friend was safe as well. The bikers weren't an issue tonight.

Realization dawned and she leaned close to Chase. "There was no reason for me to wear your shirt."

"Yes, there was."

She looked at him curiously.

"I wanted you to," he said simply.

For a man of few words, he'd just revealed plenty. Swallowing hard, she continued her perusal of the room.

Earl and his friend looked as if they'd never left their table and she decided not to put off talking to them. Sloane pushed ahead of Chase and strode up to the old man. "Hi, Earl. How are you tonight?"

"Hiya, pretty lady." He shot her his toothless grin. "You here for another whooping at my hands?" He grabbed his pool cue and perched it on the floor.

"I might be persuaded to play a game later. Right now I was hoping to buy you a drink."

"You hear that? Free alcohol," Earl called to his friend at the table. "I see an empty seat over there." He gestured to a booth that would hold about four. "Come on, Ernie. Whiskey's on the lady."

Sloane opened, then closed her mouth shut. If she wanted answers from Earl, she wasn't about to argue if he wanted to drink with his friend.

"Who's the pretty feline with you?" Earl asked Sloane, gesturing to Kendall with a tip of his head.

"Feline's a cat, numbnuts." Ernie coughed, a hacking sound that worried Sloane.

"This is Kendall," Sloane said by way of introduction, gesturing between Earl and her friend.

"She's my wife," Rick practically growled.

Sloane thanked her lucky stars he hadn't pulled his gun or revealed the weapon as a macho display of territorialism that seemed so common in this place. But Rick was a professional.

"Well, you ladies join us and we'll give our pool table to your men. How's that sound?" Earl asked.

Kendall glanced up. A muscle ticked in Chase's jaw and Rick's hand slipped to his wife's waist.

Oh damn. Sloane needed this conversation, something she knew Chase understood. "That sounds great," she said before either one could object. "Kendall?" Sloane shot a pleading glance her friend's way.

But from the excited gleam in Kendall's eye, Sloane didn't have to worry. Kendall was more than up for the adventure despite her glowering husband. "It's good by me too." She confirmed Sloane's hunch.

"We'll be over here." Chase pointed to the railing by the pool table. "*Right* over here." He aimed his dark glare and warning tone at Earl.

"I can't remember the last time we wuz seen with pretty women like yourselves." Earl grabbed her arm and led her to the table, Ernie following his friend's lead with Kendall.

Sloane shot a grateful glance Chase's way. He inclined his head and never took his eyes off her, making her feel safe and cared for.

She liked being Chase Chandler's woman.

"I don't like this." Chase nursed a beer and kept an eye on Sloane while she drank and talked with Earl and his friend Ernie.

"You think I do?" Rick gestured to the waitress for another beer. "Next time, remind me not to offer to help you out."

"Shut up." Leaning back, Chase decided to use his time wisely and to watch. He'd always been intrigued with the facets Sloane presented, though he had to admit he'd never seen the senator's daughter, only the relaxed woman. One so different than Madeline Carlisle and so at ease in his world. The one he'd wanted to see wearing his shirt for no real, rational reason.

He didn't think this Sloane was the pretense. The woman she showed the world when campaigning for Senator Carlisle, however, was certainly a facade. Sloane might be more casual and relaxed than her family, but that didn't mean she'd normally behave excessively. And the way she was doing shots with Earl and Ernie revealed a need to let herself be free. Just as she had that first night they'd met.

He told himself her rebellion was a good thing, considering she'd stifled her needs in favor of her family's for too long. Surely she'd welcome the opportunity to be on her own when their time together was through.

He folded his arms across his chest and nodded. Sloane and her situation were perfect for a man who wanted to steer clear of relationships and commitment, and even better for the reporter who wanted to be the one to break her story. So why did the thought leave him feeling hollow inside?

Sloane was dizzy. Giddily dizzy. Chances were she'd pay tomorrow with a whopping migraine, but for now, she was relaxed and hanging with Earl. And Earl had a lot of information to offer. Unfortunately, he was willing to speak up only when the women followed his answers with a shot of alcohol. She and Kendall had managed to convince the old man to substitute vodka for whiskey, saving them the more unpleasant taste, but the end result was the same.

Sloane was drunk. "So you spoke to Samson yesterday? What did he have to say?" Sloane rolled the empty shot glass between her palms. Glancing down, she saw two of them. Not two hands, which she obviously had, but two glasses, which she knew didn't exist.

"Yessiree. He called. Surprised me too, since he don't usually bother to pay for a phone call." Earl rolled his shoulders and poured his glass full. "Damn fool said he lost his house in a fire, but not to worry — he's holed up somewhere safe." Earl turned his attention to her shot glass, filling it halfway. "Did you ever do a slammer?" the older man asked her, changing Sloane's favorite subject to Earl's favorite.

"I'll get the ginger ale," Ernie said, jumping on the idea before Sloane or Kendall could answer. He headed for the bar, returning a few minutes later with a liter of soda.

"Bottles at the table," Kendall observed, her voice slurred. "Do you guys have an in with the owner?" She eyed the soda with curiosity. Obviously, she didn't know what a slammer was either, but from the gleam in the old men's eyes, they were about to find out.

Earl chuckled. "We're good customers. He don't mind giving us bottles as long as we pay for them later. And you did say drinks were on you." He glared at Sloane warily, as if she might have forgotten.

"And I meant it." She didn't mind paying for the drinks, but she was quickly reaching her alcohol limit. With any luck, another two or three questions tops and they'd learn enough to walk out of here.

"Pour and slam." Ernie filled the rest of Sloane's shot glass with ginger ale while Earl began instructing her on the finer points of a slammer. He pointed to the shot glass. "You cover the top of that-there glass with your palm, then slam the bottom against the table. It'll fizz and you down the shot." He grinned,

217

pleased with his directions. "You'll taste how much easier the alcohol goes down."

"The shot goes down easier, huh?" She met his gaze. Even his teeth blurred together and she could no longer see the space between them. "Any reason you didn't mention that about five shots ago?" Sloane asked wryly.

Drawing a deep breath for courage, she slammed the glass and consumed the drink, coughing from the fizz and bubbles until her eyes teared. But she had to admit the man had a point. "That was much better," she said when she could finally speak.

"My turn." Kendall laughed, high pitched and loud enough to pierce Sloane's eardrums. "First the questions. Where did Samson say that he was?"

With all they'd consumed, Sloane was amazed they'd been able to keep their focus on needed conversation. She owed Kendall and she'd personally deliver coffee to her tomorrow as a thank-you — if she could lift her own head off the pillow.

Somehow the two women had reached a silent understanding. In order to keep either one of them from getting too drunk, they alternated questions, hence alternated shots. Sloane couldn't imagine how she'd feel if she'd imbibed alone. She'd probably be passed out under the table by now.

Earl shrugged. "Samson didn't say where he wuz. Then again he never says much. Never calls either, so I was surprised to hear from him," he said again.

Sloane knew there was a message in there somewhere, but she was too woozy to figure out what. She tipped her head to one side and immediately regretted the quick motion. When the dizziness cleared, she forced herself to think. Samson had called Earl when he'd never called before. She wondered if he'd even had a telephone prior to the explosion.

"Why'd he call you?" Sloane asked.

"Blondie didn't drink yet," Earl said, refusing to answer until Kendall remedied her lapse.

Ernie poured and Sloane sighed, waiting for Kendall to drink so they'd get more answers out of Earl. Once he was satisfied, he did a straight shot of his own and turned back to the subject at hand. "Samson figured I'd heard about his house and wondered if he wuz dead."

Sloane cringed at the casual way Earl spoke, but at least Samson had someone to call when he'd had trouble. Even if Earl didn't seem like the warmest guy going, he was Samson's friend.

"Course I hadn't heard till he told me. I asked him if I'd inherit if he croaked." He cackled at his callous joke and she winced. "Samson said it wuz none of my business who got his money, but for my information, he had family who'd inhurt —"

"Inherit, you moron," Ernie chimed in.

Both Kendall and Sloane laughed, but Earl

ignored them, merely glaring at his friend.

Sloane grasped onto Earl's words and wondered if Samson was being his surly self in his reply to Earl or if he really had family. She wondered if he'd actually been referring to her. Her stomach churned with a combination of fear and hope, the upheaval having nothing to do with the alcohol in her system.

"Samson said I wuzn't getting a red cent," Earl continued. "But at least the damn ingrate's still living."

Despite her fuzzy brain, Sloane heard a hint of affection in Earl's voice. She refused to believe she imagined it. *Someone* had to care whether Samson lived or died, and she had to think this gruff old man was her real father's friend. After all, everyone needed someone in life who cared about them. Samson *deserved* to have at least that. A lump formed in her throat and suddenly she felt an intense longing for an emotional connection to another human being. One who cared about her.

Her gaze fell to Chase; she met his heated stare and lingered. His expression was still dark and he held up one hand, indicating she had five minutes left. Worry was obvious in his eyes and Sloane knew her heart didn't lie. *He* cared. For her.

She tugged his shirt tighter around her, feeling its warmth and accepting the sudden tide of arousal as a natural circumstance of falling in love with him.

"Hey, lady." Ernie tapped a bottle on the table. "Do *you* know who'd inherit instead of Earl?" he asked, interrupting Sloane's thoughts.

And boy, what thoughts those had been. Love? She shivered. Alcohol had a way of distorting reality. She couldn't possibly be in love with Chase Chandler. Could she?

"Hello? An answer would be nice. We've been giving you all the answers you want, but you're holding out on us." Earl folded his scrawny arms across his chest, impatient and annoyed.

"I don't know who Samson would leave his money to," Sloane said.

Which brought up another question. Did Samson really have money? If so, why continue to live like a poor man with no income? She forced a stare back to the old men at the table, the only ones who'd have any answers. "I'd heard Samson had no family."

"No friends in Yorkshire Falls to speak of either." Kendall added her knowledge, trying to help prod for information.

"That's 'cuz he's got me 'n' Ernie here." Earl tapped himself in the chest, proud of the connection to his friend.

Ernie nodded in agreement. "He don't need nobody else."

"And that's all we's saying until you drink some more." Earl followed that pronouncement with a shot of his own. There was no way she could drink any more and Sloane eyed Kendall across the table. The other woman waved a hand, indicating she wasn't drinking another shot either.

Before Sloane could think of a way to extricate herself, the Chandler brothers appeared by their table. Rick cleared his throat, but Sloane only had eyes for Chase. Tall, dark, and handsome, he was every inch her savior.

She rose, intending to tell him so. She took a step forward, tripped, and fell into his arms.

"Shit." Chase grabbed Sloane and wrapped his arms around her, supporting her weight with his body. Soft and warm, she also smelled good despite the alcohol she'd consumed and the smoke in the bar. She affected him on the most basic level, the need to protect and care for her stronger than he'd ever experienced before.

"I think I drank too much." She giggled and leaned against him.

"Really? I'd never have guessed." He silently cursed the fact that he'd allowed this situation to go on as long as it had.

Rick hauled Kendall out of her seat and into his arms. Chase figured his brother wouldn't be speaking to him for a good day or so till he cooled down.

Chase turned his attention to the old men. "Okay, boys, your fun's over for the night. If you hear *anything* from or about Samson, call me." Chase handed both Earl and Ernie a business card. Hopefully, one of them wouldn't lose it.

"Who'd have believed Samson would have people looking for him? I didn't think anyone 'cept us liked him enough." Earl shook his head and Sloane was now clinging to Chase, too out of it to realize the importance of Earl's words.

Her lips began snuggling against Chase's neck, nipping right below his ear. Keeping his mind on the search for Samson wasn't easy when she'd aroused him in an instant. Her moist lips against his skin inflamed his senses, and just the feel of her in his arms set off fireworks he couldn't believe.

"Is someone else looking for Samson?" He somehow managed to ask.

Ernie rose from his seat. "Some man was in here a few nights ago askin' questions."

"You didn't say anything about that." Sloane perked up and lifted her head off Chase's shoulder. "Why didn't you tell me?" She stepped forward but he held her tight. Her balance wouldn't be good right now.

" 'Cuz we were playin' twenty questions and you didn't ask." Earl shook his head, rolling his eyes.

"What'd he look like?" Rick asked in his cop's voice.

"Samson's ugly as sin, just like Ernie here." Earl pointed to his friend.

"There's no call to be rude." Ernie pouted like a girl but squared his shoulders, bracing for a fight.

Chase gritted his teeth, while Sloane attempted to stand up straight and pay more attention.

"Let's start over. What does the man who was asking about Samson look like?" Chase clarified his thought before he had to step between the men and break up a brawl.

"I can't remember. You?" Earl asked Ernie.

He shook his head. "Nosiree. He wasn't friendlylike and didn't want to play a game of pool or buy drinks."

"Which meant you didn't share information with him?" Chase guessed.

"Correct." Earl grinned.

Fishing into his pocket, Chase withdrew a hundred-dollar bill he'd put aside earlier. "Listen, boys." He held out the money. "I'm trusting you to call me with any information on Samson. *Anything,* do you understand? That means the minute someone comes sniffing around, you pick up the phone." He waved the greenback by Earl's face.

"Woo-wee!" The old man snatched the money. "I'll call you if'n Samson shows up and just picks his nose."

"I'm thrilled," Chase said wryly. "But if I find out you knew something and didn't call, my cop brother here will arrest you for obstruction of justice," Chase said in his most threatening voice. Neither Earl nor Ernie would realize that jurisdiction probably prohibited Rick from doing any such thing.

And Rick, who was now holding on to his

wife, discreetly displayed his holster before letting his jacket slip back to cover the gun.

Earl shoved the bill into his pants pocket and nodded his understanding. "We've got a game to play," he said, obviously wanting to get as far away from Chase and Rick as possible.

Which was fine with Chase. He'd only resorted to threats now to make sure the old men didn't *inadvertently* omit information.

At this point, he wanted only to get Sloane sobered up. He'd overheard some, but not all, of the conversation, and he hoped she'd remember the rest in the morning.

He brushed her wayward curls out of her face. "Come on, sweetheart. Time to get you home."

"So you can have your wicked way with me?" Catching him off guard, she splayed her body against his. Her breasts crushed into his chest and her lower body met his as she planted a full kiss on his lips.

Pulling her away was the last thing he wanted to do, but he had no choice. He peeled her off him and braced his arms around her so he could lead her outside.

"I'll tell you what," he said as they followed Rick and an equally drunk Kendall to the door. "Let's get you into bed, and if you're still in the mood, we'll talk about my *wicked* ways."

Chase carried Sloane into the house and up the stairs to his bedroom. He passed the answering machine on the kitchen counter and noticed the red blinking light. Damned if he'd listen to messages now. He had a soft, willing female in his arms and he wanted to be with her more than anything else.

She was compliant to the point of feeling boneless, leaving him completely aware of her sweet scent and the arousing way she nuzzled into him.

He laid her on the bed and she sprawled against the pillow, then crooked a finger his way. "I want to hear more about those wicked ways of yours," she said in a husky voice.

"And I'm all too happy to show you. After you tell me what Earl and Ernie said about Samson." He wanted her to talk before she forgot anything she might have learned.

"Earl said Samson's ugly as sin," she said. "Is he?"

He wondered if he imagined the lost-little-girl sound in her voice as she asked about the father she'd never met.

"He's . . ." Chase had never given a thought to what Samson looked like and tried to paint an accurate picture now. "He's got graying hair and he's usually tan because he spends so much time outdoors. He likes the gardens across from Norman's," he said, thinking. "And one more thing." Reaching out, he stroked Sloane's cheek. "He's not ugly as sin."

A soft, grateful smile reached her lips and he couldn't resist leaning forward to taste. As usual, one taste wasn't enough and he slanted his mouth wider over hers.

She moaned and met his tongue with hers, crawling closer, never breaking contact. Taking control, he rolled to his back, pulling her on top of him. But she obviously wasn't going to accept submission and she planted openmouthed kisses over his neck, pulling up his shirt so she could repeat the erotic licks and nibbles on his chest.

Without warning, she licked one nipple, then bit down with her teeth.

Hot sensation shot straight to his groin. "Good God." His body bucked, nearly dislodging her from where she straddled his thighs.

"Someone's looking for Samson," she said, suddenly lifting her head.

"Helluva time to focus, honey. What else do you remember?"

She shook her head. Disheveled strands curled around her face and her makeup had long since disappeared. She looked fresh and wholesome, and gazing at her, he felt emotion swamp him.

"Earl and Ernie didn't remember what the guy looked like. But they did hear from Samson and he's holed up somewhere safe. Thank goodness for small favors, right?"

"Right."

"Isn't there anyone in Yorkshire Falls who'd take him in?" she asked hopefully.

He spread his hands in front of him, knowing he had no answer to pull out of a hat that would ease her mind. "Raina would let him stay with her, but obviously we'd know if she'd heard from him. Same for Charlotte, and besides, she isn't in town. I wish I could give you the answers you want to hear, but I can't."

"Then give me something else instead."

He had no doubt what she was asking for and he was all too willing to give what she wanted. They made love twice, frenzied and fast the first time, slow and tender the next.

Chase fell asleep with Sloane in his arms and the sound of the phone ringing in his ear.

Chapter Twelve

Sloane tried to open her eyes but the pain was too great. Lifting her head was impossible. "Who hired the steel band?" she muttered, burying her face into the pillow.

"I think you did," a familiar masculine voice answered.

"Do I know you?" she asked Chase wryly, barely able to think past the reverberating drums in her head.

She felt the bed dip with his weight as he sat down.

"You knew me last night." His voice dripped with husky innuendo, and despite the hangover, a delicious warmth curled in her belly.

Still, she knew better than to attempt to laugh and groaned instead. "I can't believe I drank so much."

"It's not like Earl gave you a choice. Here. Try this," he said as he rolled her to her back and placed a cool cloth on her forehead.

She immediately felt relief. "Mmm. You're a godsend, Chase Chandler."

He chuckled. "I've got some water and aspirin for you too."

"I think I need to wait a few minutes before lifting my head," she mumbled. "What time is it?"

"Seven a.m."

"I hope Kendall doesn't feel as bad as I do," she said, recalling last night more vividly.

She'd come up empty on their search for Samson, but her heart felt full with the memory of making love with Chase. A man she wanted all to herself, yet the harsh truth remained. He didn't desire the same thing and the existence of the other woman in his life, the one named Cindy, merely validated her belief. Sloane was only a diversion for Chase Chandler until they went their separate ways.

But she didn't want anyone or anything between them now. With the compress covering her forehead and eyes, she didn't literally have to face him and it seemed the perfect time to ask. "You said Cindy wasn't simple to explain, but the longer we're together, no matter how temporary, it bothers me that you're involved with someone else."

"I ended things with Cindy." His voice sounded clear and strong, shocking her with the admission.

Sloane swallowed hard. "Why?" she asked, still not opening her eyes.

"I should think that would be obvious." Leaning forward, he touched his lips to hers.

At that moment, more memories of last night resurfaced and she recalled thinking that she'd fallen in love with him. It hadn't been a drunken thought but rather one from the heart. Opening her mouth, she greeted him with all the passion, desire, and love swelling inside her.

But the ringing telephone interrupted them, and with a groan, Chase grabbed the receiver on the nightstand by the bed. "Chandler."

Sloane waited, her head still pounding as hard as her heart, but for different reasons now. She'd fallen for this Chandler man, one who wanted no family, no future with any woman because he'd already had his fill of responsibility. He'd lived life out of order and Sloane would have to pay for that by letting him go and live his dreams when the time came.

"Mom's in the hospital?" Chase's voice halted her more selfish thoughts.

Raina was sick? Hadn't Sloane sensed as much? But Rick and Chase had insisted it was a ruse, a game to get her boys to settle down. It wasn't, and she should have insisted he look closer.

"I'll be right there," he said, slamming down the phone and turning to face Sloane. "I have to go."

She'd already figured that out. "What happened?"

"Mom had severe chest pains in the middle of the night and called an ambulance." The truth slammed into Chase's chest with brutal force. Raina had called him first, but he'd been otherwise engaged. With Sloane.

For the first time ever, he'd been too busy to check his answering machine, and stellar newsman that he'd become, he'd been too preoccupied to remember his beeper.

Family had always come first, until now. And look at the end result. He stood and reached for his pants.

"Let me go with you." Sloane sat up higher in bed and groaned, reaching for her head with her hands. "God, it's like a drummer took up residence."

He was better off going alone so he could concentrate. And regroup. "You stay. I'll call and check in," he promised.

"What happened? I thought your mother's heart condition was fake?"

"According to Rick, it was real this time. She reached him and he's been there all night."

"Why didn't he call?"

"He did." He buttoned his pants and pulled on a sweatshirt. "I was too busy to answer."

She winced, obviously catching his meaning. "I'm sorry."

"No big deal," he lied. He'd already given her too much insight, too much power over his feelings and emotions. The time had come to rein himself in.

He grabbed for his keys. "You sleep it off and I'll update you when I know more."

She nodded. If she was hurt by his withdrawal or affected by his need to shut her out, she didn't show it. And despite his deep need to fortify his defenses and keep her out, a part of him wished for the emotional reaction he struggled not to give.

He wanted to hold her and let her hold him one more time before heading over to the hospital. Instead, he waved and walked out the door.

The door slammed shut behind Chase and the sound of the truck's motor quickly followed. Then silence ensued. Any blossoming hope Sloane had held since hearing Chase admit he'd broken up with Cindy crumbled around her. He'd withdrawn and it didn't take a brain surgeon to figure out why.

She'd known the Chandler brothers for under a week but she already understood their family code of honor. Family first. Always. And Chase had defied that code last night. He'd ignored the telephone because he'd been too wrapped up in Sloane. And now he felt guilty. He probably always would. She'd be better off concentrating on her life and her problems and leave Chase Chandler and his family to their own.

Picking up the phone, she called her stepmother. Not a morning person, Madeline still answered on the first ring. "Hello?"

"Hi, Mom."

"Sloane, honey, thank God." Relief echoed in Madeline's tone. "I needed to hear your voice."

A lump rose to Sloane's throat as did a longing for home she hadn't expected. Despite the lies, she loved her family. That was one truth that her time in Yorkshire Falls was making clear. "I'm fine. And I needed to hear your voice too." To her shock, her own voice cracked and she broke down crying.

"Did you find Samson?" Madeline asked, concern lacing her tone. "Is that why you're crying?"

Sloane shook her head, answering, "No, I didn't find him. He's taken off since the house explosion, but according to people here, he's odd and his behavior isn't all that surprising." She blotted her eyes.

Still trying to keep Madeline in the dark and protected, she kept her explanation to a minimum. "When I left to come here, was Dad upset?" If Michael Carlisle were worried about Sloane, he might send someone after Samson to find him first, which might explain the person Earl said had been looking for Samson.

"No. He understands this is something you have to do."

Sloane bit down on her lower lip. "And the campaign? How is that going? Frank and Robert must be working Dad like crazy, now that they've publicly announced Dad's running for vice president." Sloane mentioned Michael's campaign manager in the hope that Madeline would inadvertently provide helpful information. After all, Frank was the one person who'd threatened Samson. The one with the most to lose, next to Michael, if the campaign were derailed by a loose cannon like Samson Humphrey.

"Actually, Frank's been in meetings nonstop while Robert went out of town," Madeline said.

"He left town now? At the height of the campaign and excitement?" Sloane asked, attempting to sound surprised.

"Family emergency. Those things can't be helped, you know." Madeline sighed. A long pause followed and then she took a sudden gasp. "You don't think they're looking for Samson to ensure his silence?"

"No! I mean, of course not. I just think Samson's an old eccentric who disappeared. In the meantime, if Robert says he has a family emergency, I'm sure he does." Sloane was also sure he'd keep himself hidden if in fact he was in Yorkshire Falls.

"Okay," Madeline said, not sounding in the least bit pacified. "At least I know you have someone looking out for you."

"Which brings me to my next point. How could you ask Chase Chandler to be my bodyguard?" she asked, calling her stepmother on her overprotective tendencies.

"I'll do whatever I have to do to keep my family safe. Chase is a good man, Sloane."

"Tell me something I don't know."

"Are you two getting along?" Madeline asked with a definite hopeful tone in her voice.

She has a lot in common with Raina Chandler, Sloane thought. "He grows on you," she said, deliberately evasive.

Madeline laughed. "Well, that's a start. Will

you call if you need me?"

"I will," Sloane promised. She hung up the phone and stared at it, her own thoughts coming back to Chase's withdrawal.

Damn the man and his mixed signals. Yes, he'd pushed her away, but she'd also seen his eyes darken with need; she'd heard him groan while he was deep inside her. No man could fake that depth of feeling. Not to mention the fact that he'd broken up with Cindy. *The hell with not reading too much into things,* Sloane thought, rising from the bed. Despite the pounding headache from last night, her mind began to clear. She had a father to find and a life to reclaim. And perhaps Chase Chandler would be a part of it.

Chase knocked once and eased open the door to his mother's hospital room. This time she'd been admitted overnight instead of being sent home from the emergency room. Guilt gnawed at his insides, and an overwhelming sense of his own betrayal flooded his system. He'd been concerned with reconciling Sloane's family instead of paying attention to the things that connected him to his.

"Mom?" Chase called out quietly in case Raina was sleeping.

"Come on in," Rick said from a chair in the corner of the large room.

Chase stepped inside, taking in his surroundings. The walls had muted pastel wallpaper covering them and a television hung from the ceiling. On mute, the picture flickered from the screen. And Raina sat up in the only bed in the large room. Eric had probably arranged for private accommodations, making certain their mother had excellent care.

Her eyes fluttered open at the same time Chase eased himself onto the edge of the mattress. He lifted her aged hand in his. "How are you?"

"Much better," Raina said, pushing herself up higher against the pillows. "I really can't believe this," she murmured, her eyes twinkling with a combination of regret and concern.

"Believe what?" Rick asked, butting in as he always did. "That Chase finally has a social life?" He looked Chase's way and winked, his attempt to lighten the mood around them obvious.

Raina laughed. "Leave your brother alone. He's allowed to have sex without you adding your two cents about it." She folded her arms over her chest, her expression and tone forbidding Rick to mention the subject again.

As if Raina's chiding had ever stopped Rick.

And she was discussing his sex life. A heated flush rushed to his face.

"Well, I think it's about time. Don't you?" Rick unfolded his body from the chair and stretched, asking his question on cue.

Chase groaned. "I'd rather talk about how Mom is doing."

"Not about what you were doing after you got Sloane home?" Rick joked.

But not even his middle brother's ribbing could ease Chase's guilt.

"Mom's going to be fine," Rick said at last, obviously reading the anxiety on Chase's face.

Raina agreed with a squeeze of her hand. "I am. But, Chase, this . . . incident isn't connected to the last one." She blushed red and her discomfort was so obvious he couldn't bring himself to express his anger at her charade.

"I know, Mom. And let's leave it in the past, okay? What's important now is your health and making sure you don't have a real relapse this time." He leaned closer, elbows on the blanket, his hand never leaving hers.

Raina blinked. "What do you mean *you know?*" Her gaze darted from Chase to Rick. "He knows?" she asked her middle son.

Rick nodded.

"I would have confronted you about it after D.C., but Sloane showed up and things have gotten out of control," Chase said. "But no longer. I have my priorities back in order." He met Rick's gaze. "What's the diagnosis?" he asked, wanting to know the worst so he could take control.

"Angina. Apparently, there isn't enough blood flow to the heart, and when she overdoes it, she experiences pain as a result."

Chase nodded, a feeling of déjà vu overcoming him as he heard this heart problem explained to him, just as Raina had once explained her last "episode." He realized now just how much information had been missing, how many clues Raina had left that she'd been faking. Clues none of her sons had picked up on because they cared only about making her better.

"Chase, we really do need to talk about what I did to your brothers, and to you." Raina blinked and a tear dripped down her face. "I was so wrong."

His heart squeezed tighter at her admission. "We have plenty of time to talk, I promise. Right now I want you to save your energy so you get your strength back." He brushed a kiss over her cheek and rose to his feet. "I'd like to find Eric and get a full explanation of where we go from here."

"He'll be back in a few minutes. I told him I'd gotten hold of you and he said he'd discuss the future with all three of us." Rick lifted his hand and looked at his wristwatch. "Roman and Charlotte will be in by tonight and Eric said we can all talk again then."

"I'm being released this afternoon," Raina added.

"Good." If they were letting her go home, things couldn't be that dire, Chase thought.

"Where's Sloane?" Raina asked.

"Home nursing a hangover, like Kendall, I'd think," Rick said, his humor tinged with annoyance at last night's situation.

"Oh, come now. Neither one of them drinks," Raina said.

"How would you know what Sloane does or doesn't do?" Chase asked.

Raina splayed her hands over the standard-issue hospital blanket. "I can read her well. She's a lovely, upstanding woman and she wouldn't do such a thing," Raina said with certainty.

"Perfect daughter-in-law material?" Rick called Raina on her obvious train of thought.

Her hazel eyes twinkled with delight. "Well, now that you mention it . . ."

"Wasn't it that kind of thinking that got you into trouble in the first place?" Chase asked her.

She shrugged. "Two down, young man. Do you really think I'm going to give up on the notion of having you settled and happy like your brothers are? My methods may have been suspect, but my motives were pure."

He groaned. So much for hoping Raina's now-precarious health would have her backing down from her quest to marry him off. "This isn't a discussion I'm willing to have."

"Because you have your priorities in order?" she asked.

He gave her a curt nod. "Exactly."

She pursed her lips and let out a sound of pure motherly frustration. "If you had those priorities in order, you wouldn't stay here with me now that you know I'm fine."

He knew exactly where she was leading, yet he was powerless to prevent the conversation. "Where would I be?" he asked resignedly.

"With Sloane."

Rick chuckled, not bothering to disguise his laugh as a throat clearing or anything else.

"Sloane can get along just fine without me," Chase muttered.

"Why should she have to?" Raina asked.

His mother's dirty look reminded him of the times he'd been caught doing something wrong as a young kid. Times that had ended quickly when he'd assumed his role as head of the Chandler house. "So I can take you home?"

"That's something Eric can do. Even Rick is going home to his wife, aren't you?"

Rick nodded. "I sure am. After I hear you read Chase the riot act about his life." With a smirk on his face, he leaned against the wall, clearly enjoying watching Chase on the spot.

"Take a hike, young man. I want to talk to your brother."

"Oh man. I miss out on all the fun," Rick said.

"Now that was a perfect imitation of yourself as a kid," Chase said, recalling the times he and his mother would have serious discussions that precluded his younger siblings. Only today, Chase's love life was the topic.

"Chase just nailed the problem. He's spent too much time being the parent to you boys and not enough time enjoying his own life," Raina pronounced. "It's not natural."

Chase blinked in surprise. That Raina would realize how unusual his life had been was shocking. "Let's drop the subject." He didn't want to delve that deeply into his psyche.

"No. I've ignored your needs for too long," Raina said in a more determined voice than he'd ever heard before.

"I'm out of here before she starts focusing on *my* needs," Rick muttered, making for the door.

"Coward," Chase called after him.

"Better a coward than the subject of Mom's analysis. See you at home tonight. Kendall and I will drop off dinner, so don't even think of lifting a finger to cook," he warned, then blew his mother a kiss and disappeared out the door.

Chase faced his mother and, in doing so, faced his past. She appeared as frail and wan as she had in the early days after his father had died. He'd seen the need to take care of her then and had stepped in without thinking twice. He saw that same need now.

His wants, his desires, didn't matter. Not in the face of a family crisis. And despite the fact that she was being released today, Raina's health was a true family crisis. Feigned or not, the last time had sent all three sons reeling into a coin toss that changed Roman's life.

Though Chase understood the severity of the situation, he wouldn't be letting Raina manipulate him this time around. "Mom, it's time to drop this subject."

"After I have my say."

Knowing she'd talk no matter what, he settled into Rick's abandoned chair. "I'm listening."

Raina turned toward the window, giving Chase the chance to study his mother some more. She'd aged but still had maintained the beauty she'd had in her youth. She'd also kept the wisdom and heart that led her to do impulsive things in the name of protecting her family. Chase couldn't imagine his life without her in it.

"I've made many mistakes," Raina said finally. "And manipulating you boys into thinking I was sick was a doozy. But it wasn't the biggest mistake I made."

Chase couldn't help it; he laughed. "Sorry, but I'm hard pressed to find a bigger one," he said

"Aah, but I can. Letting you take over as parent when your father died. That was an error I can't ever take back." She sighed, slowly turning toward him.

He could see how difficult she found it to face him but didn't understand why. "What else could you have done?"

"Sent you off to college, for one thing. Run the paper myself, for another. Raised your brothers like a single parent without relying on you, when you were just a boy yourself." She shook her head and he was shocked to notice tears falling from her eyes.

"I was more than capable of handling things," he reminded her, at a loss over what to do about her emotional state. Women and tears had never been his thing.

Which, he realized now, was probably why he'd stepped in so quickly and taken over when his father had passed on, not giving Raina the chance to make her own decisions or control their futures. He'd seen himself as the man of the house and acted accordingly. But in doing so, he'd denied all of them different paths. "What's done is done, Mom."

"I agree." She pulled a Kleenex from the tissue box on the side table and blotted her eyes. "But the future doesn't have to be a replica of the past. *That's* what I need you to understand."

He pinched the bridge of his nose, wondering how to explain. "I've come to terms with things. I have a great life. I have a great family. So what if I gave up a few things on the way? Who doesn't make sacrifices?" he asked. "But it's my time now and I intend to reach for my dreams."

"I'm glad."

A rosier glow touched his mother's cheeks and relief washed through him. He'd obviously gotten through to her and she wasn't going to worry about him when she should be taking care of herself.

"Just make sure you realize two things," Raina continued.

"And what are they?"

"Make sure those dreams are present ones, not ones born in the past. And accept the difference between helping me raise your brothers, who were already half-grown pains in the ass, and the joys of raising a family of your own." Laughter tinged her voice but didn't negate the seriousness of her point.

She wanted him married with children. That much hadn't changed. "I hear you, Mom."

"But you aren't listening, are you? Life is short. It'll pass you by before you know it, and if you let Sloane walk out of your life, you'll have regrets. I don't want you — after all you've done for us — to have regrets."

He shook his head. "No regrets. I never look back." Yet he didn't want her holding out hope that he wanted to settle down like Rick and Roman had either. "But my future's mine to determine, and like I said, I have my priorities in order."

"The Chandler way," Sloane's familiar feminine voice said from the doorway. "Family first, kids never," she said jokingly, paraphrasing his words the first time they'd made love.

Safety first, kids never.

Chase turned to see Sloane standing in the room, a strained smile on her beautiful face. After all they'd been through together, she knew him well. Though his words and thoughts wouldn't surprise her, he saw her obvious dismay. His gut churned, letting him know in no uncertain terms that he didn't like disappointing her.

He ran a hand through his hair, then stood and walked over, drawing her into the room. "What are you doing here?" he asked, unable to stop the smile on his face.

Just looking at her, pale from last night's ordeal, but gorgeous anyway, made him feel lighter and happier than he had a right to be, considering his mother lay in a hospital bed.

"I came to see how Raina's feeling, of course." Sloane stepped toward the bed and pulled a pink rose attached to a GET WELL balloon from behind her back. "I wanted to bring a box of chocolates but thought I should check with your doctor first."

"You're such a sweet girl." Raina beamed as she accepted Sloane's gift.

When it came to Sloane Carlisle, his mother was in as deep as Chase. The only difference was, Chase knew how a woman like Sloane, her desires and her needs, would conflict with his newfound freedom in life. His instinct this morning had been the right one. Withdraw and steer clear.

"I plan to continue eating chocolates to my dying day — which won't be for years. I have too much living to do," Raina said. "I want out of here."

Chase laughed. "I saw Eric walk by and wave. I'm guessing it's just another hour or so until you sign the paperwork and get sprung."

"Good. In the meantime, you two go on and leave me in peace. I'd like to nap." She closed her eyes and turned her head to the side as if she were already down for the count.

Chase rolled his eyes. "She's so obvious," he said to Sloane.

She laughed, brightening his spirits. "I know. But she means well and she's so cute."

Raina cleared her throat, but her eyes remained closed.

"Anyway, I also wanted to tell you that I planned to go by the vet and check on Samson's dog. Would it be okay if I brought him to your place? I know it's a lot to ask, but I hate thinking of him alone there, when I could take care of him and —"

"Chase loves dogs," Raina said from the bed.

"You're supposed to be sleeping," Sloane and Chase told her at the same time.

Raina merely smiled. "Great minds think alike. Married couples complete each other's thoughts. Same for couples who should be —"

Sloane let out a laugh she was obviously unable to contain, cutting off Raina's expected last word.

"Go back to sleep," Chase snapped before his mother could meddle some more. "You can bring the dog to my place," he said to Sloane. "Just ask Dr. Sterling to give us whatever we need to feed him and tell him I'll send him a check to cover the cost."

"See? Beneath that gruff exterior, he's such a softy," Raina chimed in.

Sloane reached out and caressed his cheek. "He is, isn't he?"

Her gentle touch seeped through his skin, warming him. Instead of enjoying, it made him nervous. If he let her, this woman could destroy his dreams of finally having his life to himself, no one at home to answer to, only his career ahead of him. He wasn't sure why the goal that had sustained him for years suddenly made him feel cold and empty, but he wasn't about to worry about it now.

Decision made, Chase stepped back, out of reach.

Sloane sensed his withdrawal immediately. Combined with what she'd overheard between mother and son, she understood Chase's actions were deliberate. Raina wanted him to settle down with Sloane and Chase wanted no part of her plan. He'd have no regrets. He'd never look back. He'd said so himself.

She had no choice but to find Samson, fix the mess that her life had become, and move on. She turned to Chase, determined now to play things as cool as he was.

"I can pay for Samson's dog myself, but thank you for offering," she said in a more formal, more distant voice than she'd used with him before. Was it her imagination or did he flinch at her icy tone?

"Well, regardless of who pays, Chase can go

with you. He's finished here." Raina waved her hand expansively around the room, ignoring the suddenly chilly undercurrents.

"No, I'm not. Not until I hear from your doctors exactly what's wrong and your prognosis." He folded his arms tight and Sloane had a hunch he was shutting her out more than trying to make a point with his mother.

"Ridiculous," Raina said.

He raised an eyebrow. "Is it really? You got the best of me once, Mom. I'm going to hear things from the doctor's mouth this time."

She frowned, pursing her lips in blatant disapproval, then turned to Sloane. "Well, before you drive over to the vet, at least call Dr. Sterling and make sure he's in the office. People in this town take advantage of his good nature and expect more house calls than an old-time doctor used to make." Raina fiddled with the wires connected to the heart monitor. "I want out of here," she muttered again.

"Soon enough." Chase nodded toward the phone. "Mom's right. Call the vet first."

Sloane didn't like Chase telling her what to do in that cold voice, but she knew good advice when she heard it and stepped over to the table and picked up the phone. Dialing the number Raina gave her, she listened and hung up, resigned. "You're right. I got the answering machine."

"See?" Raina smiled, obviously happy to be correct. "Now you can stay here with us." She patted the side of the bed with an unspoken request that Sloane join her.

She smiled at the older woman. "Much as I'd like to, I have an errand I have to run." Besides, Chase obviously didn't need or want her here.

"Where to?" Raina asked.

"None of your business," Chase said.

Sloane covered a shocked gasp with a cough, walking over to his mother, edging between them and patting Raina's hand. "I appreciate your asking. I'm going to visit my mother's old house," she informed Raina with a gracious smile. "I have the address you gave me."

"Oh dear. You really shouldn't go alone."

"Why not?" both Chase and Sloane asked at the same time.

Sloane only knew she wanted to get out of the hospital and away from her escalating feelings. Chase just obviously wanted her gone.

She reminded him of his failings, and apparently, Chase Chandler held himself up to higher than human standards. He didn't permit himself to have wants or desires that came before his family. She inhaled and squared her shoulders. Well, then, too bad for him. She wanted someone human in her life. Besides, she had her hands full finding her father. She didn't need to add Chase's hang-ups to her own. Much as she wanted to.

Raina clucked her tongue, as if chastising them both. "Because it's an emotional situation and Sloane shouldn't face the past alone."

"It's my mother's past. Only indirectly mine." Sloane shrugged, forcing herself to make light of the situation, at least until she left the room. "I'll be fine."

Raina expelled an exasperated breath. "But I don't need Chase here."

He shot her a glance, then leaned down on the portable tray that substituted as a nightstand and leaned closer. "All the more reason for me to stay."

"Chase has a point," Sloane said, through clenched teeth. She didn't want anything he wasn't willing to give. "He won't be satisfied until he hears you're going to be okay, and I don't blame him. I'm just going to deal with some family skeletons, try to get the dog, and then go back to Chase's. I'm hoping maybe we'll get a call from Earl or get a lead on Samson so I can settle things here and head back to D.C." She shifted her purse strap higher on her shoulder. "I want to get out of everyone's hair."

"Nonsense." Raina waved a hand dismissively. "You're not in anyone's way. But if you do get any leads, make sure you call Chase here or at my place," she said in her best dictatorial voice.

"I can't believe I'm saying this, but I agree with my mother. If something comes up, you call. Whoever's after Samson is dangerous." Concern flickered in Chase's darkened gaze, a hint of longing he couldn't hide.

But longing wasn't enough, not without his willingness to act. "Don't worry," Sloane said with a flippant shake of her head. "I can handle my life. I appreciate all your family has done for me so far, but you have more important concerns now."

Gathering her reserve strength, she walked away as if the man in the room meant nothing to her. She had no choice but to accept that unless he came to terms with his conflict, she was on her own. A place she'd been for a while now. But it was a place that was so much more lonely now that she'd known Chase.

Chapter Thirteen

Sloane was feeling brave until the moment she pulled up to her mother's old house. As she stepped out of the car, her knees went weak and she began to tremble. She'd have given anything to have Chase by her side, but he was needed elsewhere and she didn't begrudge him time with his family. Wasn't she here to learn more about hers? Though what she thought she'd find, she wasn't certain.

A cold fall breeze circulated in the air, keeping her blood pumping and her adrenaline flowing. She pulled her denim jacket close around her and focused on the house as she approached. The old Colonial looked well maintained. With the kids playing out back and the American flag hanging on the porch, Sloane figured the house was also well loved.

Not wanting to scare the kids by showing up in the backyard, she knocked on the door, intending to ask permission.

A woman opened the door. "Can I help you?" She wiped her hands on her jeans and leaned against the door frame.

Faced with the owner, a woman with bobbed hair, manicured nails, and a friendly smile, Sloane wasn't sure where to begin. "This may sound silly, but my mother grew up here and . . . Well, I was wondering if I could look around?"

The woman smiled. "I don't see why not." She opened the door wider. "Come on in." Stepping back, she let Sloane inside. "I'm Grace McKeever."

"Sloane Carlisle," she said, opting for honesty. She looked around at the floral wallpaper and dark wood floors and furniture. She had a hunch the house had been redecorated recently and had changed much since her mother resided there. "How long have you lived here?" she asked the woman.

"About eight years. From what I understand, this house has changed hands many times." She gestured around the large entryway and toward the circular staircase in front of them. "I'm not sure what you're looking for, but feel free to wander."

Small-town hospitality, Sloane thought, warmth filling her. But she shook her head. "Thanks anyway." Sloane wouldn't know which room belonged to her mother. "I really just want to see the tree house out back. I'd love to see that, if you don't mind."

Grace laughed and tucked her hair behind one ear. "Of course not. My kids spend a lot of time there. Come, I'll show you." She led Sloane through the house, to the kitchen, and out a sliding-glass door leading to a patio area in the back.

The yard spread expansively before her and she could imagine her mother playing as a child. Or maybe not, considering the repressed upbringing and strict rules employed by her grandfather. But there was no denying the fact that there were two teenage girls now — giggling, laughing, and probably talking about boys.

Just as Jacqueline and Raina had discussed the man Jacqueline loved. The man named Samson. Her father.

"Girls, it's time for Hannah to go home," Grace called.

"Can't I stay, Grace, please? I'll call Kendall and she'll say it's okay. She can't cook for beans anyway and I'd much rather eat here." A pretty blond-haired girl with a face full of makeup came skidding to a halt.

From the names tossed around in conversation, Sloane knew she was seeing Kendall's sister, Hannah. Her nonstop motion reminded Sloane of her twin sisters' actions and she held back a laugh.

An equally pretty brunette came up by Hannah's side. "Come on, Mom. There's enough food for one more."

Grace raised an eyebrow. "And you know this because . . . ? You helped cook?" she asked sarcastically.

"Because you always make a lot, and besides, Hannah doesn't eat much, do you, Hannah?"

"Nope. Honest." Kendall's sister held one hand in the air.

"It just so happens we're meeting your father at Norman's for dinner and Hannah's welcome to join us. Kendall can pick you up from there or I can drop you off on the way home. Just call and make sure it's okay with her."

"Cool, Mom, thanks!"

"Thanks, Grace."

The girls took off before Sloane could introduce herself.

"Sorry. I wish I could say they're usually better mannered, but they're teenagers and completely self-absorbed." A blush on her cheeks, Grace let out a self-conscious laugh.

"Not a problem. I have twin sisters so I really do understand."

Grace nodded. "Thank you for that. Anyway, there's the tree house." She pointed to the end of the property and the large tree in the corner. "Take your time, okay? It was nice meeting you."

Sloane smiled, liking the woman a lot. "Same here."

"I didn't think to ask where you're living, but I'm sure I'll see you around." Grace turned and headed back for the house, leaving Sloane to question why she hadn't bothered to correct the other woman's misconception that Sloane resided in Yorkshire Falls.

Delving too deeply into that question could only cause Sloane pain, and with an unknown father in her future, she had a hunch she was already in store for enough. She approached the tree house and was about to attempt the rickety ladder leading up the trunk when she heard a rustling sound from the bushes. Someone appeared to have been lurking. She glanced back toward the house, but Grace had gone inside.

Alone, Sloane's heart pounded hard in her chest. Feeling silly for being afraid in this typically friendly town, she called out in a forced but friendly voice. "Hello?"

She heard the rustling again and caught sight of a man who rose and obviously planned to run away. "No, wait." Something compelled her to stop the stranger before he could retreat.

The figure paused, then turned back to Sloane. Eerily familiar golden eyes stared back at her from an unshaven, weathered masculine face. "Samson?" she guessed.

"You look like your mother," he said — no preamble, formality, or warmth.

"Can I take that as a compliment?" She swallowed hard, shock rippling through her. After all her searching, her real father stood in front of her. That easily.

"Take it any way you please." His gaze held hers for an awkward moment; then he abruptly turned to leave.

Panicked, she called him back. "Don't go. Please."

He paused but didn't look over his shoulder.

"Why did you come here?" she asked, wondering if the same *feeling* that had brought her in search of the old tree house had also brought him. Wondering if fate did work in such mystifyingly simple ways.

He shrugged. "It's not like I have anyplace else to go."

"Your house. I'm sorry about the fire."

"Unless you lit the match, you got nothing to be sorry about."

She clenched and unclenched her fists. Obviously, somebody who worried or cared was a foreign emotion, one she chose not to delve into just yet. She hoped they'd have more time. "But why come *here?* Why now?"

"I got tired of ducking the cops."

"Excuse me?" She tamped down on the urge to step closer, afraid he'd run away.

"I couldn't go anyplace public and so I came here. I do that sometimes. When those kids are in school."

"Because the tree house holds memories?" she asked.

He merely grunted.

She took the reply as a yes. It wasn't enough that he was alone, he also retreated into the past. His story got sadder and sadder, Sloane thought, and though she was grateful to meet him now, she gained a new understanding and perspective on her own life. The chances Michael Carlisle had given her were chances Samson hadn't had.

"I have to go."

"But I want to know you." She grasped for

anything to keep him standing in front of her. "And I heard you want to know me."

He scowled at her. "What I wanted was to see you up close. To be sure. Now I can go."

Sloane had heard about his gruff exterior. She'd heard he was antisocial, but she never imagined he'd turn that harshness her way. *What were you expecting, Sloane, a warm, fuzzy family reunion?* she asked herself. She wouldn't be getting one. Samson wasn't a Chandler nor was he a Carlisle, and she had no right to put those expectations onto him. After all, she'd been warned going in.

But he was part of the blood that ran in her veins and she wouldn't go quietly out of his life. Her disappointment was hers to deal with later, but she wasn't ready to give up now.

"You wanted to be sure of what? That I was your daughter?" she asked, pushing her limits.

"Yeah." He started to reach out, as if to touch her, then dropped his hand. "You've got your mother's hair and my mother's eyes. I'm sure you're mine. Who told you the almighty senator wasn't your father?" he asked with no tact.

Samson's tone told her he was angry with the senator and didn't trust him. He was wary and she understood that. But Michael wasn't to blame and she needed Samson to understand that.

Especially if they wanted to call off Michael's men. "My father . . . I mean Senator Michael

Carlisle admitted I wasn't his," she said, attempting to put a realistic spin on the truth.

Samson's head jerked up and he met her gaze. "A few weeks ago, I went to D.C. Talked to the senator. He told me the same thing."

That news shocked Sloane. "He told you what exactly?"

"He said he'd tell you the truth 'bout me. That you were old enough to handle it. I believed him, damn fool that I am."

She narrowed her gaze. "Michael doesn't lie," she assured Samson. And she believed the senator *would* have enlightened her. Madeline had told her the same thing.

"Then why did his goons threaten me if I didn't disappear? And why'd my house blow up right after?"

Sloane blinked as more facets of the situation became clear. "Those things happened without Michael's knowledge."

"Speak English, girlie. Who didn't know what?" Samson kicked a worn sneaker into the dirt on the ground.

He'd dropped his gaze again, though remained facing her, something she considered progress. "Michael's men acted alone, without consulting him. He had no idea you'd been turned away or threatened. I'm sure of it."

"Why are you so certain? 'Cuz he's been such a paragon of virtue telling you the truth all along?"

Sloane flinched, accepting the verbal slap. He

had a point, but she still felt compelled to defend the man who'd raised her. "Michael has always acted in my best interest. Or what he thought was my best interest," she explained. "He may have kept the truth from me but he's a man of his word. If he said he was going to tell me, he was. It's his men who took things into their own hands. I'd stake my life on it."

"And was it a good one?" Samson asked, his tone shocking Sloane, and she sucked in a startled breath. For a moment, the surly old man was gone, replaced by a concerned, caring one. "Was your life a good one?"

Unexpected tears formed in her eyes. "Yes, it was a very good life."

The wrinkles around his eyes eased. "I figured that. Saw it for myself when I went back to check on your mother. She'd married someone else." Without warning, he sat down in the grass, as if the weight of telling the story was too much for him to bear.

Sloane knelt, then settled herself Indian-style beside him. "You went back for Jacqueline?" Sloane plucked a blade of grass and twirled it between her fingers, finding it easier to concentrate on the mundane than the painful history between her parents.

"In a manner of speaking." Samson squinted and looked into the sun. "I made sure she was living good. But her father said unless I stayed away from his daughter, he'd make sure the loan sharks my old man borrowed from came after him, among other threats. Your grand-father said Jacqueline was only eighteen and I couldn't support us and my family. If I agreed to his terms, he said he'd make the debts go away."

"So you took him up on it."

He nodded. "I put my family first. Before what I wanted. I had no choice."

Just like Chase, Sloane thought, drawing the unexpected parallel. Two men willing to give her up for the good of family. She realized she was being irrational — Samson hadn't known Jacqueline was carrying his child any more than Chase had turned away from her. Yet.

"You didn't know Jacqueline was pregnant, did you?" Sloane asked to make sure.

"No. But she was married to someone who had money and could give her a better, healthier life than I could have done."

Sloane tried unsuccessfully to hold back tears. "How did you find out about me?" she asked in a small voice.

"Pictures. When this presidential campaign started, I saw you on television with the senator. Your red hair blowing in the wind. I went to the library and looked up when you were born and put two and two together." He coughed and ended up laughing. "Bet you didn't know your old man even knew what a library was, but I was smart once. Before life got in the way."

Sloane lifted a hand, then feeling useless, let it fall to her side. For once, words wouldn't come.

"Once I realized the truth, I went to the high-and-mighty senator. He said he'd tell you and we could meet. A week later, a man shows up at my door and sez the senator changed his mind. He wasn't going to risk his career for the likes of me. I would threaten the campaign." He smacked his hand against the green grass. "But all I wanted wuz to meet you once. See you, talk to you, know you're mine, then leave." He rose again, intending to just walk away.

"Samson, wait." She jumped up to stop him, but at the same moment, Grace's voice called out to her.

"I'm not in the mood for people." He stepped toward the bushes.

Sloane's mouth went dry. She didn't want to part ways yet. Not when she didn't know how to reach him again.

"Sloane?" the other woman called from the deck of the house.

Sloane glanced her way. "One minute." When she turned back around, Samson had disappeared.

She let her hands drop to her sides, disappointment welling inside her at the opportunity that she'd lost.

Thinking about Samson, she made her way back to the house. She'd met her father, something she hadn't counted on happening so fast. Crossing the lawn where her mother had grown up, she shivered at the odd sense of belonging she felt in this town, at the odder connection she had for the eccentric man who'd bolted at the first sign of another person.

"I just wanted to let you know that we were leaving," Grace said as Sloane walked up the deck stairs. "The girls are in the car and I'm taking the teenagers for dinner." She feigned a shiver at the prospect. "You're welcome to hang out for as long as you'd like."

"Thanks, Grace. You've been very gracious."

"No problem. I saw you with someone. Were you talking to the neighbors?"

"You could say that." Sloane shrugged, not wanting to give Samson's hideout away. "Listen, I think I'm going to leave too."

"But you never went up into the tree house." Grace gestured in the distance. "You'd really be amazed at that place."

Sloane smiled. "Then I'll have to come back, if that's okay with you."

The other woman nodded. "Of course it is. Come. I'll walk you out."

As they headed for the driveway, Grace made small talk until they reached the cars. Sloane's rental blocked Grace's minivan. "You see? I'd have to move my car anyway so you could get out."

Grace reached for the handle on the car, then paused. "Hannah said she thought you were Chase's new girlfriend."

Sloane chuckled. "I don't know what's worse, the small-town grapevine or a teenager's perspective on life."

"You mean Hannah exaggerated?" Grace placed a hand on her heart and donned a shocked expression. "Do tell," she said, laughing.

Sloane rolled her eyes. "Let's say she's got the bare bones, not the whole story."

Grace's eyes lit with curiosity as she rubbed her hands together. "Sounds like an interesting tale."

"One that's just not worth telling," Sloane said, trying in vain to hide her disappointment at the turn her relationship with Chase had taken.

She said good-bye to Grace, then waved to the girls before climbing into her own car and pulling out of the driveway.

She fought the tide of emotion, attempting to keep any thoughts or feelings of Samson at bay. She needed time to think back on their conversation, to understand the events that had shaped the man he'd become. But not dwelling on Samson meant focusing on Chase. And that prospect wasn't any more uplifting.

Yet despite the pain, common sense told her she couldn't fault him for not giving when he'd never promised her more. She was lucky he'd helped her out when she needed it after the accident, and she should be grateful for the time they'd shared. He was a good man, one who in another lifetime would have made a great husband.

But in this lifetime, Chase Chandler had made his choices and they didn't include Sloane.

"If actions could make things happen, I'd think I caused this heart condition." Raina glanced around her bedroom, happy to be home, a little scared to really be sick, and a lot guilty for what she'd done to her boys.

Eric sat down on his side of the bed. Raina had long since redecorated the bedroom she'd shared with John, her husband, and lately she'd started to think of things here as belonging to Eric too.

"As your doctor, I can tell you that I am one hundred percent certain your charade did not cause this illness." He grasped her hand, bringing it close to his heart. "But as the man who loves you, I can say the stress you're adding to your life hasn't helped."

She nodded. "I understand. I do. I just wish Chase would see the error in his think—"

He cut her off by lifting her hand and kissing her knuckles, startling her into silence. He had the most amazing ways of shutting her up, Raina thought, warmth heating her veins and her heart rate picking up.

"I like when you touch me," she told him.

"See how easy it is to refocus your attention?" he said, laughing. "Anytime you mention the boys, I'm going to have to kiss you into forgetfulness."

Leaning against the pillow, she turned her head toward him. "I want to be married. I want you to be able to shut me up anytime you want, day or night." She reached for him, pulling him down so he lay beside her. "I want to make your breakfast every morning and let you take care of me every night."

"Why, Raina Chandler, what would the town think if they knew just how old-fashioned you really were?"

She laughed. "They'd think what I already know. That I'm lucky to have found you. And with life being so short, I don't want to put off our days together anymore."

"I was never the one holding us back."

"I realize it's been my fault and I'm the one who insisted we wait. I just wanted my sons happy."

Eric reached out and stroked her cheek. "And they are, Raina. You raised them well. It's time to let them go."

"Now? Before Chase has settled his turmoil?"

He graced her with a gentle smile. "What better gift could you give them? What better gift could you give yourself than to let their good judgment and fate take over?"

"Quite frankly, Chase's judgment is wonderful when it comes to his family, but it sucks when it comes to his personal life."

Eric burst out laughing. "I do love you, Raina. Now, how about setting a date?"

A buzzer rang, preventing Raina from answering.

"That's dinner. I've been heating the meal Izzy sent over. I have to go check it before it burns," Eric said, rising from the bed. "But don't think I've forgotten where we left off."

"Of course not." She waited for Eric to disappear out the bedroom door. He had no idea how fortunate the interruption was. Because Raina wasn't getting married until Chase proposed to Sloane.

Where was she? Chase had gotten his mother settled at her house hours ago, leaving her in Eric's capable hands. He'd come home expecting to find his guest, but instead the house was empty. The way it should be.

So why didn't he feel better?

Because he was worried about Sloane. Because he wanted her by his side. He kicked his foot against the carpeted floor in frustration.

He grabbed his keys and started for the door at the same time she slowly walked inside, as if she had no idea he'd been pacing the floors in concern. He wanted to demand answers, to know where she'd been way past dinner, but the lost, dazed expression on her face stopped him.

Sucker punched him, in fact. He stepped back from his anger and exhaled hard. He knew she'd gone to her mother's old house, but if anything urgent had come up, she'd have called. She'd promised.

Or had Raina just asked her to check in? He no longer remembered. "Where have you been?" He studied her, wanting to be certain he didn't miss any clues to what she might be thinking.

She shrugged. "Around." Swinging her hands at her sides, she started past him.

Without meeting his gaze. "You said you were going by your mother's old place. Did the memories there upset you?" Drawn back to her despite his better judgment, he wrapped an arm around her shoulders and pulled her close.

He sensed her struggle not to give in, to maintain the distance he'd begun in his mother's hospital room. But just as his deepest feelings pushed him toward her, she came to him.

Her body molded to his, her light weight leaning against him. "I found Samson," she said as her legs went weak beneath her.

"You what?" He turned her around, not letting her fall and providing the support she needed.

Wide eyes met his. "I found . . . my father. My real father."

Her voice cracked, and so, he thought, did his heart.

"I walked out back to the tree house and —" She placed her hands out in front of her, wide and imploring. "There he was. As if he'd materialized from thin air."

That was Samson, Chase thought. He came

and went, no one close enough to him to notice or care. He appeared and disappeared on a whim. But after the explosion and his obvious vanishing act, Sloane finding him today was no accident. He'd obviously sought her out. If not, he'd come to the tree house for the same reason she had, solace and peace. He wondered if either of them had found the answers they sought.

"So now you know where I've been." She straightened her shoulders and righted her stance.

Body language indicated she no longer needed him. Chase knew better. He saw the longing in her eyes and it matched the desire pulsing through him. Not just a physical ache that needed satisfaction but an emotional one only this woman could fill. For him, it was an all-consuming need to be a part of her and take away her pain.

"I need some rest." She started past him, but he stopped her with a simple touch on her arm. Turning, she raised an eyebrow in question. "Is something wrong?"

Hell yes, he thought. Everything was wrong. From his mixed-up emotions to the overwhelming desire to pick her up and drag her to bed and make love to her — no discussion, no questions. And that would solve nothing. Not his problems and certainly not hers.

From the pain in her eyes, he saw she had plenty. "You said you saw your real father for the first time, and in the next breath, you said you needed to rest. Don't you think you left out something important in between?"

"Nothing I can't handle." Her gaze darted from his, letting him know in no uncertain terms she was excluding him on purpose.

"You don't need to handle things alone," he reminded her, his words at odds with his own needs.

She slanted her head to one side, a defiant tilt to her chin that boded no good. "Oh really? Since when did I start sharing my life with anyone in particular?"

"Ouch." He winced. "You know I'll be there for you."

"Yes, I do," she said, her eyes glazing over as she spoke. "Because you're Chase Chandler, everyone's white knight."

Sloane bit down on the inside of her cheek, fighting against the urge to do as he suggested, to lean on him and let her problems seem more manageable for as long as he held her and made her feel safe.

"So let me do what I do best," Chase said.

One look at his lopsided grin and endearing wink and she was tempted to do just that. But Chase specialized in riding to the rescue for one reason only. He felt obligated. "I wish I could give in as easily as you." Sloane forced herself to meet his gaze. "You're here for me one minute; you're pushing me away the next. Don't get me wrong, I understand why —"

"Then you understand a hell of a lot more than I do," he said, interrupting. He ran a hand through his hair before pinching the bridge of his nose in a gesture she'd come to recognize as one of intense contemplation.

One that never failed to endear him to her even more. Dammit. "Look, it's been a long day. Between your mother's sudden illness and my father's return, well, we don't need any more drama in our lives."

"No, but right now I need you." His voice dropped a husky octave and Sloane had no doubt he meant what he said. *Right now.* And that was what bothered her.

But despite her misgivings, it also freed her. Chase's attitude hadn't changed from the day they'd met. Hers had. She wanted the happily-ever-after Raina hoped for. And she wanted it with Chase. Knowing she could never — would never — have it, she decided she'd take one last time with him instead.

After the meeting with Samson, Sloane was at her most vulnerable. Swallowing her pride, she held out her hand and admitted, "I need you too."

Chapter Fourteen

Thank God. Maybe he was selfish, but damned if Chase wouldn't take what Sloane offered. Even as he placed his hand inside her softer palm, he looked into her eyes and saw the finality there. A finality he refused to deal with now.

Not when he could have Sloane and comfort her at the same time. He admitted to himself he wasn't sure which pleased him more. He also understood the implications that his heart was involved. But his heart couldn't dictate his future or else he'd give up his dreams. Again. And this time he was on the verge of uncovering a story that would jump-start his career. No matter that it was at Sloane's expense.

He pushed aside all thoughts in favor of more pressing desires to satisfy. And those were all about Sloane, the woman who beckoned to him like no other, the one who understood him like no other.

First he checked the lock on the door leading downstairs to the office, then the outside entrance. Only after he was certain they wouldn't be interrupted, he returned to Sloane. He sensed this was going to be their last time, and if that was true, it was damn well going to be one they'd both remember.

Sloane leaned against the wall, a determined, come-hither look in her eyes. She held out her hand and Chase came willingly. He didn't know who kissed whom first, but once he tasted those moist, damp lips, he wanted more and wasn't about to wait.

Between deep sensual kisses, they made their way to the bedroom, where they shed their clothes along with inhibitions that were already long gone. Before he knew it, Chase had joined Sloane on the bed, hovering over her lush, naked body, which just waited for his undivided attention.

Bending his head, he lavished his attention on one plump breast, kneading her full flesh in his hand while drawing one distended nipple into his mouth, pulling on the damp, pointy flesh. Arching her back, she moaned her delight; then she suddenly pushed on his head, letting him know she wanted equal attention paid to the other breast.

Happy to oblige, his tongue trailed a moist path across her chest. "Mmm," she said, a purr coming from her throat.

He encircled her other nipple and grazed lightly with his teeth, while plumping one breast with his hand. He wanted to continue feasting on her flesh, but his body was straining, begging for release, and it wouldn't be denied.

He spread her thighs, and while her dilated eyes locked on his, he thrust inside her, discovering her full, wet, and completely ready for him. And even as he found his release, sex was the furthest thing from his mind, as unexpected, overwhelming emotion swamped him.

The sound of the telephone ringing woke Sloane out of a deep, sated sleep. She hadn't realized how exhausted she was, but she'd slept through the night without waking once. She rolled over at the same time Chase answered the phone beside her.

"Hello?"

Sloane shut her eyes and let the sound of his deep voice wash over her. Knowing she was minutes away from rising and walking out of his life forever made these last minutes bittersweet. But she had no choice. Sloane didn't want to be Chase Chandler's obligation anymore. She wanted to be his equal, or she didn't want him at all.

"Hey, Roman. Where are you?" Chase asked.

Sloane propped herself up on her side and listened.

"So stay at Mom's," he said. Meeting Sloane's gaze, he explained. "They're running late, but they're on their way to Yorkshire Falls. His place is being painted and the fumes are no good for Charlotte."

She nodded and he spoke to his brother once more. "Eric's car's in the driveway? So go to Rick's," he muttered. From the frustration evident in Chase's tone, he didn't want to invite his brother and sister-in-law to stay over.

Apparently, didn't want *them* interrupted. Or he just thought Sloane already occupied his guest room. Either way, he was wrong.

She was out of here. "Chase, let them have your guest room." She sat up in bed, pulling a sheet up to cover her exposed breasts.

He held up one hand, signaling she should wait, not paying attention to her words. "Don't Pearl and Eldin have an extra room in the guesthouse? That should help Charlotte avoid stairs."

He listened, then frowned.

"What's wrong?" Sloane asked.

"Apparently, Charlotte's been having early contractions. The doctor said extra rest and no stairs," Chase explained. "What's that, Roman?" he asked, his attention called back to his brother's call.

Sloane waited.

Chase ran a hand through his hair and groaned. "Pearl and Eldin what?" he asked, his voice rising in disbelief. "What kind of guest could that old couple have? Besides Kendall, no one's visited them in years. And if they had company, we'd know. Pearl tells us all of her business."

Sloane chuckled. "Remember the extra bags of groceries?" she reminded Chase. "They obviously have someone staying with them."

And suddenly she knew who it was. Her father. Samson was hiding out with Pearl and

Eldin, which explained why he was tired of *ducking the cops*. He was attempting to elude Rick at every turn while living under his nose. It would have been funny if the situation weren't so pathetic.

"I know I have stairs too," he said. "Come over and we'll figure something out."

Which was perfect, Sloane thought, because once she was gone, Chase might just appreciate the company Roman and Charlotte would provide.

His voice brought her back to his conversation with his brother. "Pearl and Eldin don't pay rent. Now they're housing guests. Don't you think they're taking advantage?" Chase listened, then said, "Yeah, see you soon" before he slammed the phone down, still muttering to himself.

"You're in a foul mood this morning." Sloane eyed him warily.

He exhaled a long and deep breath. "Then come make me feel better." He held his arms out, expecting her to roll into his embrace. But as she met his gaze, she recognized the same wariness in his expression that she felt in her heart.

It was time.

She shook her head. "I can't. We both needed last night, but we've come to the end, don't you think?"

He sat up straighter in bed, arms folded across his chest, a barrier she couldn't let deter her.

"Your choice," he said.

She laughed, but the sound was bitter. "Not really." She rose from the bed, grabbed for one of his T-shirts, and pulled it on. At least she'd be covered until she got back to the guest room, showered, packed, and moved on. "It's *your* choice," she said softly.

He raised an eyebrow but said nothing.

"I'm sure of myself and sure of my feelings, Chase. Despite everything that's going on in my life, I *know*. I love you."

He flinched. She hadn't imagined it, but to her surprise, his expression softened. "I love you too, Sloane."

The words warmed her heart despite the fact that she knew they wouldn't change a thing. Still, shock and a jolt of hope filled her veins.

"For a man of few words, you do choose them well."

She took a cautious step toward him, but he held out one hand to stop her. "I love you, but I can't follow through on commitment any more now than I could when we first met." Pain etched his expression, but she heard the definitive tone in his voice.

She forced a smile. "You've already raised a family."

He nodded. "Been there, done that," he said too lightly. "And I haven't begun to reach for my professional dreams."

"You want more for yourself than to run the *Gazette*," she said knowingly. "You need to prove yourself and the story of a lifetime's hovering just within reach."

"You know me well." A wry smile lifted his lips.

She laughed despite the pain in her heart. "Yeah, I do."

"My entire life has revolved around other people — keeping the paper going for the town, maintaining my father's legacy, supporting the family." He shook his head. "Don't get me wrong, I love what I do, but I've always dreamed of more." He folded his arms across his chest. "I've always wondered what having my freedom would be like."

She nodded slowly. "Then you need to find out. Chalk us" — she gestured between them — "chalk us up to a case of bad timing." She swallowed over her disappointment and sought to find the words that would allow her to depart with dignity. "I knew where we stood from the beginning," she finally managed with a flippant shake of her head. "Which is why I'm making this easy. I'm leaving."

He swung his legs over the side of the bed and she forced her gaze away from his bare chest and naked body. Forced herself to focus on ending things, not getting caught up in sexual attraction that would lead to nowhere but heartache.

"You aren't leaving this house. Not until we know you're safe," he said as he stood.

"I'll be fine." She glanced over to see Chase

shoving his legs into jeans before walking around the bed and coming up beside her. So close she could inhale and smell the masculine scent that settled inside her and made her want so much more than he could give.

"You're not going anywhere I can't keep an eye on you," he said, shoving his hands into his back pockets.

"It's not like you have a choice in the matter. I don't want to be your obligation anymore." She opted to spell things out in language he'd understand. "But if it makes you feel any better, I'm going to my father."

"Samson sure as hell isn't safe." Chase narrowed his gaze. "And since when do you know where he is?"

She shrugged. "Since five minutes ago. I think Samson's staying with Pearl and Eldin."

"Just when did you plan on telling me?" he asked, his voice rising.

She shrugged. "I'm not sure that I was. I mean, he's my father; it's my problem."

A muscle ticked in his jaw. "The last place the man stayed exploded and now he's living in my brother's backyard. I think that makes it my problem too."

She winced, knowing she couldn't argue. Worse, she realized she hadn't even thought in those terms. "God, I'm sorry."

His eyes, which had darkened with anger, immediately softened as he reached for her. "There's a lot going on. Too much to take in all at once. But there's also the fact that I care about what happens to you." His hand grazed her forearm and his grip was soft as he caressed her skin with his more callused thumb.

His husky voice and honest admission could be her undoing if she let it. "I only just figured out where Samson was staying while you were on the phone with Roman," she said. "And now that I have, it's a solution, don't you think? I can stay with him and that will guarantee nothing happens to either Samson or Rick and Kendall, since my father's men wouldn't hurt me."

"That's not a guarantee and it sure as hell isn't a bet I'm willing to lose."

"Well, to increase the odds, I'll call Michael and ask him to come up here. To fix things somehow." She spread her hands wide. "And I'll be out of your hair. Easy solution, all the way around."

He stared at her for a long minute, his hot, devouring gaze never leaving hers. "Go shower."

"What?" She shook her head, unsure why.

"Go shower and I'll take you over to Pearl and Eldin's," he said, feeling resigned.

So he was letting her go. Pain cramped her belly, but what had she expected? That he'd beg her to stay? With regret, she pulled her gaze from his and walked out of the room. Out of his life would come later.

Chase followed Sloane to Rick's house in his truck, which was a good thing considering

Sloane didn't think she could be in close quarters with him and still walk away. After pulling up to the curb, she insisted they first talk with Samson before telling Rick that he had the man staying in his guesthouse.

Sloane's legs shook as she made her way to Pearl and Eldin's, partly because she wasn't sure of her reception and mostly because she knew this good-bye to Chase would be final.

She knocked on the door, rapping quickly with her knuckle, before she could change her mind.

The door opened a mere sliver. Considering Pearl's reputation for friendliness and her tendency to welcome people with open arms, this secrecy cemented Sloane's certainty. Samson was inside.

"Pearl?" she called. "It's Sloane. We met at Norman's the other day and I was hoping I could talk to you."

Silence followed, but the door widened a little bit more. Taking advantage, Sloane tipped her head closer. "Pearl, please. I know you have Samson in there and I need to speak with him."

The admission had the opposite effect as the door slammed shut in Sloane's face. She jumped back and barreled into Chase. His arms came around her, steadying her before she could fall or knock him over. Unfortunately, they didn't let go either. And despite the weight of her jacket, she felt his body heat and the security that always came with Chase Chandler.

"Looks like you're right," his husky voice said in her ear. "She's hiding something."

His warm breath caressed her skin and she shivered. "Small consolation when they won't let me inside."

"I think a visit by Officer Chandler might do the trick," Chase suggested.

Sloane stiffened and tried to turn around, but Chase held her in place. "You can't turn my father in," she said, panicked by the thought.

"He's not wanted for anything serious, Sloane. Rick just wants to ask him a few questions and protect him at the same time."

Why did anything that came from Chase's mouth sound so rational, so certain, so right? "He obviously doesn't want protection," she said, refusing to be swayed by emotion.

"Sometimes what people want and what they need are two very different things."

His husky voice sent tremors of awareness rippling through her body, as did the dual meaning behind his words. But she knew that his desires wouldn't change his actions. She needed to get away from this man and the effect he had over her. "If you insist on telling Rick, then I'm going to talk to Samson first, so why don't we split up and do what we each need to do?"

His arms tightened around her instead, his lips hovering at her neck. "You make the simplest things so damn hard," he muttered.

"You're fighting yourself and I refuse to pressure you." Sloane forcefully wriggled out of his grasp. He'd come to her on his own or not at all.

Chase nodded in agreement, stepping back. He had more self-control than anyone she'd met, damn him.

"Rick needs to know what he's up against. So we'll play this your way," Chase said. "You handle Samson and I'll go see if Kendall and Rick are home."

"Okay." She waited until Chase disappeared around front and turned back to the guesthouse, knocking once more. "Pearl, it's Sloane and I'm alone."

Finally the door opened wide. Pearl grabbed Sloane by the wrist and pulled her inside. "Good Lord, girl, do you know how hard it's been keeping this secret?" Pearl patted her bun. "Come eat."

Sloane blinked. From foreign intrigue to food. "Pearl, where's Samson?" She glanced around the small entryway, from the fresh, bright paint to the older but immaculate couch and chairs in the living room.

"He went to get his dog from Doc Sterling."

"Won't that be like announcing his presence?" Sloane wrinkled her nose.

"He's just gonna take him. Doc doesn't lock his doors," the older woman said. "No one in town does."

Sloane merely blinked at that. "But I'm sure

he'll figure out that Samson has him."

"But he won't know where Samson is. Unless you tell him." Pearl leveled her best glare on Sloane, which wasn't worth much since sweetness oozed from the older woman's voice.

"Pearl, Chase is telling Rick as we speak. This isn't a safe situation for anyone involved," Sloane said, coming to a decision. "Can I please use your phone?"

"Oh surely. Are you going to tell Chase to keep that reporter's mouth of his quiet?" She leaned closer, obviously enjoying the intrigue.

Sloane laughed. "No, but I am going to put an end to this once and for all." Following Pearl to the kitchen, Sloane picked up the phone and called Michael Carlisle.

He answered his private line on the first ring. "Carlisle."

"Hi, Dad. It's me, Sloane."

"Sweetheart, I have been so worried." Her father's voice dropped an octave, the relief he felt on hearing her voice evident.

A little girl's need to have her daddy rose up along with adult respect for the man who'd raised her and loved her. "I need you, Dad." Her voice cracked and she didn't care, didn't bother holding back the tidal wave of emotion.

"You don't have to ask twice. You never did. Madeline said you're in Yorkshire Falls. I can be there by tonight."

Turning away so Pearl, who was obviously eavesdropping and watching with eager eyes, couldn't witness everything, Sloane blotted her eyes. "I love you."

"I love you too."

She hung up, realizing she didn't have to make peace with Michael Carlisle's decision not to tell her the truth about her parentage. She already had. She could forgive him because he loved her and had shown her that in so many ways over the years. But because she now knew the truth, she understood herself better too. And hopefully, now she'd have the time to get to know the eccentric man who'd sired her.

"I think this occasion calls for a brownie, don't you?" Pearl asked.

Sloane turned back to face her hostess. "Sure." She might as well eat while she was waiting for Samson.

As she shared a chocolate square and hot tea with Pearl, the man Sloane sought finally arrived.

Samson walked in through the back, his pug following close behind. "Had to run from the cops, avoid a reporter, and that damn man who kept asking directions. Then Dog here had to make a run for it when that dumb-ass mongrel Rick and Kendall call Happy came bounding round the side of the house," Samson grumbled, not looking up or noticing Sloane. "What the hell kind of name is Happy for an animal, anyway?"

"I suppose *Dog* is better?" Sloane couldn't help asking.

Samson frowned, glancing from Sloane to Pearl. "What's she doing here?"

"I'm looking for you." Rising from a chair in the kitchen, Sloane rubbed her damp palms against her pants.

"And I couldn't very well leave her on the doorstep, now could I?" Pearl put a hand on Sloane's shoulder. "It's wintertime."

"It's not quite winter yet. Anyway, how'd she find me?"

"Any reason you don't just ask me?" Sloane said.

His scowl deepened. " 'Cuz if I ignore you, maybe you'll go away."

"Samson Humphrey, you apologize this instant," Pearl said before Sloane could react. "I won't be putting up with rudeness in my house. Just ask Eldin. We speak with respect here, or we don't speak at all."

"Then there must be a lot of quiet time 'round here," Samson grumbled.

Sulking, Pearl folded her arms over her ample breasts, then lowered herself into the chair Sloane had vacated.

This wasn't getting them anywhere. Although Sloane knew better than to be insulted by Samson, who treated everyone with the same surly disdain, there was a part of her that wished he'd look at her differently and talk to her like the little girl he'd lost. But that was a lot like wishing Chase would treat her like the woman he loved and wanted to raise a family with. Neither wish would be coming true.

At this point, she'd settle for being allowed to stay with Samson during the little time she had left in Yorkshire Falls. And she didn't think he needed to know Michael Carlisle was on his way here either.

"Look," she said, coming up to Samson. She scooped up the pug for good measure and petted his head. "I need a place to stay, and since we want to get to know each other, I thought I could stay with you," she told Samson.

It wasn't until she'd spoken the words aloud that she realized she was afraid he'd say no. Reject her. She curled her fingers into the fur on the dog's back.

"The sofa in the family room pulls out," Pearl said at the same time Samson growled at her.

"You ain't staying here. I said I wanted to know if you was mine, but I didn't say I wanted no kid in my life."

Sloane shut her eyes, but his words remained out there. "It would just be for a day or two. Until I'm ready to go home."

"Stay with your boyfriend. There's no room here," he said, a defiant tilt to his chin and an uncompromising tone in his voice.

Even Pearl, whose eyes had opened wide, merely remained silent.

"Chase only wants me when I'm some damsel in distress," she admitted aloud for the first time. And the notion hurt.

Samson's head jerked up and he met her gaze.

Eerily familiar eyes stared back at her, reinforcing a family resemblance she hadn't acknowledged until now. But he glanced away just as quickly, severing the connection. Apparently, two men were about to turn her out of their lives, but she forged on, determined not to make it easy on Samson. "I can stand on my own two feet just fine."

"Maybe you can, maybe you can't. Depends on what kind of stuff you're made of."

"I'm made of *your* stuff," she shot back. "And apparently, you're not that much of a recluse if you've heard the gossip about me and Chase." Sloane straightened her shoulders, holding her own with him.

"Yer shacking up with the man. How could I not know?"

She sighed, not wanting to let him get off track. "I think we have some things to discuss, like my mother, for one, and where you're going to live, for another."

He waved a hand, dismissing her. "I don't remember saying I wanted or needed you in my life. I can handle things without your help, thank you very much."

She bit down on her lower lip. "What if I want to know you?"

"Then you're flat out of luck. Now give me my dog." He grabbed his animal out of her arms and turned away.

She told herself it was fine. He hadn't been a part of her life until now and she didn't need him in her future.

She'd ensure his safety from her father's men and be gone. But her emotions didn't match her thoughts and the pain she felt was raw. Her chest hurt and her throat grew full. She swiveled toward the front door, but instead of an escape from the hurt, she found more.

Chase stood at the open door, along with Rick and Kendall, and a couple she'd only seen in pictures but recognized as Roman and a very pregnant Charlotte. All witnesses to her humiliation.

Oh, she didn't need this now. Unable to deal with the embarrassment, she walked past them without meeting anyone's gaze and headed for the street. Her rental car beckoned like the haven she didn't have, and ignoring the voices calling her back, Sloane unlocked the car, slid inside, and drove away.

Where was she headed? She had no idea.

After Sloane's departure, the quiet in the small guesthouse was palpable. No one dared speak, but Chase wasn't afraid of breaking the silence. He'd never forget the pain and humiliation in Sloane's eyes and he knew who was to blame.

"Samson." Chase barked at the older man.

Sloane's *father* ignored him, muttering under his breath as he stroked his dog's head, giving the animal the affection his daughter craved.

"I'm talking to you." Chase strode to the man's side and grabbed his arm, forcing him to look up and acknowledge him.

In his eyes, Chase saw the same hurt he'd witnessed in Sloane and that observation gave him hope that his gut feeling was correct. That the man had a reason for rejecting the daughter he'd initially sought out.

"What do you want?" Samson asked.

Behind him, Chase heard Rick whispering to Pearl and Kendall, no doubt giving orders about who'd be staying where until the threat to Samson was eliminated. Now that they knew where the man was, Chase and Rick agreed no one should be living with a walking target. Kendall would take Hannah to Raina's, along with Charlotte. Rick and Roman would stay here in the hopes of preventing further disaster. It had been quiet since the explosion in Samson's house, but they'd missed the older man once. Chase had no doubt another attempt on Samson's life would be coming.

"I know why you rejected Sloane," Chase began. "You wanted her away from you and any potential danger. Nice sentiment, but wrong way of handling things." He released his grip before he took out his anger on Sloane's father.

"So now you're a mind reader as well as a reporter." Samson snorted.

Drawing on his patience, Chase inhaled deeply before tackling the stubborn old man once more. "How about we play this one straight? No games, no smart-ass answers, and no pretending to be some dumb backwoods hermit. We both know you're smarter than you act."

"I don't want her around me because I don't want her getting hurt. I don't want Pearl and Eldin at risk either, but I had nowhere else to go." Samson spread his hands wide, looking more like a dejected man than a sullen, angry hermit. "So I'm here, but I'm not going to bring anyone else into my life. At least not until it's safe." He confirmed Chase's hunch.

"Why not stay in Hampshire? Earl or Ernie would have taken you in and you'd be far enough from Yorkshire Falls to make your trail even harder to follow." Chase paced the floor, still uncertain of how to handle this man, with his unexpected moods and curious way of thinking.

"Because then I couldn't keep an eye on my daughter." His voice cracked at the admission.

Chase paused in his walk across the floor, stunned and unsure how to react. As much as he'd figured Samson was looking out for Sloane, he'd never given any thought to the older man's feelings. He'd never acted as if he had any before.

"She looks so much like her mother, it hurts to see her," the man went on, still stroking his dog. "I had to let Jacqueline go, but I'd never have done it if I knew she was pregnant. I lost

Sloane's mother. Then I lost seeing Sloane growing up. I'm not going to risk her life now." He swiped a hand across his eyes, refusing to look at Chase. "Even if I just drove her away for good, at least I'd know she wuz alive."

Chase nodded, understanding. "You did the right thing, not letting her stay here. But after this is over, you damn well better make things right," he muttered. "She doesn't deserve to think you're rejecting her."

"Not any more than she deserves the way you're treating her, Mr. High-and-Mighty Chase Chandler." Samson put the dog on the floor and circled around the sofa until he invaded Chase's personal space, taking him by surprise. "She's *my* baby girl and you hurt her just as much as I did. That much is obvious, even to someone as antisocial as me."

Chase winced, knowing Samson was right. "We both knew the score going into the relationship." But his words sounded lame to his own ears. Because knowing the score only meant something on their first night together.

Once Sloane came to Yorkshire Falls, things changed. The explosion that rocked Samson's house also rocked Chase's world and things hadn't been the same since.

"You're a grown man. If you ask me, you should start acting like one," Samson said. "Take responsibility for your actions. Decide what you want, once and for all. I made my choices all those years ago and I have to live with the regrets now. If you want to let her go, then wave good-bye and don't look back. Don't hang around playing her savior when it suits you and pushing her away when it don't," he said, reverting back to normal Samson-speak.

"For someone who's been hiding out, you seem to think you know a lot about me and Sloane."

He shrugged, but there was an arrogance in the gesture Chase was coming to notice more and more. At least when it came to Sloane.

"I've seen and heard a lot more than you realize," Samson said. "And I don't care if your last name *is* Chandler; the way you're acting is a disgrace and my little girl deserves a lot better than you."

On that parting shot, Samson settled into the couch, back in his surly mood, ignoring both Chase and Pearl, who was trying to catch his attention.

Chase couldn't forget Samson's words. They echoed in his head even as Rick directed Pearl and Eldin to pack their bags and move in with Raina. Samson would stay and hopefully draw out the men after him with Rick keeping watch. But Chase had no time to think or draw parallels between his life and Samson's until the threat to Samson and, indirectly, to Sloane and the rest of Chase's family blew over.

Chapter Fifteen

"Last time we were all together like this, one of us had to get hitched." Roman folded his arms across his chest and laughed, reminding the brothers of their coin toss more than nine months earlier. A time when Raina's heart episode had been nothing more than indigestion, but the brothers hadn't known that then.

Raina had used the incident as the beginning of her illness charade, begging for one of her boys to settle down and give her grandchildren before she passed on. The three single Chandler brothers had tossed a coin to see who would get married and give their mother a grandchild first. Roman had lost the toss and his reunion with his long-lost love, Charlotte, had begun.

"It hasn't been all that long, and now two of us are married, leaving just one bachelor," Rick said, leveling a glance at Chase, who didn't find the topic of discussion at all amusing.

The situation was sadly ironic, though, since now Raina really was sick, and Chase would do just about anything to see her well. Except that his getting married to suit Raina's needs wouldn't do anything to help his own.

Not even his brothers seemed to realize that

fact. "Do either of you two morons realize you fell right into Mom's trap? Trying to escape her meddling, you gave her exactly what she wanted." Chase glanced out the window of Rick's kitchen, the one that overlooked Pearl and Eldin's house in the back.

At one time, Pearl and Eldin lived in the house while Kendall had stayed in the guesthouse, but the older couple's health and Rick and Kendall's marriage made swapping houses the perfect solution.

Meanwhile, all appeared quiet in the backyard while everyone from the guesthouse packed to leave. Only Samson remained inside the guesthouse, refusing to leave.

Roman shrugged, then headed for the refrigerator. "Soda?" he asked his brothers.

Both grunted "no."

"Suit yourself." He pulled out a bottle of Coke and started rummaging through cabinets.

"What the hell are you looking for?" Rick asked.

Roman slammed a cabinet and opened another. "Drinking glasses."

"The door next to the microwave. And by the way, feel free to make yourself at home," Rick said.

Roman chuckled, apparently not the least bit offended. "Back to basics," he said, seating himself on the Formica counter. "Did *you* realize that the way things turned out, what Mom wanted was in our best interest, after all?"

"Kendall's going to kill you if that counter cracks," Rick said.

"Naah. She's going to kill *you*." Roman grinned, then raised his glass in a mock toast, before guzzling his drink. "So when are you going to give in and admit Sloane's the woman to give you a kick in the ass?" he asked Chase.

Chase let out a groan. Just because Roman and Rick had opted to marry and have families didn't mean that doing the same was in Chase's best interest. "We all have our own paths to follow."

"And you can't follow yours and be with Sloane at the same time?" Roman lifted an eyebrow. "Seems to me I said the same thing. I can't have my career and settle down with Charlotte. I was wrong."

"*You* were a foreign correspondent and willing to change positions in order to accommodate both of your needs. I'm going to write an article that'll get picked up by every paper out there and decimate Sloane's father's political career. That's hardly being a decent *partner* in marriage."

"We're talking marriage?" Rick asked. "Woo-hoo!"

Chase leveled him with his sternest glare. The one that had worked when a sixteen-year-old Rick had threatened to take Chase's car if he didn't choose to lend it to him. At almost nineteen, Chase had felt more like thirty and hadn't trusted his middle sibling behind the wheel.

Rick merely shrugged. "You said the dreaded word first, not me."

Obviously, now that Rick was thirty-five, Chase's anger didn't mean much anymore. Not when Rick thought himself right.

"Would you two behave?" Roman said, attempting to be the voice of reason.

Rick chuckled, but sobered quickly. "The kid's right. We've got more immediate concerns, for now. What about Sloane?"

"What about her?" Chase asked, deliberately playing dumb because he wasn't in the mood to deal with his siblings.

"She sure as hell doesn't need to be alone after what Samson just pulled on her."

Chase rolled his shoulders before giving his brothers the answer he'd been trying to make himself believe for the last hour. "Sloane needs time to sort through her feelings about Samson."

"How about protection?" Rick asked, falling back into cop mode. "We already made sure the rest of the family, Pearl, Eldin, and Samson were safe. Doesn't Sloane deserve the same?"

"As long as Sloane's not with Samson, she's fine. We already agreed on that. And Samson's holed up in the guesthouse."

"She may be physically safe, but what about emotionally?" Rick shook his head, treating Chase to a look that told him he was pathetic at understanding the opposite sex. "All women like to have that strong shoulder to rely on in times of need," he said cleverly.

"And you would know." Chase slanted his head to one side and met his middle brother's amused gaze.

"Can I help it if I excel at rescuing damsels in distress?"

"It got you married in the end."

Rick shrugged. "What of it? I didn't marry any old woman Mom shoved in my face. I married Kendall, the right woman for me, not Mom. So did Roman. But you, big brother, are still running."

"That's a crock of shit," Chase muttered. "I haven't run from a damn thing in this lifetime, starting with my responsibilities to the two of you."

"Those are long finished, Chase. But they're a damn convenient excuse for you to use every time you want to avoid thinking about your feelings for Sloane." Roman cleared his throat. "And it's those responsibilities you're running from."

"What was your major in college, again?" Chase asked, not hiding his sarcasm. "Because I don't recall you taking psych."

Roman rolled his eyes. "It doesn't require a rocket scientist to figure you out."

"Oh, boys!" Pearl's high-pitched voice interrupted their conversation as she burst through the front door.

"I thought you were at Raina's," Rick said, watching as Pearl made her way up the stairs and into the kitchen.

"I am, but you had rushed me before and I forgot my plate of brownies." She perched one hand on her full hip and wagged her free finger in front of Rick's nose. "What kind of houseguest doesn't bring a thank-you gift to her host? Raina's putting up with me in her not-so-healthy condition, so I came back here for my brownies. Because I'm grateful," she continued rambling. "And because Charlotte's so very pregnant and craving chocolate."

"So where are the brownies?" Rick asked, eyeing her empty hands.

Chase figured Rick was angling for food.

"In the car out front. With Eldin, who's waiting." Pearl gestured outside. "But you should know, Samson's gone. He's not in the house where you told him he should stay. And when I realized he was missing, I didn't want to be arrested for being an accessory to a crime, for not reporting his disappearance." She nodded her head, certain she'd done the right thing.

Which she had, Chase thought. Even if her reasons made no sense and were completely skewed.

Rick placed an arm around her shoulder and started walking her toward the front door. "You did the right thing," he assured her.

She nodded again. "There's one more thing I should have mentioned earlier."

Rick tipped his head to one side and stopped in his path. "What is it?"

"Samson's been mentioning that someone keeps asking him for directions. The same man popping up in different places where he's been. When we suggested he tell you, he said he wasn't concerned. That the man had had many chances to *take him out,* if that's what he wanted to do." She twirled her fingers into her housecoat. "But Samson's stubborn and doesn't trust people to help him. He hasn't for years." Hanging her head low, she said, "I just thought you should know."

Chase sucked in a deep breath, then forced a calm release. While Rick walked Pearl to the car, Chase was forced to admit two things. His brothers' lectures had distracted him from watching the window and the guesthouse to make sure Samson didn't sneak out on them. And with Samson on the loose, Sloane could no longer be alone. It wasn't safe.

Because if her father went looking for her, Sloane, like Samson, would be a walking target.

The smell of fall permeated the air in the old tree house. Wood walls prevented the biting wind from whipping around, but a small window let a cold draft inside. And Sloane was freezing. Not that it mattered. She had no place she could go, and so she'd been alone here for the last few hours.

Curling her legs beneath her, she shut her eyes and leaned back, when without warning, the sound of someone climbing the rickety ladder leading to the tree house took her by surprise.

So did her visitor.

Samson eased his body into the small doorway and sat down beside her. She eyed him warily, unsure why he'd seek her out after rejecting her earlier. Refusing to make any overture, she tightly hugged her knees and waited.

"You deserve better than someone like me to be your father."

She clenched her hands at her sides. "It's not up to you to decide what's best for me. And besides, we don't determine our gene pool. Fate does that." And she'd take the man *fate* had provided for her.

He wore an oversize army-green jacket and wrinkled khakis. His straggly white hair was windblown and his bearded face possessed the ravages of a life that hadn't been kind to him. But in his eyes, she saw a depth of emotion and caring she hadn't noticed before. He was obviously a man who hid his emotions well, letting them out only when he trusted the response.

And since Sloane had already reached out to him, maybe he trusted her now.

"So you're stuck with me." He shoved his hands into his jacket pockets and rocked in place.

"That's one way to look at it." Sloane's lips lifted in a grin. Drawing a deep breath, she decided to extend the olive branch once more. "I prefer to think fate has blessed me with two different but very good men as father figures. You've just come to me later in life, that's all."

He tilted his head to one side. "Why are you being so nice about all this? About me?"

"Why wouldn't I be? Besides the obvious reason that we share bloodlines, we also missed out on a lot. I want to catch up. Get to know my real father."

"And what a stand-up man he is." Samson gestured to himself in disgust. "Can't compare to the senator, can I?"

She shook her head, noticing yet again the self-deprecating way he spoke about himself, making her wonder about a life that had beaten him down so badly. But she also noticed his change in tone, manner, and speech. No longer the country bumpkin with incorrect grammar, he spoke to her like a more educated man would. *The kind of man Jacqueline would have been attracted to,* Sloane thought.

"I never thought to compare you to Michael any more than I like being compared to my sisters or my stepmother. We're different people. I came looking for you and I'm not disappointed in what I found. Are you?" She met his wary gaze.

"Of course not."

Giddy relief flowed through her, but she wasn't about to ruin the moment by throwing herself into his arms. Yet. They still had too much to learn about each other. She'd discovered enough about Samson to know that if she got emotional, he'd bolt. So she decided to switch subjects.

"What's with the country-bumpkin act? One minute you're talking like you barely finished elementary school and the next minute you're civilized and speaking to me like a proper gentleman." She leaned toward him. "Why the cover?"

"It should be obvious," he muttered. Reaching into his pocket, he pulled out what looked like a pack of gum. "Want some?"

She shook her head. "No, thank you, and it isn't obvious to me."

"Your mother and I had dreams. We'd both finish school; she'd work until she got pregnant; I'd get a job with an antiques dealer until I could start a business of my own and support us." He shifted, the nylon jacket he wore making a loud, crinkling noise in the otherwise quiet tree house. "I was majoring in art history, you know."

"I didn't realize." No one had given her his background or history and she hung on his every word.

"No reason you should. I gave up those dreams when I gave up your mother. The day her father arrived, proof that my father was indebted to a loan shark in one hand and the solution in the other."

"What do you mean?" His last explanation had been in gruff Samson-speak. Sloane wanted to hear the truth now. All of it.

And Samson seemed willing to provide the answers. "He offered me a check to pay the loan shark off. My father agreed to sign the house over to me if I took the deal. What could I do? My mother wouldn't live in fear of losing the roof over her head anymore. My father wouldn't have his kneecaps blown off." He shook his head and let out a rough rumble that resembled a laugh.

But Sloane didn't find the story amusing and neither could he. "Nobody blows kneecaps off anymore," she said.

"No, they just blow up houses." He lifted his gaze from the warped wood floor. "You grew up sheltered, thank God. That's one of the reasons I took the money and let Jacqueline go. To protect her from my family and my life."

"Not to mention the fact that my grandfather made that one of his conditions, right? The money in exchange for letting Jacqueline go?" Sloane asked through gritted teeth.

"As it turned out, it was an excellent deal for your mother. She had a wonderful life. Short as it was."

This conversation had turned more emotional than she'd planned. But Samson didn't seem to be running away, so Sloane pressed her advantage. "How do you know Jacqueline wouldn't have had a better life with you? The man she really loved?"

Samson shrugged. "She didn't have a choice and neither did I. Your grandfather made it clear that if he didn't supply the funds to pay off the loan shark, my father would probably be found dead in an alley. The bank would take our house and we'd be out on the street." He ran a hand through his already windblown hair. "Added to that, my mother had cancer. We couldn't afford treatment and she was going downhill fast. I wanted to make her final days comfortable ones at least. I needed more money for that."

Sloane swallowed over the lump in her throat, unable to believe the painful saga he was revealing. "Please don't tell me you told my grandfather about your mother's illness and he used that as leverage."

Samson nodded. "He added to the check without blinking and told me to stay the hell away from Jacqueline. What else could I do except take it?" Samson rolled his shoulders in a nonchalant gesture, as if the story were old news, but the ravaged look in his eyes and his life history told her he'd never gotten over his decision.

"You said earlier that you went back for Jacqueline, in a manner of speaking. What did you mean?" She wiggled her ice-cold fingers, trying to get the blood flowing again. Her entire body had grown cold.

"At first I didn't go back. Didn't look in on her at all. I had my hands full with my mother's illness and I needed every last penny your grandfather had given me. I couldn't afford to rile him. And then my mother passed away."

"I'm sorry." At the mention of a grand-mother she'd never met, Sloane swiped at the tears falling from her eyes. So much of her life she'd never known about and would discover only secondhand.

All because of one man's selfish need to con-trol everything around him. She wondered if her mother's father ever had regrets for altering and playing with the lives of everyone around him.

But nothing could change the facts, so she turned back to Samson. "So what happened then? Your mother was gone and your father —"

He cleared his throat. "Had disappeared anyway. He wasn't one for taking care of people, in sickness or in health. He bailed on my mother in her last days."

She opened her eyes wide. "He had a funny way of showing gratitude, considering what you'd done."

"He thought creating me meant I owed him."

She shook her head but knew words of sym-pathy would be meaningless. "So your parents were both gone. Why didn't you go back for Jacqueline?"

"Your grandfather was a senator and a very smart man. He made me sign a loan agree-ment. I had to take the bastard's word that he wouldn't come after me to pay him back. Un-less I went after Jacqueline." He shook his head, dejection and regret evident in the slump of his shoulders and the raw pain emanating from him in waves. Pain for things he'd done — and not done. "And let me tell you, that was one whopping sum of money I took. I wouldn't have been able to pay it back in ten lifetimes."

Sloane exhaled, realizing for the first time her breath came out in visible puffs. *Drat the open window,* she thought, rubbing her hands up and down her arms. Not even her jacket made a difference now.

"You need to know that money threats couldn't have kept me away from Jacqueline." Samson seemed focused on their conversation, oblivious to the chill. "But when I went to check on her, she was married. She looked happy and I knew she was well cared for. All things I couldn't give her. Not anymore." He, too, wiped his eyes with one sleeve. "So I came back home."

"And withdrew from life." Sloane understood him now. Understood everything about him and why he'd turned into a recluse.

"It was easier not to be around folks in this town." He slashed his hand through the air, as if cutting people out of his life. "But they persisted. Pearl brought brownies by and Izzy and Norman sent food after my mother died. But I didn't want their sympathy. And when polite manners didn't do the trick, I started turning them away with gruff, rude talking." He jutted out his chin. "It worked too. Pretty soon, everyone left me alone."

Despite the pride in his voice, Sloane sensed how false his words sounded, how hurt he must have been to have lost Jacqueline first, then his entire family.

"You must have been lonely." She tipped her head to one side, waiting for him to protest his independence and need for no one and nobody.

The man was a recluse who didn't want emotion given to him, nor did he desire to provide any in return. But his next words surprised her. "It was a life I wouldn't wish on anybody," he muttered, and stood pacing just past the window. "But I got by and I'm fine. Darned if I'm not." He straightened his shoulders, ever the solitary man he presented to the outside world.

"I know you're fine, but at least admit you could be better." Sloane followed his lead and rose to her knees, grateful for the excuse to move and get her circulation flowing again. "You've got family now and you're stuck with me," she said, echoing his earlier words.

He would learn Sloane Carlisle wasn't a woman easily deterred. Samson might not want tender emotion, but he was going to get some anyway. Sloane was his daughter, the only flesh-and-blood person he was connected to in this world. It was time he acknowledged her in an embrace. And she intended to enjoy her first real father-daughter hug.

Standing, she moved forward, past the open window, and turned to reach for Samson at the same moment a loud noise sounded from outside and a burning sensation seared through her left shoulder. The impact propelled her against the wall as she cried out in surprise. She grabbed for her shoulder while white flashes and bursts of light circled around her.

"Damn, girl." Samson reached for her, easing her to a sitting position before kneeling beside her. "Easy." He moved her hand so he could check her shoulder.

Sloane glanced down. Was that her blood on her hands?

"You've been shot," Samson said in a shaking voice.

Sloane's vision blurred badly. She thought Samson was pulling off his jacket. Thought he muttered, "Gotta stop the bleeding." She couldn't be sure.

But when he put pressure against her shoulder with that jacket, a searing, burning, unbearable pain shot straight through to her heart. She rolled her head to one side and shut her eyes to escape the agony, but there was no getting away from her own body.

Other outside noises intruded. . . . Footsteps, maybe? Voices, definitely. Without a doubt, she heard Samson speaking. She wished Chase were beside her, doing his white-knight bit, but he was with his family. His primary obligation. She'd walked out of his life. Or had he walked out of hers? Nausea threatened to overwhelm her along with the disorienting sensation of losing her balance.

Go with it, she told herself. If she did, she'd escape the pain and nothing mattered more, she thought as she allowed herself to fall into the oblivion that beckoned.

"You should have let me drive," Chase muttered.

"You're too upset," Rick said, slowing down for a yield sign.

He glared at Rick, who, after hearing Samson had disappeared, had snatched his car keys and ordered his brothers around like the cop he was. He didn't want the man wandering around town alone, unprotected.

He hadn't turned on Chase for not going after Sloane when he had the chance, but that was fine since Chase had enough self-recrimination without his brother's lecture. His gut feeling told him father and daughter were together and the end result couldn't be good.

"Step on it, will you?" he told his brother.

Rick ignored him, while Roman reached out from the backseat and put one hand on Chase's shoulder for support. "We'll be at the McKeevers' house soon enough."

The old tree house, where Sloane had met Samson for the first time, was the only place Chase could think of that Sloane would go to be alone. Lord knew she wouldn't return to Chase's house. He'd done his best to freeze her out and drive her far away from him.

Damn.

Finally, after what seemed like half an hour but in reality wasn't more than five minutes, Rick pulled up to the curb in front of the sprawling Colonial. No car in the driveway told him the McKeevers still weren't home, which he'd figured since they hadn't answered the phone when Chase had called from the car on the way over.

"We could be panicking for nothing," Roman said in an obvious attempt to reassure Chase.

"Yeah, I'd like to hear you say that if it were Charlotte we were looking for."

Roman scowled at him. "Don't go borrowing trouble."

Chase jumped out of the car before Rick even shut the ignition. He took off toward the backyard, rounding the house with his brothers not far behind. His blood pounded in his ears and his mouth ran dry. He didn't know what he'd find and didn't care if he barged in on Sloane like a crazy man, only to find her alone in the old tree house. Just so long as she was okay.

Dried leaves crunched beneath his feet, making more noise than he'd like and probably announcing his approach, but there was nothing he could do about it now. An indecipherable, muffled noise sounded from nearby and Chase came to a halt alongside a large blue spruce, his instincts suddenly telling him to tread cautiously.

"What's wrong?" Rick whispered.

Chase shrugged. "I don't know. Something just seems off."

Rick motioned for Chase to remain where he was. "I'm going to approach from behind," he said, gun in hand, as he pointed with his other hand to the tree house and the lone window visible from a distance.

Without warning, a solitary figure broke the silence and ran through the trees, crunching leaves in his wake. At the same time, Samson stuck his head out the window. "Call 911," he yelled at them.

"I've got it," Roman said, pulling his cell phone out of his pocket at the same time Rick ran after the escapee.

Chase took off for the tree house, panic engulfing him. He didn't remember climbing the stairs, but he was damn well aware of easing himself into the old structure and seeing Sloane passed out cold on the floor. Blood seeped through Samson's old jacket, which now acted as part tourniquet, part bandage, to stem the blood flow.

His gut clenched and fear struck a blow to his heart, his pulse pounding with racing speed. "Rick called for an ambulance," Chase told Samson before kneeling beside Sloane and taking her ice-cold hand into his own.

A distraught-looking Samson paced the floors, muttering to himself.

"What happened?" Chase managed to ask, though his mouth had grown dry as cotton.

"What does it look like, genius?" Samson aimed a scowl Chase's way. "We don't need you here."

"That's a point I'm not going to debate now. What happened? Besides the obvious, I mean," he asked again, impatience in his tone and anger in his blood. Anger at himself and at fate for taking advantage of his own stupidity for leaving Sloane alone.

Samson ran a weary hand over his eyes, and for the first time, Chase felt sorry for the man who was obviously suffering as much as he.

"I came to find my daughter," Samson said. "She'd been here awhile, but whoever shot at me didn't know that because they'd probably been following only me."

Chase swept a strand of hair out of Sloane's face, concerned when she didn't flinch. Without turning to look at Samson again, he asked, "Is this a guess, or do you know for a fact you were followed?"

"I know." The old man turned a deep crimson shade. "Someone's been after me, hanging around, watching my movements."

Chase gritted his teeth, fear consuming him as he looked once more at Sloane's pale face and cataloged her lack of response to anything, including him squeezing her hand or whispering in her ear. "Any reason you didn't report this to the police? Or at the very least tell Rick earlier today?" Chase raised an eyebrow in question.

"I don't trust nobody. I thought I covered my tracks coming here. *You* didn't know I'd gone. Least not right away." Samson raised his chin in a gesture of defiance that didn't fool Chase.

Not when his eyes were damp and his mouth trembled when not arguing his point. The man was near to a breakdown with guilt and concern, and though Chase wanted to lace into him, Chase agreed he bore much of the same blame.

They'd both failed Sloane. "Listen, man. Maybe it's time you start trusting, before she suffers even more."

Samson snorted, his sarcasm obvious. "As if you're an expert."

Blessedly, ambulance sirens sounded in the distance, growing closer and preventing the argument from escalating. It wouldn't do Sloane any good, and if Rick caught the shooter, not much else mattered, Chase thought.

Except Sloane, the woman he loved. And the one he might lose, if she lost any more blood. He ran a shaking hand down her cheek, trying not to look at the patch of red seeping through the old jacket. It looked like so much blood. And she was still unconscious, he thought, fear lodging in his throat. The overwhelming panic hadn't left him since he'd realized Sloane was with Samson, and had only magnified with each passing minute.

Because he'd left her alone, putting her in harm's way, he might not have the chance to tell her that he was sorry. That he really did love her. That he didn't want to lose her.

Yet, what did that mean for the future he'd envisioned? The one without family or responsibilities. He shook his head, his own desires mocking him, as his mother provided enough responsibility and would continue to, even if she married Eric. Old habits died hard. He'd never be completely free of his responsibilities.

Nor, he was coming to realize, did he want to be. The one thing he didn't want was to end up old and alone. And if Sloane died, that's exactly where he would be.

Chapter Sixteen

A shoulder wound. The bullet had passed clean through, or at least that's what Chase thought he heard an emergency-room doctor say. Needing confirmation, he walked over to a fresh-out-of-med-school-looking guy and tapped him on the shoulder. "Excuse me. I need to see Sloane Carlisle."

"She's with the doctor," he said without glancing up.

But that doctor wasn't Eric, Chase thought, because he hadn't arrived yet. "How is she? Last time I saw her, she was unconscious and there was too much blood." He involuntarily trembled at the memory.

"Are you family?" the guy in green scrubs asked, barely glancing up from his chart. "Because I can release patient details only to family."

"Yeah. Yeah, I'm family," Chase muttered, the lie slipping too easily off his tongue.

In reality, he had no claim on Sloane other than a sudden overwhelming desire to possess her as his own, and to never let go.

"You're her . . . brother?" the young resident asked, hazarding a guess as he finally looked up.

Stupidly, Chase shook his head no because he wanted to say he was her husband. He couldn't. There were too many people in this hospital who knew him, knew his background, knew how proudly he'd always touted his bachelor status. Especially once he'd become the last remaining single Chandler man.

The resident met Chase's gaze, compassion filling his eyes. "Okay, buddy, you want to get in to see your girlfriend. I get it. But not until she's conscious and can okay your visit." He patted Chase's shoulder in what must be his best practiced bedside manner. "I'm sorry."

"Thanks." Chase turned away, pissed at the other man but mostly pissed at himself.

As a journalist, he'd often fudged his status to get closer to a story, admittedly not possible that often in a town that knew everyone's business. But he'd had no compunction doing it when he could. Yet with Sloane lying in the other room, her status unknown, he could barely think enough to hold himself together and get in to see her. Some hotshot reporter he turned out to be, unable to get near the most important person in his life.

His heart was pounding double time and adrenaline raced through his veins, making him forget common sense and reason. Which cemented his feelings. As if he'd had any doubt. He didn't. Not anymore. He had no doubt about how he felt and what he wanted — Sloane, in his life forever. But he'd start with seeing her open those gorgeous eyes.

Glancing at the clock, he realized only ten minutes had passed since he'd followed the ambulance to the hospital, feeling useless and more frightened than he ever remembered being. Including when he'd been eighteen and his father had passed away, leaving him as the man of the house and completely unprepared for all that status had entailed.

Chase groaned. Ten minutes wasn't nearly enough time for the doctors to really patch up Sloane. It wasn't enough time for Rick to drag the suspect's sorry ass down to the station and see to it he was processed correctly. But Rick had in fact captured the man, gun in hand, tackling him on the neighbor's property before he could make it to his truck, which he'd left on the corner. At least Chase could trust his brother to take care of police business.

In the meantime, he forced himself to sit in a chair near the emergency-room doors through which they'd wheeled Sloane earlier. Forced himself, through gritted teeth, to wait for Eric instead of barging into the ER and demanding answers and the right to see Sloane. Something Chase couldn't do until Eric arrived and helped him get past hospital security and restrictions.

Suddenly the double doors swung wide and a woman doctor strolled through. Chase recognized her as the one who'd taken charge of Sloane from the minute the ambulance drivers unloaded her stretcher.

He jumped up from his seat. "How is she?"

The doctor eyed him, a combination of wariness and compassion in her professional gaze. "Stable," she said, as if she weren't sure whether to trust him with the information. "She's groggy, but she wants to see her father."

Relief swelled inside his chest. Sloane was awake enough to talk. Thank God.

"Do you know if her father's here?" the doctor asked.

Chase tried to speak, but the lump in his throat made it difficult. "I haven't seen him." After sitting by Sloane's side in the ambulance and seeing her safely to the hospital, Samson had disappeared.

Damn the man.

Chase glanced around once more, but the eccentric was nowhere to be found.

"Can I see her?" Chase asked, unable to disguise the hope in his voice.

The businesslike brunette shook her head. "Once she's settled in a room, if she wants to see you, then we can arrange it." The doctor shoved her hands into her white jacket pockets. "In the meantime, I promise she's in good hands."

The doctor placed a hand on his shoulder. *The gesture must be practiced in Family Care 101,* Chase thought, frustrated.

"Well, if Ms. Carlisle's father shows up, be sure to tell him his daughter is asking for him."

Before Chase could reply, an imposing man

in a suit and tie — none other than Senator Michael Carlisle — strode up to the doctor. "Did you say Sloane's looking for her father?"

The young woman nodded. "You're —"

"Senator Michael Carlisle," he said with the air of authority that had helped him rise quickly in the political world. "I want to see my daughter now."

Madeline stood by her husband's side, tears in her eyes. She looked neither left nor right, and she didn't notice Chase standing right next to her. Understandable, considering how upset she was. And since Chase had been instructed to watch out for Sloane and to keep her safe, he would be the last person Madeline would want to see right now.

Regardless, Chase wanted to talk with the senator — not just about Sloane, but about his campaign managers and this whole situation. Including who was the best reporter to cover the story. The only reporter capable of protecting both Sloane and the senator's interests at the same time. Chase, however, knew better than to interrupt the man before he'd checked on his daughter.

Instead, he watched with frustrated impotence as the senator led Madeline Carlisle, his hand on her back, through the double doors to see their daughter. She had the family who'd raised and loved her here now. They'd make sure she got the best care possible. Something Chase hadn't been able to do.

He kicked the old linoleum floor with his foot. Frustration filled him, but so did resolve. Sloane was alive and he had his second chance. He couldn't wait to tell her. He couldn't wait to begin his future.

As long as Sloane didn't move her body, she didn't feel too much pain. The drugs administered by the doctors were starting to do their job, she thought, leaning her head against the pillow. She still hadn't gotten past the shock of what happened, and once the pain had begun to subside, she'd asked first about Samson. The news was good, but his whereabouts weren't. He hadn't been shot or injured, but after being assured Sloane was okay, he'd departed for parts unknown.

No surprise there, Sloane thought. She wouldn't be getting any warm, fuzzy parental moments from him. Although, for a brief moment back at the tree house, she thought she was close to reaching past his hard outer shell. Something she wouldn't be able to attempt again unless she was released from the hospital.

A knock on the door startled her and she jumped, immediately regretting the impulsive motion when pain surged through her bandaged shoulder. She reached to support the injury with her good hand, resting her palm against the thick bandages.

Before she could respond, the door opened wide and Madeline and Michael strode through.

Sloane had already seen them in the emergency room, but this was the first time they'd had a moment alone without doctors and nurses hovering over Sloane. She smiled, motioning with her good hand. "Come on in."

Madeline came in first and sat on the bed, while Michael chose a chair on the other side.

"I am so relieved you're okay. So are your sisters. They send their love and begged to come, but I wanted them in one place and safe until we knew you were." Madeline grabbed her hand and held on tight. Her bright eyes shimmered with unshed tears. "Sweetie, when I said you could come to Yorkshire Falls, I had no idea there was actual danger involved."

"That's because I didn't tell you. I didn't want to worry you unnecessarily." Sloane sighed.

She vividly remembered the day she'd overheard her father's men discussing her parentage, yet it seemed so long ago, considering all that had happened since. Especially the emotional effort she'd invested in both Samson and Chase. In that respect, Sloane felt old beyond her twenty-eight years.

Madeline wagged a finger at Sloane. "What you really mean is that you didn't want me to forbid you from coming to meet your real father. Not that I could do that anyway, since you're an adult."

"No, but you could have sent me here with a bodyguard. And that wouldn't have gone over well with the nosy good people of Yorkshire Falls." Sloane laughed, but sobered quickly as she recalled that Madeline *had* sent her with a bodyguard. A man named Chase Chandler, and though he'd done his best to protect her body, he'd stolen her heart in the process.

Shoring up her defenses wasn't easy, but Sloane managed. She couldn't allow Michael or Madeline to know she was in more emotional pain than this gunshot wound could ever inflict, and the oldest Chandler brother was the cause.

Apparently, her father had been informed of the situation with his aides by a Yorkshire Falls police officer who'd met him at the airport at the request of Rick Chandler. Sloane knew Michael was probably reeling from the news, even if he refused to show her his distress.

She forced a smile their way and continued with the family part of the conversation. "Besides, Samson wouldn't have responded well to any kind of official bodyguard tagging along with me."

Michael scowled at the mention of the man's name. "We'll deal with Samson in a minute," he interjected, the voice of authority she'd known all her life. "First, I need to know you're okay. The doctors said the bullet passed clean through, and they're treating you more for shock now than anything else. But how are you really?" He leaned closer, brushing his lips over her forehead the way he'd done many times when she was a child.

The gesture was warm, familiar, and comforting, the way a father's caress should be, Sloane thought with gratitude in her heart for this man who'd given her such a good life. Especially compared to the one Samson had lived.

"How are you in here?" Michael asked, tapping on his chest, above his heart.

She smiled at his innate understanding. Just hearing his strong, caring voice told Sloane all was right with her world again. She should never have doubted it. Or doubted him. If she'd come to him when she'd learned the truth about Samson, they all would have been spared a lot of grief. "I'm fine. Really."

"I don't call getting shot fine." He rose and began pacing the floor in the small, confined space. "I don't call being betrayed by the men I trusted most, being fine," he said, his voice rising.

Obviously sensing his agitation and fury, Madeline stood and walked to his side, placing her hand inside his. "Sloane was shot, but she's going to recover." She spoke in her most reassuring tone, the one that had comforted Sloane when she'd been sick at night or after a scraped knee or a fight with a friend. "The rest of those problems are yours, Michael. Not Sloane's. She *is* fine. And you will be too. *We* will be. It's just going to take time."

Sloane shifted in bed, but her shoulder immediately rebelled. Wincing, she asked, "What will you do about Robert and Frank?"

"String them up by their goddamn —"

"Michael!" Madeline admonished in her strictest tone.

He chuckled, despite the serious subject.

Ignoring him, her stepmother turned to Sloane. "Robert was arrested by Rick Chandler, gun in hand. And Frank was picked up for questioning in New York. To say they've been fired is an understatement."

Sloane swallowed hard, knowing how much pain Michael must be in. "Have you confronted them?"

He shook his head. "Not yet. But the police told me about their initial interview. At first, Robert stonewalled like the coward he is, but when he found out he'd shot you and not Samson, it shook him up badly."

"You mean he has a conscience?" Sloane asked. "That's hard to believe after he tried to kill my father," Sloane muttered, speaking of Samson. Then, realizing who her audience was, she felt a burning flush sear her cheeks, and tears welled in her eyes as she met Michael's pained gaze. "Oh, Dad, I'm sorry. I didn't mean —"

He waved a hand, dismissing her apology. "There are a lot of things we're going to have to deal with. Terminology's the least of our problems, honey." But he turned away, wiping his eyes with the sleeve of his dress shirt.

Sloane bit down on the inside of her cheek.

She didn't know what to say.

Michael, seemingly more composed, grabbed a seat by the bed once more. "You asked if Robert developed a conscience, and I guess it depends on your definition." He seemed determined to pick up normal conversation. "Regardless, he confessed to firing the shot that hit you, though you weren't the intended target."

"So the threat's over." Sloane exhaled, allowing the realization to wash over her.

Michael nodded. "You're safe. So is Samson. I take it you two have met?" A smile of acceptance curved his lips and Sloane knew he understood her need to meet the man who'd sired her. He also knew she loved him, Michael Carlisle, faults and all.

"We've met." Sloane idly smoothed her good hand over her bandages.

"What was it like for you? I know he's different."

She tried to explain, but what words described a man who named his pet Dog and talked to himself? "Samson's . . . eccentric. But he seems to care about me in his odd way."

"He wanted to meet you and risked a lot by coming to me now, in the middle of a campaign. And those threats he issued to Robert — well, I knew they were harmless. He just wanted to see you." Michael spread his hands wide. "How could I deny him that pleasure? It never dawned on me that Robert or Frank would try to harm him. My plan all along was to make things public and deal with the fallout. I never got the opportunity."

Confined to bed, she was unable to do more than nod.

"But I can tell you the man's harmless or I wouldn't have let you come up here," Michael assured her.

Sloane sat upright — or tried to — and immediately suffered the consequences. Tears poured down her eyes as the pain robbed her of breath.

"Oh damn." Michael wrapped an arm around her, holding her until the agony subsided.

"I'm okay," she finally whispered.

He released his tight hold but remained by her side. He reached out and tapped her nose. "You know I have to keep tabs on all my girls."

She smiled through her lingering tears.

Madeline squeezed Sloane's good hand. "How could I not tell him where you were? He'd have killed me. Besides, your father and I don't keep secrets."

Sloane's eyes opened wide. "Oh, I get it. You just keep secrets from your children. That's quite the double standard." She regretted the sarcastic words as soon as they passed her lips. Embarrassed, she leaned her head back on the pillows and stared at the old cracked ceiling. Okay, so maybe the resentments weren't completely gone, she thought. But still that didn't give her the right to be cruel. "I'm sorry."

"Don't be," Madeline said.

"We're the ones who are sorry." Michael knelt down before her, and Sloane had no doubt he meant the gesture as supplication and apology all wrapped into one. "I had no right to keep something like that from you. Adopted children have the right to know they were adopted, and you deserved to be told and to judge whom you want in your life."

Sloane met his gaze. "But I understand why you didn't tell me. I'm an adult now. You were dealing with a child and you made your choices accordingly. It's done now. We need to go on."

"I love you as much as if you were mine," Michael said as he stood once more.

She smiled, her tears returning. "I never doubted that. Ever. That's why we can go on," she assured him. "But we need to talk about —"

Before she could finish her thought, the door opened wide and an unfamiliar young woman wearing a business suit walked in, clipboard in hand. "I'm sorry to interrupt, but this is important."

"That's okay; come in, Kate." Michael turned to Sloane. "This is my new personal assistant, Kate Welles."

Sloane smiled and the other woman acknowledged her with an apologetic nod before turning her attention to Senator Carlisle, her boss. "The press is getting antsy. What they know so far is that you're here because your daughter's been admitted. They don't know why. They don't know about the shooting," she said, lowering her voice to a hushed whisper.

"It's okay, Kate. Everyone in this room knows what happened," Madeline said, laughing. She glanced at Sloane. "She's new," she whispered.

Sloane grinned, but one look at the efficient Kate reminded her that they had a serious issue on their hands. The press had sniffed out a story and wouldn't be satisfied until they knew all. And in small-town Yorkshire Falls, the entire town would be happy to oblige with information about Sloane, Chase, and their exploits. With heaven knew what kind of elaboration.

Unfortunately, they didn't need embellishment. The truth was enough to derail a political campaign. Sloane's stomach cramped with the knowledge she could destroy everything her father had ever worked for.

"It's not your fault," Michael said, reading her mind. "It's mine for keeping a secret I knew had explosive potential."

"But blame won't get us anywhere, so let's work on strategy instead." Madeline sat on the edge of Sloane's bedside and motioned Kate over.

The young woman pulled up a chair, while Michael leaned against the wall, clearly in thinking mode.

Kate clicked her pen, clearly ready to work. "The police put a lid on the story, but honestly, I don't know how much longer we can hide the truth."

The senator nodded his understanding. "Well, I say what I've always said. I should go public and deal with the consequences. I've already spoken to Kenneth," Michael said of the current president, his running mate. "He knows what's coming. I offered to withdraw before going public, but he insists on standing by me."

"Dad —"

Michael shook his head. "No arguments. It's about time I accept responsibility for what I did — to you, to Samson, and to the public. If the constituents can't value honesty and apologies, then that's that." He spread his hands out in front of him. "I am who I am."

"I'm proud to be your daughter," Sloane told him. "And that will never, ever change."

"So we agree?" he asked the people in the room. "We hold a press conference?"

"No." Madeline spoke up. "We can't."

"Why not?" Sloane asked. "Dad's right. It's the logical answer."

Madeline shifted, crossing, then uncrossing her legs. "I agree with the idea of revealing the truth, but I have to alter the means by which we do so. I've already promised a certain reporter an exclusive story."

She refused to meet Sloane's inquiring gaze, something that gave Sloane all the information she needed.

"Oh really?" Michael raised an eyebrow. "And who deserves the scoop of a lifetime?

That is, if you don't mind sharing the answer with me, your husband, the person from whom you don't keep secrets."

Sloane followed the byplay, looking from her stepmother to her father. Like Michael, she waited for Madeline to speak. Unlike Michael, she already knew the answer.

Madeline flushed but didn't flinch, nor did she seem particularly concerned about her husband's reaction. "I promised the exclusive to —"

"Chase Chandler," Sloane said, the knowledge settling inside her. "You promised Chase an exclusive in exchange for looking out for me. Right?" she asked, but didn't need confirmation. Gut instinct was enough.

Though Chase had already admitted Madeline asked him to watch over her, he'd never mentioned any kind of quid pro quo. Sloane should have known that Chase the reporter had something in it for him. Her shoulder hurt, her heart hurt, and now her head hurt as well.

"It seemed prudent at the time." Madeline glanced down at her skirt, waiting for the jury to pronounce her fate.

To Sloane, it didn't matter. What was done, was done. Besides, nothing could have changed the outcome between her and Chase.

Michael let out a long breath. "Considering you were protecting our daughter, I say bravo." He clapped his hands. "It seems we owe the man a story."

Sloane shut her eyes. She'd known this was coming. One way or another, Chase was going to write Sloane's story, expose her parentage, and obtain the scoop of his career. Once he did that, once he validated himself as the reporter he'd always wanted to be, he'd be free to live the life he'd only dreamed of before. Big stories and no time for family or responsibility.

Just the way he'd always wanted. She just wished that in being the vehicle to his success, she didn't have to lose him in the process.

"Set up a meeting with Chase Chandler," Michael told Kate, oblivious to Sloane's inner turmoil and pain.

From the slanted look her stepmother gave her, Madeline knew exactly what was going on in Sloane's mind. Or rather, her heart. Not that it mattered. This was something not even a mother's hug could cure.

Another knock on the door interrupted them and Eric walked inside. With his white coat, stethoscope, and concerned look on his face, he appeared every inch the doctor and nothing like Raina's relaxed suitor. "Everything okay in here?" he asked.

Sloane nodded, then launched into introductions. When they were through, Eric faced Sloane. "There's someone who's been asking to see you. And now that you've had time with your family, if you don't agree, I'm afraid he's going to do some serious damage to our hospital."

"Chase." Sloane didn't have to ask. She already knew.

"Yes," Eric said with a fatherly, kind smile on his handsome face.

"I'm not sure she's ready," Madeline said, stepping between the doctor and Sloane. Madeline knew how her daughter felt about Chase, and perhaps she was responding to his absence. In any event, she was playing protective parent and Sloane realized she and her stepmother had some serious catching up to do.

"Sloane?" Eric asked over her stepmother's shoulder, patiently awaiting her decision.

"My family has some business to take care of," she said pointedly to Madeline. "You need to be by Dad's side through all this."

And they all knew what *this* meant. "You two go discuss strategy and let Eric send Chase in." She drew a deep breath. "I can handle him," she said with more confidence than she felt. Especially with the drugs making her exhausted and the pain wearing her out.

A few more protestations by Madeline and reassurances by Sloane, and Michael finally led his entourage out of her room, leaving Sloane alone. Alone to compose her words and find the strength to say good-bye to Chase.

Chapter Seventeen

Chase waited until after Sloane's family left, then gave her a few minutes alone before walking toward her room. It wasn't easy, being patient, but he hoped the reward would be well worth the anticipation. Knocking once, he stepped inside, his pulse pounding a mile a minute and his heart in his throat. There wasn't a cliché he wasn't feeling at the moment and his gut told him all these rare and extraordinary emotions were normal. After all, when was the last time he'd laid his heart at a woman's feet?

Swallowing hard, he looked at Sloane for the first time since seeing her passed out on the floor, blood splattered everywhere. Now she lay in the bed, a vision against the standard white hospital sheets. Though her face was pale, her copper hair gave her a vibrant look, warming his heart.

"Hi, sweetheart." He stepped forward, pulling out from behind his back the flowers he'd bought at the concession downstairs. "You sure know how to scare a guy."

Sloane laughed, but he knew her well enough to recognize the strain in the sound. "There's nothing wrong with keeping you on your toes."

She did that. In spades. Which was probably

one of the reasons that this woman affected him so deeply, when so many others had tried and failed. Sloane didn't have to try. From the day he'd laid eyes on her, he'd been a goner. He just hadn't known it at the time, and had fought it every day since.

But the more he learned about Sloane Carlisle, from her strength and resolve, to her determination and loyalty, the more she had an impact on him. He wanted her in his life and was damn glad he'd realized it at last. Walking to the bed, he eased himself beside her, placing the flowers on a bedside tray.

"You didn't need to bring flowers." But she smiled gratefully.

He shrugged. "I had nothing else to do while waiting for permission to see you."

Sloane burst out laughing. "You're such a charmer."

"I do try." He grinned, grateful to see her back to her normal, teasing self. And as long as he didn't focus on the bandage, he could almost convince himself she hadn't come close to dying.

He sucked in a shallow breath. "Much pain?"

"No. The morphine pretty much covers that." She gestured to the IV attached to her arm.

He winced, shaking his head. "I wish it were me lying there."

"I'm really okay," she assured him.

He curled his hands into tight fists. "But I'm

not. I should have been with you."

"And then Samson wouldn't have been. I was really connecting with him, Chase." She placed her good hand over her heart. "I mean, I was getting to understand him better. That wouldn't have happened if we'd had an audience."

He gritted his teeth, accepting her answer. But he still blamed himself for letting her go off alone. "I promised you'd be safe."

"Promised who? Madeline?" she asked.

And wasn't it just like Sloane to return to the heart of the matter, Chase thought. "No, sweetheart. I promised myself." Reaching out, he brushed a lock of hair off her forehead, taking advantage and letting his fingertips trail down and stroke her soft cheek. "I failed you."

"And that's unacceptable for Chase Chandler, white knight?" Her voice held a tinge of resentment as she nailed his biggest flaw.

"Is there something wrong with that?" he asked.

She shook her head slowly. "Of course not. How can I find fault with the traits that make you an exceptional man?"

"I wouldn't canonize me just yet," he said wryly. "Especially since nothing changes the fact that I want you so bad, I ache. I want to bury myself inside you and prove to us both you're alive." He didn't seek to shock her as much as to state the bald truth.

She laughed softly. "No, I wouldn't nominate you for sainthood either." She placed a warm hand over his. "And I want you too. Very much. Probably too much, considering. And I always will. That's the problem."

Relief hit him with intense force. He obviously hadn't driven her away, no matter how hard he'd foolishly tried. "I don't see any problems."

She squeezed his hand tighter. "I've done the affair thing. I've lived in the moment, telling myself I'd take what I could get with you and then deal with the letdown later, once I was home. But I just got shot." She shook her head, then had to release his hand to pull her hair off her face.

He missed her warmth and hoped it wasn't a prelude of a bigger withdrawal to come.

"I learned life's too short to settle for less than everything," she told him, meeting his gaze.

"Then I have to repeat myself. I don't see a problem. Because I've come to the same conclusion myself." His heart beat out a rhythm he'd never felt before — fear, excitement, and adrenaline combining to put him on edge. "I told you once before, I love you, Sloane. I meant it then, but I'm ready to act on it now. I want to spend the rest of my life with you," he said, attempting to breathe and yet holding his breath as he waited for her to reply.

Her eyelashes fluttered closed. A lone tear dripped down one cheek. He caught it with his thumb, tasting the salty moisture and drawing strength from making her a part of him in such a tiny but intimate way.

"You're ready to spend your life with me. Now, after almost losing me." She exhaled a long sigh. "Of course you are," she said, no joy in her voice. No excitement.

"Sloane?" he asked, fear filling him where once completeness and satisfaction had been. "What's going on in that beautiful head of yours?" Because whatever it was, he was going to have to talk her out of those negative thoughts.

She wet her lips before speaking. "You're known for your family loyalty, Chase. Your need to protect. I've seen it in action and it's strong. Admirable, even. And of course, guilt would follow if you felt you failed in any way."

He narrowed his gaze, opting to let her finish before beginning any counterargument.

Her hand ran circles over her bandage, as if soothing herself while she spoke. "Like when your mother got sick. You felt so guilty for not being there that you planted yourself beside her, at the hospital and then at her house. You didn't want me with you. In fact, you froze me out, remember?"

Again, he merely nodded. Let her make her point, he told himself, and then he'd counter every one. But his gut cramped and fear insidiously crept inside him, making him wonder. What if he couldn't sway her?

No, he refused to believe that. He *would.*

"What are you afraid of, honey?" he asked softly. After all, she'd been shot, and now she was questioning everything about her world, about him.

Her damp gaze met his. "It's not fear. It's certainty. I believe you love me."

"That's a good sign."

She managed a laugh. "Well, no guy says that twice if he doesn't mean it."

He ran a hand through his hair, still confused. "So what's wrong?"

"You're letting guilt push you into going that one step further. Making you think *I love you* has to mean you want forever. You don't, Chase. That's the guilt talking."

"No —"

"Let me finish," she ordered in an un-Sloane-like voice. "Chase Chandler, the white knight. That's the role you play best. I've seen it many times since we met. But it's never been a life-or-death situation before. You weren't there when I got shot. And because of that, you think you need to be with me forever. To protect me from everything that might ever happen." Her voice rose, her language clear; she meant business.

And every word from her luscious lips dripped of serious certainty. She wouldn't be swayed with platitudes, and Chase understood; he'd given her every reason to distrust his words. "Okay, to a certain extent, you're right. I want to protect you and be with you forever.

But not out of guilt." He rose and began pacing the floor. "I know my own feelings," he said, insulted she'd think otherwise no matter what he'd said or done in the past.

She sighed. "Chase, you stepped in and raised a family out of necessity. You said yourself you were finished with those days. *Been there, done that* might have been your exact words." She folded one arm across her chest. "Nothing's changed except my brush with death. And like your mother's brush with death, it's sent you into an I'm-not-leaving-you mode. Don't worry, it'll pass," she said, sounding too jaded for his peace of mind.

"What makes you so sure you know everything?"

"Not everything. Just you."

He rose over her, bracing his hands on the pillows behind her and leaning in close. So close he could bury his face in her hair, but instead he towered over her to make his point. "I know me too and I've changed."

"It's temporary," she insisted, her bottom lip pushing out in firm resolution.

"There's no way *this* can be temporary." He captured her mouth with his, not accepting hesitance or arguments, immediately drawing her lush lower lip into his mouth and tasting her. Her warm, moist mouth told him she was alive, that he hadn't lost her, nor would he.

Determined to make his point, to make her *his*, he deepened the kiss, his tongue taking command and swirling inside the damp recesses of her mouth. Only after he was certain he'd made his mark on every delectable inch, he softened the kiss, arousing himself even more by merely enjoying the sensation of his lips rubbing sensuously against hers.

Then he reluctantly broke the kiss. "We're meant to be, honey." He leaned his forehead against hers.

"For as long as you feel obligated. And I won't have you saddled with a wife you feel too guilty to leave." She inhaled, then uttered the words that were his undoing. "Good-bye, Chase."

Operating on autopilot, Chase walked out of Sloane's room. Out of her life. It wasn't permanent, he told himself, but he wasn't convinced, unsure how to win her back or counter the feelings she had. Feelings he'd worked hard to cement in her mind.

Those same thoughts circled his head as he returned to the *Gazette* offices for the first time all week. Avoiding the stares of his employees and ducking Lucy before she could question him, he holed up in his office, ignoring phone calls. He was so focused, he didn't hear his name being called until Madeline Carlisle tapped her manicured fingernails on his old desk.

"We need to talk, Mr. Chandler," she said in a no-nonsense tone, one he was sure she used with her children and husband with success.

Too bad he wasn't in the mood to comply. "Shouldn't you be at the hospital with Sloane?"

"You don't mince words or waste time with *hellos*. I respect that." She laughed, obviously undeterred by his forthright question.

Because of his mood, he'd abandoned etiquette and immediately regretted being curt with Sloane's mother. "Excuse my manners," he said, rising. "Please sit down." He swept the air with his hand, gesturing to the chairs in the room.

She shook her head. "No, thank you. I've sat during our traveling. I'm happy to stand, if you don't mind?"

"Can I get you something to drink instead?" He pointed to the old refrigerator and side-by-side liquor cabinet his father had installed during his tenure here.

"No, thank you." She gripped the wooden handles of her clutch bag and met his gaze. "We have business to discuss."

He swallowed hard. If that business included how he'd hurt Sloane, he didn't need the lecture. He could still see the pain in her eyes and feel the reluctant but determined good-bye in her kiss.

And if Madeline wanted to discuss how he'd failed in his bargain with her by not keeping Sloane safe — well, he didn't need that particular lecture either. He'd beat up on himself enough.

He rose and paced his office, determined to get this discussion over with as quickly as possible. "What can I do for you?"

"First, I'd like to thank you for keeping your end of our agreement. I respect a man of integrity and honor."

Chase stopped in his tracks, turned, and stared at the woman, certain he'd lost his mind and his hearing. When he caught sight of what seemed like a warm, genuine smile gracing her lips, he figured his sight had gone too. Yet, he detected no sarcasm to Madeline's words or expression.

"Excuse me?" He narrowed his gaze, attempting to figure out what was going on. "Have you forgotten that your daughter is lying in a hospital room right now because of me?"

She placed her purse on his desk and leaned against the old wood. "Unless you fired the gun, and I know you did not, I suggest you get rid of the blame you're carrying. Robert and Frank were determined to get to Samson. There wasn't anything anyone could have done to prevent what happened. Including you."

Easy for her to say, Chase thought. She obviously didn't have all the facts. Sloane had probably spared her.

"Now let's get down to business before the rest of the journalists figure out what's really happening. I owe you an exclusive and I'm determined to keep my word."

His stomach cramped with guilt that she'd

still want to give him their family story after all he'd done. "I'm sorry, but I wouldn't feel right accepting the exclusive," he said.

Had those words really passed his lips? Had he just turned down the story of a lifetime? The story he'd wanted at any expense? And why did doing so feel so damn right?

Madeline shook her head, determination blazing in her eyes. "Don't be a fool. There are dozens of reporters who'll take this story and run with it, no questions asked. This is a career-making opportunity and you've earned it. Why turn it down now?"

Chase walked up beside her, taking her hand. "You're a kind woman, Madeline, but you know as well as I do, *I* should have been with Sloane when she was shot. At best, I might have been able to prevent it. At least, I would have been there."

She arched one delicate eyebrow. "Did I ask you to glue yourself to Sloane's side or merely to look out for her? Which I hear you did quite well."

Was that a sly smile she possessed? And why did it remind him so much of Raina at her meddling best? Chase shook his head. "I blew it."

"Guilt is a wasted emotion in a lifetime of uncertain duration," Madeline said as she expelled a frustrated breath. She picked up a yellow legal pad and pen, then turned, handing him the writing utensils. "Right now I suggest you listen and take notes. Then later you can examine why you're so hard on yourself. After which, you'd better damn well get over it. My daughter deserves more than a man who's wallowing in the past."

Despite it all, Chase wanted to applaud her performance.

"Now." She sat down and crossed her legs, her feminine movement at odds with her harsh, determined words. "My husband will be here soon to add his side to the story, so it's time for you to take notes." She leaned back in her seat, glancing his way. "Unless you'd prefer a tape recorder?"

Chase chuckled. "You ought to meet my mother."

"I'm sure we'd get along extremely well. And there's plenty of time for introductions. Another day."

Hours later, after Chase had secured the story from Madeline and the senator himself, the revealing details that would provide an exposé and journalistic opportunity of a lifetime, he sat down to write the story.

It was a story of love and loss — Samson's, Michael's, Jacqueline's, Madeline's, and now Sloane's. It was a story that would either sway voters to side with Senator Michael Carlisle, a good, decent man who'd done right by a young woman in need, or convince them he'd used that same woman for political gain. In the end, Chase believed that whatever Michael's political reasons for marrying Jacqueline, he'd loved her too. And in the end, he'd saved her from her father, who would have emotionally destroyed her.

Chase's slant was unbiased, but even in the unbiased version, Chase felt Michael's side was not just well represented, but understandable. Samson had contacted Chase too, backing up the senator's story and supplying his own painful tale for the world to read. But he no longer resembled the sad, misunderstood man the people of Yorkshire Falls had come to know.

Just as Chase no longer resembled the heartbreaker his brothers jokingly called him. And they both had Sloane to thank. The difference was, Samson had Sloane in his life, while Chase was still alone, ironically finding no satisfaction in the story of a lifetime or the career he'd insisted was so important.

Sloane was his future, but how to convince her of his sincerity? Irony came to play once more, as he decided that his mother's matchmaking talents might be useful, after all.

Sloane awoke with a start. Considering she was still in the hospital, she'd slept well, or at least in between being woken up for temperature and IV checks. She wasn't sure what had roused her from sleep, but something had. She opened one eye and realized she was facing the window and the aluminum blinds let a hint of sun slip through the horizontal slats. Morning already. She tried to move and winced, realizing how much of a beating her body had taken and how much pain she was actually in.

She buzzed for the nurse, determined to take only half the amount of painkillers they'd administered yesterday. She wanted a clear head for her last hours in Yorkshire Falls. Her parents were taking her home today.

A muffled sound caught her attention and she turned her head gingerly toward the door, expecting a nurse with a hypodermic needle. Instead, she saw an unfamiliar man wearing a dark suit, sitting in the chair beside her bed, watching her in silence.

"You'd better be more careful next time you pass by open windows, young lady," he admonished in a gruff but familiar voice.

"Samson!" His rough outer exterior might have changed, but she'd know that gravelly tone anywhere.

"What's the matter? You don't recognize your old man?" he asked in that Samson-type language she'd come to know. But his expression softened as he continued. "I'm guessing this look is what you'd have preferred to find when you came looking for the man who sired you?" He gestured up and down, taking in the fitted suit, shirt, and tie. A deep crimson stained his clean-shaven cheeks, but to his credit, he didn't glance away.

Sloane immediately noticed the gleam in his

eyes, more apparent now that his face was visible and his hair freshly washed, cut, and styled. He accepted who he was — then and now. He was about to find out, so did she.

A lump settled in her throat, but she forced herself to speak over it. "I didn't care what you looked like," she said truthfully. "I just wanted to meet my father."

He treated her to a warm smile and she was struck for the first time just how handsome and distinguished-looking he actually was.

Reaching over the blanket that covered her, he extended a shaking hand. "Your father's right here."

Sloane met him halfway, and using her uninjured arm, she placed her palm inside his larger, callused one. When she looked at him now, she saw a different man from the gruff one she'd met; she saw the one Jacqueline, her mother, must have fallen in love with, the one who'd sacrificed his entire life for his gambler father and sick mother. And though he had his share of regrets, he never admitted them to the outside world.

Sloane was scared to ask the question that hovered in her mind, because now that she'd found this man, she didn't want to say goodbye. "Where do we go from here?"

"That's up to you."

She smiled, realizing that like Chase, he might be a man of few words, but also like Chase, Samson would, in fact, be okay. He wasn't going to push her away anymore, which meant she now had this gruff, enigmatic man in her life. Relief and happiness washed over her, making her almost giddy.

A knock sounded at the door and a nurse walked inside, tray in hand. "I have your morning medication, Ms. Carlisle," she said in an efficient voice that set Sloane's nerves on edge. She wanted out of here.

"Can you come back in a little while, please?" Though she'd called for medication, she needed absolute clarity while she and Samson talked.

"Are you sure?" he asked. "It's no crime to accept a little weakness."

Sloane laughed while the nurse hovered, waiting for an answer. "I'm sure. And I promise that when we finish talking, I'll take the pain-killers. I'm not going to be a martyr. I just want this time with my father."

Samson glanced over his shoulder at the nurse. "You heard my daughter," he said with pride. He looked back to Sloane, the need for her approval so obvious in his eyes.

Happy, she squeezed his hand, giving him everything he'd asked for. But he hadn't answered her question. They'd established a biological bond and had just begun to make an emotional connection.

Where *did* they go from here? she wondered. "Where will you live?" she asked him when the nurse walked out. She still vividly recalled the ashes and destruction that were the remains of his home.

His gaze darted back and forth, nervousness evident as he pulled his hand back and twisted his fingers together. "What I have to say is going to shock you," he warned.

"I can't imagine how," she said. "Life's thrown me so many curves, I'm used to them."

"Oh yeah? I'm wealthy." As he made his statement, he locked his stare on her face.

He'd been right. He'd floored her, she thought, and sucked in a startled breath. He certainly didn't live or act like he had money. "You're *what?*"

"Wealthy," he repeated. "I have money saved."

"But . . . how? And what about the run-down state of your house before the explosion? The mooching sandwiches from Norman's? The ratty clothes?" Her head spun.

But even as she asked the questions, she recalled Earl and Ernie discussing Samson's money and who'd inherit after he was gone.

He sighed. "Remember how I explained it was easier to keep people away from me by being surly and nasty, by dropping refinement and pretending I was the low-class bum everyone wanted to believe I was?"

She nodded, still stunned.

"Once I established myself, people ignored me without guilt. The human psyche is an amazing yet sad thing." He shook his head.

"Anyway, I figured if I was going to use the poor-Samson bit as a pretense, why not live that way too? At the time, I didn't give a damn about anyone or anything. And who was left in my life to impress?"

Sloane wanted to answer, to say he should have wanted to impress himself, but she couldn't. Through his slumped shoulders, his embarrassment was already clear. So she swallowed hard and remained silent.

"Much as I hate to admit it, I began to wallow in the truth I created. The truth the town accepted."

"I understand the motivation." And it saddened her. "But the money? Where did that come from?"

"A few months after your senator grandfather died, an envelope arrived at my house."

Sloane's eyes opened wide. "And?"

"Your grandfather had provided enough money to compensate me for my sacrifice. At least that's what the low-life snake's letter said. Fat good the money did me after he stole your mother and ruined my life." Though he sounded bitter, he'd also accepted the way life had turned out.

Which, Sloane supposed, was the story of his life. "But you refused to spend his money?" she guessed, since he said he was wealthy.

Samson shrugged. "Why give the man any satisfaction? He thought he could rule the world, even from the grave. Sent me blood money when it was too late, when your mother was already gone. It certainly wasn't like I could go after her then. So I just invested and let it build up."

"So Grandfather Jack had a conscience," Sloane said bitterly. "One he defined by his own terms, as usual."

"Exactly."

Tears filled her eyes, yet she couldn't waste time worrying about the past. "But you're willing to use his blood money to rebuild your house?" she asked Samson.

He nodded. "I want a place my daughter can come visit and be proud of. A place she can bring her own family," he said, hope lacing his gruff voice.

She glanced down, unable to face him, knowing she'd be disappointing the man who'd already suffered so many letdowns. "I wouldn't get your hopes up on the family angle," she told him. She looked at him from the corner of her eye.

He squared his shoulders, obviously upset. "Does that Chandler boy have rocks in his head? I told him to get off his ass and see what's in front of him before it's too late. I told him life's too short to waste with regrets and could-have-beens." He let out a low growl. "He doesn't have a lick of his mother's sense, that much I can tell you."

"Whoa," Sloane said, realization dawning. "Back up. You *told* Chase to go after me?"

"Of course I did. Do you think I want you or him suffering the same fate as me? I told him what it's like to live life wishing things could have been different," Samson said, clarifying, his eyes glittering with satisfaction that he'd done his daughter a good turn.

She didn't want to know when he and Chase had had this conversation. Nor could she bring herself to tell him that he'd merely played on Chase's innate guilt and white-knight complex. Samson had helped push Chase into Sloane's arms, offering proclamations of forever, but Chase needed to come on his own, without being prompted. Without guilt. He needed to opt for a future with her because it was what he wanted, not what he thought he owed her, or what he thought she needed.

But Samson had performed his first parental duty on Sloane's behalf and she loved him for it. She crooked her finger and Samson came forward, and this time, no bullet flew as she received her first father-daughter hug from Samson.

Chapter Eighteen

Chase paced the floor of the hospital waiting area, along with the rest of the family. Charlotte's water had unexpectedly broken, nearly a month early, and she was inside, in labor. Thank God all signs indicated nothing was seriously wrong except for the baby's rush to join the Chandler clan on its own schedule. Charlotte's parents were on their way back from L.A. and the rest of the Chandlers were gathered here together. Waiting.

"You are one pathetic human being," Rick said to Chase as he leaned against the wall.

Although everyone was nervous for Roman and Charlotte, that wouldn't stop Rick from ganging up on Chase in the meantime. And since Rick knew Chase wouldn't leave until the baby was born, he had Chase cornered. "So *I'm* pathetic, huh?"

"That's what he said." Hannah came up beside them, bouncing from foot to foot, excited beyond belief at the prospect of being crowned baby-sitter.

"Go away, squirt. I'm trying to talk to my brother," Rick said.

Hannah shook her head. "There's no talking to Chase when his mind's made up about something. At least that's what you always say." The pretty fourteen-year-old grinned, laughing wickedly.

Rick groaned. "You're not helping."

"Oh, I think she is." Chase leaned closer to Hannah and whispered, "What else does Rick say about me?"

"Hmm." She twirled a long strand of hair around her finger and pursed her lips in thought. "He says you've been a pain in the ass since Sloane left. That you should have gotten down on your hands and knees and begged." She paused to giggle. "But it probably wouldn't have mattered, since Sloane got out while the getting was good." She nodded, apparently satisfied she'd hit on all pertinent details.

"Tsk, tsk." Rick said, winking at Hannah. "There's no allowance for you this week, kid."

"Hannah, you get over here and leave Rick and Chase alone," Kendall called from across the room.

Rick rolled his eyes. "Too little, too late," he informed his wife.

Kendall shrugged. "I tried." Then she turned her attention back to Raina, who was sitting on the couch, browsing through a magazine.

Chase dug one sneakered foot against the linoleum floor, wondering how much to tell Rick about Sloane leaving him. "I never figured you had much of a brain, but I have to admit you nailed things with me and Sloane."

Rick raised an eyebrow. "What happened?"

he asked, all signs of joking and laughter gone from both his tone and expression.

When things got serious, the brothers were there for one another, ribbing and kidding put aside. "I did ask her to stay. In a manner of speaking. I told her I'd changed my mind, that I wanted a future."

"And she left anyway," Rick said.

The reminder caused an ache in Chase's already empty heart. "That much is obvious."

"But you don't know why."

Embarrassed to be discussing both his failures and his love life, Chase merely nodded.

"Need me to spell out Sloane's reasons for you?"

"Might as well start." How else could Chase fix things? He'd come up empty on his own.

"Sloane knows you well." Rick pulled up a chair and straddled it, settling in. "Probably as well as Roman and I do, and considering how short a time you've been together, that's saying a lot."

Chase snorted. "You call this analysis? Tell me something I don't know."

Rick shrugged. "Relax. I'm getting there. I'm guessing Sloane thinks you wanted an affair. Short term by definition. No commitment."

Folding his arms across his chest, Chase eyed his middle sibling. "Again, so far I'm not impressed. This is all obvious."

"I'm just getting started." Rick rubbed his hands together in anticipation. "She thinks these things because you used your famous saying: *Safety first, kids never.* Am I right?"

Chase rubbed a weary hand over his burning eyes. "That about sums it up." It was the same lecture he'd given his brothers over the years, when being forced to perform the fatherly duty of safe-sex discussions. "So?"

"So women have memories like elephants," Rick explained. "Sloane's not likely to forget you said that."

"You'd think she'd appreciate the fact that I looked after her," Chase muttered.

"She appreciates it, all right. Then she fell in love and all that appreciation flew out the window. Now she wants the house, the white picket fence, the kids," Rick said, his eyes drifting to his own wife, who sat holding Raina's hand.

Chase sighed. "I told her I want all those things too."

"*After* she'd seen Chase Chandler in action. She's seen you with your family, seen how you put Mom first. If I had to guess, she's seen you step up in a crisis and pull away in the aftermath." Rick slanted his head toward Chase, awaiting an answer.

"What the hell makes you think you know me so well?"

His eyes opened wide. "I grew up with you, the model of perfection. You never once bailed on a responsibility. But when you're alone and quiet, you withdraw. I'm sure that wasn't easy for Sloane."

"Yeah, well, she loves me in spite of it," Chase said defensively.

"Yet she's in D.C. and you're here. What gives?" His brother raised an eyebrow, his challenge obvious.

"She doesn't believe I love her. Oh shit, that's not true." Chase kicked the wall, grateful afterward he was wearing sneakers and caused no damage. "She believes I love her; she just doesn't believe I want those things you mentioned." He paced the floor. "Can't a man change his mind? Women do it all the time and we're forced to accept it."

"Women are their own breed. They can do whatever they want and, like you said, we men accept it. It's our lot in life."

"I heard that," Kendall called from across the room, making Chase realize she and his mother had grown silent, listening to Chase's problems instead.

"And I love you even when you're eavesdropping," Rick called back, then faced Chase once more. "Did Sloane have a reason to believe you changed your mind about marriage? Women need proof."

"Would you quit lumping us all into one broad category?" Raina suggested, getting involved for the first time. "Every woman is an individual. I'm certain Sloane needs proof because she doesn't want to feel she trapped you into marriage."

Chase slapped his head with one hand.

"When did this become a family conversation?" he muttered. "I have nothing to prove. I love the woman. I want to spend the rest of my damn life with her and she thinks the need will wear off! Have you ever heard anything so ridiculous in your life?"

Raina put down the magazine she'd been thumbing through. "She must have a valid reason."

He glanced at his mother, annoyed with her attempt to be the voice of reason, and he gritted his teeth. If it weren't for the fact that dissecting *his* life took the focus off waiting on Charlotte, he'd walk out on this farce of a conversation now. Hannah, thank God, had gotten engrossed in television and wasn't paying attention.

"*She must have a valid reason,*" Chase mimicked. But when he let himself think, he was forced to admit the truth. "She does," he admitted aloud. "Sloane thinks I've got this *white-knight complex.* That I feel guilty I wasn't there when she got shot."

"Do you?" Kendall asked softly.

"Of course I feel guilty. But I wouldn't saddle myself with a wife or even consider having kids just because I think I failed her."

"I hope not," Raina said.

He glanced at his mother, a woman on the verge of getting her first blood-related grandchild and saw a glimmer of hope in his dim future. "If you mean that, put your matchmaking skills to work and help me get Sloane back," Chase said to Raina, picking up on the idea he'd had the other day.

"I can't." Raina glanced down at her hands, obviously unable to meet Chase's stare.

"Why the hell not?" he asked in shock. "You've spent how many years playing match-maker against our will? And now when I'm asking . . . no, begging you to help me out, you're saying no?"

She nodded, eyes still lowered. "That's right. I've learned my lesson. I'm getting married and I'm going to have a life of my own."

From the doorway came the sound of ap-plause. Eric clapped, obviously proud of Raina and her new leaf. "I just wanted to let you know, Charlotte's doctor said it shouldn't be much longer."

Raina glanced at Eric, and her cheeks glowed. Chase's gaze traveled between Kendall and Rick, and he witnessed the same adoration. Goddamned envy consumed him. Yeah, he was happy for his mother and siblings, but his en-tire family possessed what he desired. With Sloane. And he'd struck out.

He turned back to his mother. "Can't you learn this lesson after you help me?"

"I'm sorry, son, but she's out of the match-making business. And as soon as I get my ring on her finger, where it belongs, I'm going to keep her too busy to meddle. That much I can promise all of you." With a wave, Eric took off for the delivery room once more, the only person with access other than Roman, who wouldn't leave his wife's side.

"Shit," Chase muttered.

"Would you watch your language?" Kendall asked, placing her hands over her sister's ears.

Hannah laughed. "Like I don't hear worse in school?"

"Look, Rick's got a point," Kendall told Chase. "I've stayed out of this so far, but I'm female and that gives me some wisdom. Add to that, I've dealt with a Chandler man who possesses a white-knight complex. I'm more than equipped to give you a few pointers." She tucked her hair behind her ears and watched him, waiting for permission.

He let out another groan. "Might as well give it a shot. Everyone else has."

"That's gratitude for you," Rick said.

Kendall ignored him, focusing on Chase. "As much as I hate to admit this, Rick's right. If you love Sloane, and I believe you do or you wouldn't be so miserable, you're going to have to convince her you've changed."

"And how do I do that?" he asked Kendall, needing this advice more than he needed his next breath.

Before she could reply, Eric came in to announce to the family that another Chandler had been born. Lilly Chandler, a healthy five-pound, eight-ounce, eighteen-inch baby girl, had come into the world. And Roman, who'd witnessed battlefields and wars up close and personal, had nearly passed out, needing a paper bag and coaching by Eric to resuscitate him.

While the rest of the family headed for the glass doors of the nursery to wait for their first glimpse of the baby, Kendall pulled Chase aside.

"You gave me advice once. I just want to return the favor." She smiled at him, accepting him for who and what he was.

"I'd appreciate it."

She placed a hand on his arm. "Look inside yourself and see what made you the man you were. The man who didn't want a family. Then figure out why you suddenly do. When you can explain it to yourself, you can pass that wisdom on to Sloane. That's all she'll need to believe." She shrugged as if it were simple.

But why didn't it feel that way?

Sloane had been in Yorkshire Falls for only a brief time, yet she missed both the town and the people. At home in her Georgetown walk-up, she dressed for her first day back at work with a shirt that let her cater to her bandaged arm, and a determined attitude of renewal.

When she'd taken time off, she'd closed down her small storefront office from which she ran her interior-design business and called her most immediate clients to explain she'd had a family emergency. Though many of her existing clients were antsy, if her overly full answering machine was a judge, there were none who couldn't be soothed with a phone call and rescheduled appointment. This morning, she had a legal pad full of phone calls to make, consisting of basic things ranging from overdue furniture deliveries to scheduling a pickup on a wall unit a client decided she wasn't happy with, after all. *Easy enough,* Sloane thought.

She was a people person, something she'd probably learned — she could no longer say inherited — from Michael. Meeting with her clients while trying to combine their needs with her vision normally gave her a great deal of satisfaction. But since her trip to Chase's hometown, everything here felt bland. Dull. Lifeless.

She tapped the pen on the desktop, reminding herself she lived in Washington, D.C., the nation's capital. A swinging town at night and a bustling city during the day. So why did the sleepy upstate New York town and its eclectic citizens draw her so? Or was it just Chase who pulled at her like a magnet? She missed him so bad, she ached.

Shake it off, Sloane. Life goes on, she reminded herself harshly. She'd let him go so that he could experience the rich life he'd envisioned, the one of a single man who found ultimate success as a journalist. A life no longer tied to family or obligation. She'd never have forgiven herself if she'd accepted his words of love and tied him to a future, only to see regret and longing in his eyes later on.

The jingling of bells signaled she had a visitor and Sloane glanced up.

Her friend Annelise walked in the door, two cups of Starbucks coffee in hand and a scowl on her lips. "Well, well, well, look who came home." Annelise handed Sloane a *grande*-size cup. "What kind of friend disappears without a word? Doesn't call? Leaves me to worry?" She sat down, coffee in hand. "I called Madeline and she said you were taking some breathing room," Annelise said, her voice rising. "Wouldn't a real friend know if you needed breathing room?" Her pout was as real as her concern.

Sloane's guilt rose to the surface and she winced. "I'm so sorry." From the moment she'd overheard Robert and Frank admit Michael wasn't her father, forcing her to find solace in Chase, Sloane had been single-minded in her pursuit of Samson. And protective of her time with Chase Chandler. All at the expense of her job, her friends, her life.

Yet here she was, back home, engrossed in work, being berated by a concerned friend, and all Sloane could think of was the people she'd left behind. This life no longer felt like hers. In fact, she hadn't thought about it once since she'd taken off for Yorkshire Falls.

Annelise rapped on Sloane's desk with her knuckles. "You're not paying attention to anything I've been saying."

Her friend deserved better. "Annelise, I really am sorry," Sloane said. "I've just been through a major life crisis and . . . I guess I had to do it alone." She expelled a long breath. "I'm still coming to terms with some changes."

"I know." Reaching into her purse, Annelise pulled out the newspaper Sloane had avoided, not wanting to know when her life became public and she'd lost Chase to success.

Annelise pushed the paper in front of Sloane. "Michael Carlisle's not your real father; some man named Samson is. And what a scandalous history is involved in that story," she said, but her voice had softened, no hint of anger in her tone. "I had to read about it in the paper. I wish you'd felt you could confide in me." She sounded more hurt than angry.

Sloane centered the front page to read the headlines. FATHER FRAUD OR FATHER FIGURE? SENATOR MICHAEL CARLISLE REVEALS HIDDEN FAMILY SKELETONS. "Ugh," she muttered. But as she scanned the contents of the article, she read not just an unbiased accounting of the facts, but a rosy picture of the life Sloane had led and the reasons behind it, no dirt heaped on the senator or his character.

And that, Sloane realized, was because the author was Chase Chandler, the article having been picked up by the major newspapers, the *Washington Post* included. Headlines and innuendos weren't of his choosing, she was sure.

Pride swelled inside of Sloane as she accepted he was living his dream at last.

He'd broken the story of Michael's secrets, Sloane's parentage, and her shooting in a way that dignified everyone involved, including Samson. She chuckled, imagining how difficult Chase had found that particular task. Still, the story was out now, she thought, and said a silent prayer that Michael's career didn't suffer because of decisions he'd made in the past.

Slowly she met her friend's gaze. "It's been a wild ride," she admitted, patting her shoulder softly. "Sometimes a dangerous one."

Annelise nodded. "And I can see how something like this would send you reeling."

Sloane sighed. "That's an understatement. I'm not sure I could have shared or explained this to anyone. I'm glad it's all public now." She spread her hands in front of her. "And thank you for understanding."

Annelise nodded. "I'm your friend, Sloane. And that means I'm available for discussion. If you ever decide you want to talk about this guy you're mooning over, I'm here."

"What makes you think I'm mooning over a guy?" Sloane asked after pausing to join her friend for a sip of coffee. The drink was too sweet and she grimaced. "Am I that readable?"

"You sure are. Your emotions are plastered across your face. You're miserable and it isn't family issues bothering you, and before you ask how I know . . . Well, I can just tell." Annelise leaned forward, her elbow brushing fabric swatches laid out on the table. "By the way, I like this pattern."

"It's called a trellis." *Like some of the hangings on Norman's bird-filled walls,* Sloane thought.

And that was another weird thing. The little hole-in-the-wall diner with no real sense of style appealed to Sloane far more than the places she frequented in D.C. The ones who paid the finest decorators to create an atmosphere customers would want to return to. Sloane missed the tacky birds.

"Okay, your body may be here, but you are still lost in thought." Annelise picked up her purse. "Call me when you want to talk, okay?"

Sloane nodded. "Will do. And thanks again."

Long after Annelise walked out the door, Sloane forced herself to work her way down the list of phone calls, accomplishing some things and crossing them off her list, and leaving messages on others, with follow-up notes on her pad. By the time her cell phone rang, she was ready for any distraction that wasn't decorating related. "Hello?"

"Hi, sweetie."

Madeline's voice came through over the phone and Sloane was so happy to talk to her with no secrets, no problems between them. "Hi, Mom. Where are you?"

"In the mall, taking your sisters shopping. Or actually, chauffeuring your sisters while I pick up a few things myself. I just wanted to hear your voice, so I thought I'd call." Madeline laughed, but the shakiness was obvious.

A brush with death would do that to even the strongest person, Sloane thought. "I'm fine," she assured Madeline, even though her step-mother hadn't asked. Madeline wouldn't want her to know she was still worried. "I'm trying to get back into the swing of things at work."

"And are you?"

"No." Sloane laughed. "Not in the least."

"Then come visit. I still have those letters of Jacqueline's I promised to show you, and of course your sisters want to see for themselves that you're okay. Hold on."

Sloane heard some static and then Madeline's voice. "Girls, bare backs are fine, but that much cleavage is *not*. Different dresses," she ordered.

Sloane chuckled. "Christmas fund-raiser?" Sloane asked knowingly. She'd attended enough of those to figure out what the twins were shopping for.

"Of course," Madeline said. "And you can't imagine the slinky getups Eden and Dawne just tried to get me to agree to let them wear."

Sloane rolled her eyes. "They figured you were distracted and would just nod. Then when you yelled at home later, they could blame you."

"Exactly. Now, would you come home? We can discuss your attending that fund-raiser then. There are many new men I can introduce you to who'll help you get over what's-his-name in no time," Madeline said.

Sloane stiffened in her seat. "His *name* is Chase Chandler, which you very well know." Chase was unforgettable.

He'd never lied to her, never given her less than what he'd promised, and had always delivered more. She loved him even more for that.

"I know his name, honey. I just wasn't sure how you were feeling about him these days."

Great, Sloane thought. Patronized by her own mother. "We're better off not going there. It wouldn't do any good."

"Did you know Charlotte had her baby?" Madeline asked softly. "A little girl?"

Sloane shook her head. No, she hadn't known. She'd missed the occasion, missed seeing Chase's expression when he saw his niece for the first time. And she'd missed it all because she'd let him go. He'd offered her a future and she didn't trust that it was what he really wanted.

Had she been wrong, after all?

"Sloane? Are you there?"

She wiped a tear that began dripping down her cheek. "I'm here. And no, I didn't know about Charlotte." She swallowed over the lump in her throat. "I'll have to send a gift."

"I'm sorry, honey."

"Yeah. Me too." She gripped the receiver harder in her hand.

"Come home and let me take care of you. I

thought you should take a few more days off to recuperate anyway."

Sloane smiled, suddenly finding the thought of Madeline's care and her sisters' chatter appealing. But the notion of Yorkshire Falls was even more inviting. "Let me think about it, okay?"

"No, it's not okay. Either you call for a flight or I'll schedule one for you. I don't want you alone. You still need family around you."

Sloane groaned. "You're determined. But it wouldn't work unless I wanted to come. I'll call and schedule a flight. I can be home tonight." And in Yorkshire Falls tomorrow, if she chose to be.

"We're not going to be home tonight. Your father and I have plans and your sisters are sleeping at a friend's house, but you have the key, right?"

"Yes." She jangled the key chain that held all her keys. "I'll just see you in the morning."

"Wonderful! Don't forget to put your flight information on our answering machine so I have it," Madeline instructed. "Well, I have to go. The girls are coming back with armloads of dresses. Let me go weed out the trashy from the trashier. I'll see you tomorrow."

Sloane hung up, feeling better than she had since leaving Yorkshire Falls. Tomorrow she'd be home with her family. Okay, so it wasn't the same as being with Chase, but it was a start.

Sloane stepped off the plane and walked down the runway. Albany Airport wasn't busy, and since she had only a carry-on bag, she walked straight outside to grab a taxicab. A cold wind whipped through the night air and she shivered.

Before she could wind her way through to the taxi line, a dark truck pulled up beside her, passenger window open. "Need a lift?"

Sloane recognized Chase's deep, rumbling voice and her stomach flipped over in surprise. "How'd you find me?"

"Madeline called and said you needed a ride home from the airport."

Sloane narrowed her gaze. "That match-making, lying, sneaky —"

"Those used to be my sentiments exactly, back when my mother used to exercise her skills. But that was before you came along." He laughed. "Come on and get in. It's freezing outside."

Without waiting for a reply, he opened his door and stepped into the street. Ignoring her protests and questions, he walked around to put her suitcase into the back of the truck.

Sloane rubbed her now free hand over her shoulder and eyed him warily. She *could* take a taxi anyway, but he'd driven half an hour to the airport to pick her up, and Yorkshire Falls was in the opposite direction from her parents' house, so he'd gone out of his way. Just to see her.

And it was *so* good to see him. Even if Madeline had obviously set her up. But *why* had Chase been willing to go along? She wouldn't get answers unless she joined him, so when he opened the door, she slid inside without hesitation. The heat blasted around her, warming her from the outside in. When he settled into the driver's side, the temperature in the truck spiraled upward.

His darkened gaze met hers, telling her he felt that instant connection too. Warning herself to tread carefully, she shifted in her seat, trying to think of neutral conversation.

"How's the shoulder?" he asked as he pulled onto the road leading out of the airport.

She leaned her head back against the seat. "It still hurts some. I'm down to taking Tylenol only."

"I'm glad."

She wasn't ready to tackle anything about *them,* so she went for the obvious choice. "I heard from Madeline that Charlotte had her baby."

"She's incredible." His grin was infectious; his adoration for the baby so obvious, it tore at Sloane's heart. This reaction from the man who didn't want children of his own? Once again, Sloane was forced to reexamine her own reasons for pulling back and not trusting in Chase's proclamation that he'd changed his mind.

Could the fact that her life was in turmoil

have played a factor? The people she'd always trusted, Madeline and Michael, had betrayed her in the most fundamental way. Chase had offered her his heart along with the things she'd told herself she wanted.

Yet, she'd turned him away. "How is Charlotte feeling?" she asked.

"Better by the day."

"I wish you had called to tell me." Sloane forced out the words that would draw them into an emotional conversation, not knowing where things would lead.

One hand on the wheel, Chase rested his other arm on the headrest behind her seat. "I didn't think you wanted to hear from me."

She sighed. "Did I say that?"

He slanted his head her way. "*Good-bye, Chase,* spoken loud and clear. But I decided to ignore your words and go with my gut."

"Turn off at the next exit," she instructed, catching sight of the thruway signs.

Instead, he passed right by her parents' exit. "Chase?"

"I know where I'm going. You're going to have to trust me, sweetheart. Can you do that this time?"

She let out a wry laugh. "That's a good one. When did I ever not trust you?" She'd trusted him with her life and he'd delivered, every time.

"When I told you I loved you and you pushed me away," he said bluntly.

"Touché." Just as she'd begun to suspect, she

really had contributed to messing things up between them. He wasn't solely to blame. She rolled her head to the side, glancing out the window into the dark night. "Chase?"

"Yes?"

"I pushed you away and you didn't think I wanted to hear from you, right?"

"Right."

The truck drove over a bump in the road and her shoulder took the brunt of the turn. She winced, ignoring the pain. "Then what are you doing here now?"

"I want to be here." Chase glanced over and immediately noticed the strain in Sloane's face, the exhaustion evident by the dark circles under her eyes.

She still hadn't completely recovered from the shooting incident, but she had returned to work after merely one weekend of rest. Not enough in Madeline's opinion, nor in Chase's. Which was why he was kidnapping her, so to speak. Raina may have given up matchmaking, but Madeline had been only too happy to provide him with easy access to her stepdaughter.

Chase couldn't read Sloane's reaction to his words. She hadn't turned back to face him and remained quiet for the duration of the trip, until he parked in a graveled parking lot by a small inn.

"Where are we?" She turned to him at last.

"A place where you can rest." He strode out

of the truck and walked around to her side, opening the door for her.

She glanced up at him. "Do I have a say in this?"

"If you say you'll follow me inside, then yeah, you have a say." He pointed toward the renovated dairy barn that now served as a luxurious inn.

"Very funny."

"I'm not laughing." He lifted their suitcases out of the back and shut the door. He ignored the urge to back her against the truck and kiss her until she stopped talking, stopped arguing, stopped doing anything except loving him. But he'd tried that last time and it hadn't worked. He wasn't about to make the same mistake twice.

Since he'd already checked in earlier this evening, he didn't have to bother with paperwork now. Instead, he led Sloane up a short flight of stairs and down a narrow hallway to their dimly lit sitting room. There was a fire crackling in the fireplace, adding to the atmosphere he'd wanted to create for her. Intimate, private, and solemn.

Once they were inside, she glanced around, taking in the paneled walls and old-world charm. "This place really is beautiful."

He helped take her jacket off, careful not to hurt her shoulder. A bandage still covered her wound and the thick padding stuck out from her shirt. "My parents came here on their honeymoon and every anniversary after."

She turned around, obviously startled. Her pupils dilated, the significance of their surroundings kicking in at last, he hoped. He wasn't sure he could take much more anticipation, not knowing what she was thinking or feeling.

"I take it you brought me here for a reason?" she asked. "Besides me needing rest?"

He grunted. "You *do* need rest. And I'm going to see that you get some." He caressed the dark skin beneath her eyes with the pad of his thumb.

At his simple touch, a soft moan escaped her throat. Acting on instinct, he wrapped his hand around the back of her neck, invading her personal space and bringing her squarely into his.

To hell with leading into things slowly. "I love you, I missed you, and I want you in my life. Forever," he said gruffly.

A smile lifted her lips. "Keep talking."

"You were right not to believe I was ready for commitment," he said, explaining what he'd only just come to understand.

She blinked, her eyes wide and comprehending. "I never wanted you to look back and resent me or feel like I trapped you during a weak moment." She shrugged with her good arm. "I'd rather know you were happy without me than miserable with me."

"Not a chance," he growled. "But I do have a lot to tell you."

"Then do you think we can sit down? I'm still kind of weak."

Taking in her pale face, he agreed. "Sure thing, sweetheart." Chase lifted her into his arms and settled her down on the couch across from the fireplace. Feeling more hopeful than when he'd surprised her at the airport, he joined her. He wanted to see her face as he explained his past, his present, and their future, and how he'd come to the realizations that he'd reached.

Sloane licked her dry lips, waiting in silence, wondering what Chase had to say. She understood it was serious and knew he'd put a lot of thought into where, when, and how to share his feelings with her. She understood too that whatever he had to say would determine their future, and her heart pounded hard in her chest.

"Talk to me." Reaching over, she grabbed his hand, needing to feel his heat and strength.

"Remember I told you my dad died and I took over all aspects of the family?" His eyes dilated as the memories overtook him.

She nodded. "Of course I remember."

"Well, I was sitting and holding Lilly, Roman and Charlotte's baby, and marveling at how this little person had already wormed her way into my heart."

She shivered at the imagery he'd given her — Chase, his big, strong hands holding a baby — and she wished it were their baby he was holding. Wished and hoped that's what he desired too. "And?"

"And I started thinking about how she was another person for me to protect. Then it dawned on me." He met Sloane's gaze. "She wasn't my responsibility. She's Roman and Charlotte's. But I still had this initial, instinctive need to protect her."

Sloane smiled, her grip on his hand tightening. "That's because you're special."

"It's because I'm a controlling son of a bitch," he countered, laughing at his self-imposed description. "And while holding that little baby, I realized why."

Sloane resisted the urge to curl into him, to kiss him, to tell him the whys didn't matter. Because they did. She'd pushed him away once before and now he was giving her what she needed to trust him, the reasons for his sudden change of mind. If he understood why he was ready for a one-eighty change in his future, then he'd never look back and regret it.

She leaned forward, wanting to hear more.

"I guess this need to be in control of the people I care about, their lives and their well-being, started when my father died. It was damn obsessive, but my mother was too grateful to care, and Rick and Roman were strong enough to find their own way despite me." He shook his head, his laughter self-deprecating.

"No, Rick and Roman were strong enough to

find their own way *because of you*," Sloane countered.

"Well, it doesn't change the fact that I developed that white-knight complex you mentioned because it gave me the illusion of being in control. The illusion of safety."

He drew a deep breath, and Sloane waited, wanting him to feel no pressure, only support.

He leaned his head against the back of the couch, staring at the ceiling. "In my misguided mind, I figured if I controlled my family and was always there for them, I wouldn't lose them . . ." He paused as his voice cracked. Then clearing his throat, he continued. "I wouldn't lose them the way I lost my father."

His admission struck Sloane in the heart. She'd only thought she understood this often silent, mostly enigmatic man, but she hadn't known his deepest pain.

She did now and she regretted forcing him to dig so deep that he had to suffer. "I'm sorry. I pushed you away when I should have realized you understood yourself well enough not to offer more than you could give. But I was afraid too. I'd just been through a betrayal with Michael and Madeline and it affected me more than I'd been willing to admit to myself." She shook her head. "But I shouldn't have pushed *you* away in order to fight my own insecurities. I'm sorry."

He brushed a strand of hair off her forehead. "Don't be sorry. In the end, you brought us back to each other."

She shook her head. "Then why do I feel so selfish?"

"You're not selfish. You're honest and real. And obviously we both had more things to work out than we were aware of at the time." He shrugged. "That just makes *us* honest and real."

Her eyes filled with tears.

"Besides, you were right. I *did* feel guilty I wasn't there when you were shot. But more because I could have lost you than because I wanted to be in control of things. I want you in my life, Sloane. Now and forever. I'll never look back and wonder *what if.*"

"How can you be sure?" She bit down on her bottom lip, hating the fact that she had to ask.

Chase turned his head to the side. "Sweetheart, I wrote the article of a lifetime and it left me cold and empty inside because I didn't have you."

Sloane released the breath she hadn't been aware of holding. More than anything, *those* were the words she needed to hear. That she added to his life and didn't take away from it. "I read the article and it was masterful, Chase. You did such a professional job, yet protected my family in a way no other reporter would have."

A smile twitched at his lips. "I couldn't exactly trash the family I want to marry into, now could I?"

Ignoring the pain in her shoulder, Sloane

came to her knees and threw herself into his arms, pushing him back down against the couch. She stared into his deep blue eyes and knew there was no place she'd rather be for the rest of her life than with this man whose love and caring ran so deep. "Say you're sure."

"I'm sure." He laughed, shifting his position to accommodate her. He managed to maneuver her beneath him, so he straddled her hips. "I am one hundred percent sure I want to be with you for the rest of my life."

She raised an eyebrow. "Married with children?" she asked, certain she knew the answer. "Because when you talked about holding Lilly, all I could think about was you holding *our* baby in your arms."

"Honey, there's nothing I want more."

Sloane exhaled hard, finally able to breathe. "I love you too, Chase." She wrapped her good arm around his neck and pulled him toward her. "Now kiss me."

"With pleasure," he said, and sealed his lips against hers, this time knowing nothing would come between them. Not fear, not mistrust, and not the past.

He slipped his tongue inside her mouth, making love to her at the same time his lower body rode in insistent circles, pressing his groin hard against hers.

"Want to try making that baby now?" Sloane asked, breaking the kiss and breathing hard.

"Right here?" He reached down and unsnapped the button on her jeans. "Right now?"

"Yes. Oh yes." Her hips jerked upward as she tried to help him, hindered by the use of only one hand.

Chase took over, undressing her, pausing to arouse and stimulate each and every inch of her luscious skin. He lowered the zipper and helped her wriggle off her pants and lace undies all at the same time. He started fondling her with his hands and followed with laps of his tongue and nips of his teeth. So that by the time he came down on top of her, bare skin against bare skin, her damp, wet body was more than ready for his heated flesh.

And he entered her, here and now, in a perfect attempt to create their future.

Epilogue

Raina wrapped her hands tighter around Eric's waist and let him lead her around the patio. She was dancing at her own wedding. They'd decided to have a small, intimate family affair at Raina's house.

By Yorkshire Falls' standards, that meant a revolving door of more than one hundred people at any given time, pets included, passing through and giving good wishes. But what mattered most to Raina was family. Hers and Eric's, gathered here together for the first time.

Roman stood by Charlotte, who held their baby in her arms. Oh, Lilly had captured Raina's heart and she would break the hearts of many men in her lifetime. Raina chuckled at that thought, as only a grandmother could.

And then there was Rick and Kendall. Their family had begun with Hannah, Kendall's sister, who was now charming the teenage boys and keeping them on their toes. Raina laughed. She and Hannah had developed the most wonderful relationship, as if they'd been grandmother and granddaughter all along. And Raina had a hunch Hannah would soon be joined by another child in the house. Considering the full waist of Kendall's dress, Raina would guess that a little one wasn't more than seven or so months away. But she knew better than to ask.

Rick wouldn't answer personal questions. He was keeping his personal life private — something Raina finally not only understood, but also accepted. She was willing to wait for whenever Kendall got pregnant, no pushing from Raina. Even if her real heart scare did make grandchildren feel more urgent, it was up to her son to decide. But another baby, close in age to Lilly, would be wonderful. Another generation of Chandlers growing up in Yorkshire Falls, Raina thought proudly.

Ending with Chase and Sloane's children? Raina glanced over at her oldest son. He'd never seemed happier. Even if he was yet another of her children who wasn't divulging many details of his personal life, except for the fact that he and Sloane were going to be married in Washington, D.C., next month. Though Raina wanted to help, they refused to let her overdo. Sloane and Madeline Carlisle were handling the actual wedding planning, working around the senator's busy schedule on the campaign trail. But they consulted Raina whenever possible, making her feel at home and welcome, and she was grateful. She had no doubt — babies would follow.

"You're awfully quiet," Eric said, tightening his hand around her waist. "Feeling okay?"

She smiled up at him, her good fortune overwhelming her. "I'm just at a loss for words."

"Should I tell Chase to stop the presses?" he asked, laughing.

She shook her head. "Don't tease me. I'm too afraid all these good things won't last."

He slowed their step, leaning his head closer. "Any reason why they shouldn't?" He rested his cheek against hers and a warm fluttering rose in her stomach.

He made her feel safe and secure, and, she admitted, so did the setting around her. "No, no reason at all. I've got my children, their families, and you. What more could a woman ask for?"

He grinned. "Not one single solitary thing."

She laughed because he was right. Raina had learned many things since she'd begun her charade, the most important being that life was what you made of it. And with the Chandler men, they'd make all things good and most things possible. Eric sweetened the deal.

Raina's family had a lifetime of possibilities ahead of them, and she intended to enjoy each and every one.

About the Author

New York Times best-selling author **Carly Phillips** is an attorney who has tossed away legal briefs in favor of writing hot, sizzling romances. Her first single title contemporary romance, *The Bachelor*, captured a spot as the third pick of the "Reading with Ripa" book club on *LIVE with Regis and Kelly*. The announcement launched Carly into the number-one slot on both Amazon.com and Barnes&Noble.com within just a few hours and for a six-week stay on the *New York Times* list. The follow-up to *The Bachelor*, *The Playboy*, also hit the *New York Times* list its first week.

Carly currently lives in Purchase, New York, with her husband, two young daughters, and a frisky soft-coated Wheaton terrier who acts like their third child. When she's not spending time with her family, Carly is busy writing and promoting (and playing on-line!). Carly loves to hear from her readers. You can write her at: P.O. Box 483, Purchase, NY 10577, or e-mail her at: carly@carlyphillips.com. To discover more about this quickly rising star of romance, all the Chandler men and Carly's upcoming books, visit Carly's Web site at: www.carlyphillips.com.